JOURNEY THROUGH HELL ALMOST TO HEAVEN

A young doctor experiences the horrors of the Civil War with the emergence of modern warfare and the entry of modern medicine

Mel King

Journey Through Hell Almost to Heaven
By Mel King

First Printing-September 2018
ISBN-13: 978-0692180815
Library of Congress Control Number: 2018910573

A Special Thanks:

All Battle field maps are courtesy of Hal Jespersen cartography services.

Formatting and graphic art were done by Daniel Cervantes.

TABLE OF CONTENTS

INTRODUCTION

A ccording to recent reports of nations' educational systems, the United States ranks only eighteenth in the world. That's not surprising, considering that nearly one-fourth of high school graduates in our country are capable of reading only at a fifth-grade level, and that their performance in science and mathematics ranks somewhere below that of at least fifteen other nations. Although many young people can recite verbatim the words of popular songs and rap, the majority are often unfamiliar with history. Unless corrected, those deficiencies in our educational system could have disastrous effects on the future performance of our nation in an increasingly competitive and dangerous world.

Why is knowledge of history important? Since at least the mid-1500s, scholars have recognized the truth of the proverb: "History repeats itself." If people are not aware of the events of the past, if they continue to succumb to human frailties of bigotry, greed, self-interest, desire for power, and if they lack knowledge of past mistakes, then they are destined to repeat them. The aftermath of the Civil War provides us with an example of this.

Beginning with South Carolina in 1861, eleven southern states seceded from the Union and started a war with the North, primarily to preserve the evil institution of slavery. Some revisionist historians have claimed that "states' rights" was the main reason, but the following historical facts disprove this:

1. The Confederate Constitution protected slavery. Confederate Vice President Stephens and other Southern politicians referred to slavery as "the cornerstone of the Confederacy."
2. When South Carolina seceded from the Union in 1860, it declared that the "immediate cause" was the Northern States

failing to return fugitive slaves, and northern abolitionists who incited slaves to rebel.

3. The Georgia Secession Convention of 1861 declared that a separation from the North was the only thing that could prevent abolition of slavery.

4. During the War, the Confederate troops massacred surrendering black Union troops, General Lee shipped to the South free blacks his army captured in northern Virginia and Maryland, and the Confederacy treated captured blacks as 'escaped chattel'.

5. At time of secession, the only mention of 'states' rights' was made by the North, which declared that the Southern states "had no right to secede."

Although less than one-fourth of the white residents of the Confederate states owned slaves, the vast majority of Rebel foot soldiers, who did most of the fighting and dying, were poor whites, who never owned slaves. The wealthy class made up most of the officers. Yet they convinced the poor whites that it was their patriotic duty to fight the North to preserve slavery.

After the War, some Southern historians began referring to the Confederacy as the great "Lost Cause"; revisionist historians referred to it as a war for 'independence', extolling the virtues, deeds and character of many Reb generals and the South's troops in victorious battles. What they failed to emphasize was the enormous cost the South paid for starting that War: the devastation of many of its cities, towns, and villages; the death or permanent disability of hundreds of thousands of young men; the destruction of its agriculture, especially 'King Cotton'; the impoverishment of its people. The square-shaped battle flag of General Lee's Army of Northern Virginia, with its blue cross containing thirteen white stars, all on a background of red, became known as the Confederate Flag. Over the next hundred and fifty years, that flag was revered by hate groups like the Ku Klux Klan and white supremacists. Beginning in the mid-1950s, the Civil Rights movement advanced and the Supreme Court ordered desegregation of schools, which the South did its best to avoid. The majority of southerners, who had, from an early age, been taught to hate blacks and/or that they were an inferior race, vigorously—and often violently—opposed integration and equal rights. It was not coincidence that a number of Southern states adopted the Confederate flag as part of their state flag, or raised Lee's battle flag in a prominent location in their state capitols. Blacks and liberal whites unsuccessfully objected to this government display of a symbol of the era of slavery. It was not until July, 2015, after the brutal murder of nine black churchgoers by a bigoted young white man, that the governor of South Carolina signed a bill passed by its legislature ordering the removal of Lee's flag from the capitol grounds. Other Southern states followed suit.

In this novel, I have attempted to show the true cost of the Civil War to both sides, especially the South. Instead of simply praising the accomplishments of Confederate General Lee, I have depicted him 'with warts and all', relating his costly errors and callously ordering thousands of troops on a suicidal mission. I have not spared some Union Generals from similar criticism.

I have also attempted to show that the War changed medical science and treatment from a prewar condition that had changed little in many hundreds of years, to the first steps forward into modern medicine, with a recognition of the importance of sanitary conditions, the use of anesthetics during surgery, and the keeping of detailed medical records. This is revealed as the reader follows the life and deeds of a fictional character, a young medical student who joins the Union Army and experiences the horrors and successes of the War as a surgeon in the Medical Corps.

And now, on with the story.

CHAPTER 1:

THE APPROACHING CONFEDERATE DEFEAT BRINGS HOPE FOR FREEDOM TO THE PRISONERS

Henry Freeman walked outside his tent early in the morning of March 30, 1865. He stretched his arms towards the sky as the brilliant golden sun seemed to rise above the pine forests on the east side of Andersonville Prison. As he breathed in the morning air, he thought:

"What a beautiful morning if it were not for the stench of decaying dead bodies in the shallow trenches outside the stockade, and the putrid odor arising from the maggot and other vermin-infested waste covering so much of the ground in the stockade."

He noticed the prison commandant, Capt. Heinrich Wirz, approaching him. Stroking his thick black beard and moustache with his left hand [his right hand and arm were virtually useless as a result of a wound sustained in battle], Wirz said:

"Henry, you should have much less workload today, since we completed the transfer of more than 25,000 of our prisoners to prison camps far south of here several months ago. We no longer have several hundred dying daily and thousands in need of medical treatment. We finally have almost enough food to give each prisoner one meal per day.

"You call that swill of mashed corn cobs with small pieces of fermented bacon, food? After you rebels lost the City of Atlanta, which General Sherman burned to the ground, and his troops marched about 150 miles to the sea, capturing Savannah two days before Christmas, you should have realized the war was lost, and let the prisoners go free."

"That's easy for you to say. But I am, for better or worse, a Captain in the Confederate Army. It was risky enough when I failed to obey the order of General Winder, my superior, to construct earthwork defenses around the stockade. When General Sherman captured Atlanta a few days later, we began transferring most of the prisoners to a new camp farther southeast, so the additional fortifications became unnecessary. But to set the prisoners free—that would have been treason. I would have been promptly court-martialed and executed."

"So, Captain, to save your own skin you continued to hold the remaining prisoners in deplorable conditions, where many of them were certain to die of starvation and disease".

Wirz's face turned a bright red as he angrily faced Henry Freeman. "Be careful what you say, you fuckin' ingrate. Instead of treating you like all the other prisoners, I gave you a tent with a wood floor and a straw mattress to sleep on; gave you the same food as the guards; and privileges like being able to roam free outside the stockade."

"Yeh—but not out of the goodness of your heart. I had to agree to work long hours every day, providing medical treatment—including surgery, if necessary—not only to prisoners, but to the Confederate guards and officers. My only pay was the slightly better treatment I received from you, you son of a bitch."

"Henry, you don't seem to understand. You were a prisoner of war, and I had a duty as a Confederate officer. I appreciate what you did. Do you recall when, several months after the fall of Atlanta the Governor of Georgia ordered the Georgia Militia to leave the Confederate Army and return home to help pick the crops so that the people of this state and the army could be provided with food? That's when I realized that the war was lost, and shortly after that I offered to parole you so that you might return to your home in the North. Why did you refuse my offer of freedom?"

"I could not leave the poor wretches who had fought so bravely for the Union, to die without any medical aid in your stinkin' prison."

Wirz put his hand on Henry's shoulder and faced him with what appeared to be an admiring glance. "You are a better man than I, Henry. I'm not sure that I would have made the same choice had I been in your shoes. Well, I guess we've spent enough time chatting. We both have work to do." The Captain turned and walked towards his office, and Henry walked to the prisoners' hospital—a large tent—to see what medical services awaited him for the day.

As he walked from one patient to the next, he had to brush off the sand fleas that kept jumping onto his shoes from the sand and dirt floor, which was infested with fleas, ants, roaches and other vermin. Except for bedpans, sanitary facilities were almost non-existent. The only anesthetics were a gallon of chloroform, a half-gallon of alcohol, and a dozen pints of bourbon, stored in a wooden cabinet at one end of the tent. Although there was a stream with fresh water outside the prison, when Henry made his rounds of the POWs incarcerated inside the prison walls, the only source of water was a creek polluted by human waste that flowed through the middle of the stockade, which water Henry boiled for several minutes before using it for the patients. He supplemented this with rainwater collected in several open barrels during the frequent rainy days. It was no surprise that, during the 14 months the prison camp was in operation, nearly one-third of the 45,000 Union soldiers imprisoned there died of starvation, disease, and wounds sustained in battle.

As he made his rounds to the sick and wounded prisoners, he tried to encourage each with a ray of hope, saying:

"It looks like you'll be free in a little while. Most of the Rebs in Georgia have been defeated, their army crushed. And word has it that Lee's army in Virginia is nearly surrounded by General Grant and his troops. We expect the war will be over any day now."

What Henry didn't say was that he was afraid most of the POWs, including the sick and wounded in the makeshift hospital, wouldn't survive more than a few weeks longer.

Late that night, after completing his work for the day, he retired to his tent. As he lay on his mattress, he thought of his parents, his childhood, his wife, and how he came to be at the Hell-hole called Andersonville.

CHAPTER 2:

HENRY'S FATHER, HORACE, BECOMES A DOCTOR AND MOVES WEST

During the 1800s, prior to the Civil War, the state of medical knowledge and treatment were abysmal, primitive. Doctors did not know the causes of infection and were totally unaware of the existence of bacteria or that those microorganisms caused disease. They were not aware of the necessity for sterility during surgery, and antiseptics were not used, nor was their importance even understood. In fact, it was considered by many to be a mark of a good surgeon to wear a blood-stained apron. Charles D. Meigs, a prominent obstetrics surgeon and medical school professor, opposed the use of anesthesia in surgery and, as late as 1856, wrote that it was not possible for surgeons to transfer disease on their hands to a patient during surgery because "Doctors are gentlemen and a gentleman's hands are clean." It was not until 1865, when an English doctor named Joseph Lister read of Louis Pasteur's theory that microorganisms [bacteria] cause infections, that Lister realized the importance of using phenol [carbolic acid] as an antiseptic in amputation surgeries, thereby reducing the fifty percent mortality rate from sepsis to fifteen percent. Bloodletting by the use of leaches on sick patients was common. Washrooms with soap and running water were not even available near operating rooms in hospitals. Medicine remained in the same primitive state it had been in for several hundred years.

In the United States, there were maybe a dozen medical schools. [Although there were perhaps fifty more so-called medical schools, many of them were just auditoriums in which doctors offered lectures at a fee of about twenty-five dollars, had few or no regular students, few courses, and awarded few if any degrees]. Many doctors never even went to those schools. They simply trained as an apprentice with a practicing physician or surgeon, sometimes for as little as a couple of weeks to as much as several years, and then held themselves out as doctors. In some frontier territories, barbers with little or no training, served as surgeons. The result was high mortality rates. For example, as many as one out of every three surgery patients died from infection.

It was during this era that Oliver Wendell Holmes, Sr. received his M.D. degree from Harvard in 1836. He was determined to improve the state of medical knowledge and practice. One year after graduation, he received an award from Harvard Medical School for a paper on the benefits of using a stethoscope [as of up until then an unheard-of instrument in America] during physical examinations. With three fellow M.D.s, he established the Tremont Medical School above a drug store on Tremont Row in Boston. One of the first young men to enroll in that school was Horace Freeman. He and eleven other students were the first graduating class from that medical school in 1840.

After graduation, Horace moved to Ohio, where, with three thousand dollars inherited from a deceased uncle, he bought a small farm outside of Cleveland, which at that time had a population of 6,100. He turned the barn into an office and operating room, and opened a medical practice. Less than a year later, he married Elizabeth, a nineteen year-old girl he met at church. As the city's population doubled to nearly 12,000, Horace's medical practice thrived, and in 1844, their son, Henry, was born. In 1861, when Henry was 17 years of age, Cleveland's population had reached more than 43,000. Horace began teaching his son medicine, hoping that he would one day become a surgeon. Henry was an eager student, reading all the medical journals he could get his hands on and closely watching his father's diagnosis and treatment of patients. Horace had an excellent reputation as a surgeon, so Henry enthusiastically agreed when his dad asked if he would like to assist Horace during surgeries.

The first time Henry assisted his father in an operation, Horace handed him what looked like a butcher's apron.

"Put this on, son. Surgeries can get pretty messy at times."
As Henry followed his father's instructions, he noticed Horace putting on a blood-stained apron.

"Dad, why aren't you putting on a clean apron?"

"Son, a blood-stained apron is a mark of a good surgeon. It shows he's had lots of experience."

Although only minutes earlier, his father had fed some chickens they were raising, Horace did not wash his hands. When Henry asked why, his dad repeated Dr. Meigs' saying that "gentlemen have clean hands."

A new medical school, Cleveland College of Medicine, had recently opened. Henry asked his father if he could borrow the horse and buggy to go the school to see if it would allow him to read some of its medical books and journals. Encouraged by his son's interest in following his profession, Horace agreed. Henry arose early the following day, readied the horse and buggy, drove the four miles to Cleveland College of Medicine, arriving at 9:30 a.m. He opened the door of an office on which was a sign "REGISTRATION AND INFORMATION" and introduced himself to a woman seated at the information desk.

"My father is a local doctor/surgeon, Horace Freeman. I'm interested in becoming a doctor and he suggested that I ask if you have a library with some medical journals that I might read."

"We do have a medical library with over five hundred books, journals and other medical papers. If you'd like to enroll as a student, I'd be glad to help you."

"For now, I'd just like to read some stuff about the practice of medicine, to help me decide if that's the career path for me."

"Our library is down the hall on your right. Our librarian is Elizabeth Ashley. She's very familiar with the medical literature we have, and I'm sure she'll be glad to help you."

Henry walked down the hall, opened the library door, and observed a pretty young woman with long blond hair seated at a desk to his right side. He stood motionless for several seconds.

"Can I help you, sir?"

"I'm looking for the librarian, Elizabeth Ashley, m'am."

"I am the librarian. You seem somewhat surprised."

"It's just that I didn't expect to see someone so young and…and, if you'll pardon me for being kind of forward….so pretty. The lady at the information office said the librarian was very familiar with all the medical literature…."

Elizabeth rose up from her chair. Henry thought: "Wow. She's got a beautiful hour-glass figure."

"I may be young—just turned seventeen. But my father is a physician, an obstetrician. He's also an instructor here. For years I've been interested in medicine, read his medical books, magazines and journals. I wanted to become a doctor, but he said there's only one woman- doctor in the entire country, Elizabeth Blackwell, who graduated from Geneva Medical College in upstate New York. Dad said she was enrolled there as a joke. The Dean told the students that he'd leave it up to them as to whether to enroll her as a student, and that he would only do so if the entire class agreed. They all thought he was joking, so they unanimously told him to enroll her as a student."

"That's not a good reason for your father to discourage your ambition."

"He said that even if I did get into medical school, I'd be subjected to prejudice from male doctors and be shunned by most patients. Dad suggested I become a nurse, but that kind of compromise did not interest me. When I learned this College would be opening, I volunteered to make the rounds of doctors and hospitals in Ohio and gather whatever medical literature they were willing to donate to the school's library. To show its gratitude, the college appointed me librarian."

"My dad is training me to be a surgeon. But he operates wearing a filthy blood-stained apron, doesn't wash his hands or clean his instruments. I questioned him about that and he quoted me something from a Dr. Meigs about a doctor being a gentleman and gentlemen always have clean hands."

"Oh, I'm familiar with that stupid belief. My dad is an obstetrician. Among the medical writings he donated to the library is the article by Meigs with that dumb statement. Meigs wrote that in response to a well-researched and scientifically sound article by Dr. Oliver Wendell Holmes, contending that puerperal fever is an infection in women shortly after childbirth that can be avoided or reduced if the surgeon purifies his instruments. Wait a few minutes and I'll find those articles for you."

A couple of hours later, before departing from the library, Henry invited Elizabeth to a picnic at his house next Saturday afternoon. She happily accepted the invitation. As he was about to leave, she said:

"Your father seems like most doctors. They get set in their ways and don't keep up with improvements in medical treatment. You should consider attending this college. It's always open to new ideas and better methods of treating patients."

"I'll think about that. It might be better than just training with my dad."

When Henry arrived home, he told his father of the article by Doctor Holmes, reminding Horace that Holmes was one of the founders of the Tremont Medical School, where Horace had obtained his medical education. Annoyed at his son's attempt to teach him about medicine, Horace angrily said:

"Let's get one thing straight, son. You are the student. I am the teacher, the one with years of experience. If you insist on criticizing me or trying to instruct me, you can go somewhere else to learn about the medical profession."

A couple of months later, a surgical repair of a compound fracture of the forearm was performed on a seven-year old boy. His bone was broken, splintered, and his skin was torn. As usual, Henry's father put on his blood-stained apron and did not wash his hands prior to surgery. His father did wash the wound thoroughly with clear water, but after setting the bone he tugged at the broken skin with his bare hands to stretch the torn skin into partially overlapping flaps to cover the wound. He then took a needle on which there were spots of dried blood from prior use, into the eye of which he inserted a thread, the end of which he had moistened with his spit and rolled tight with his fingers so as to make it easier to pass through the eye of the needle. Henry's father then stitched the flaps together. The operation seemed successful, but a few days later, pus appeared, which Horace said was "laudable pus, a good sign of healing". Within a few weeks, gangrene set in and the boy died of an infection that Henry believed had been contracted during surgery. Recalling the article by Dr. Oliver Wendell Holmes, Sr., that he had read recently, Henry asked his father:

"Dad, could the boy's death have been prevented if you had used an antiseptic to purify your instruments and the needle, not used your saliva to moisten the thread, and washed your hands before surgery?"

"Nonsense," his father said, repeating Dr. Meig's statement that gentlemen have clean hands.

It was at that moment that Henry decided to enroll in Cleveland Medical School and receive formal training in medicine, beginning with the next semester, in January, 1862.

CHAPTER 3:

THE WINDS OF WAR THEATEN TO INTERRUPT HENRY'S MEDICAL EDUCATION

During the next twelve months, Henry spent long hours studying and attending classes and laboratory work at Cleveland Medical College. Much of his free time was spent courting Elizabeth Ashley. But the Civil War had begun between the free states of the North and the slave states of the South. At first, the North thought the war would be over shortly. But events like the week-long battle in Virginia in June of 1862, in which the Confederate Army under General Robert E. Lee defeated the Union Army, and the Second Battle of Bull Run, Virginia, in which the Confederate troops defeated much larger Union forces, caused it to realize the struggle would be long and costly. The ill wind that brought often discouraging news from the front lines began to cast a shadow over Henry's education and his love life.

From colonial days up through the Revolutionary War the importation of slaves from Africa and the use of slave labor were common, especially in the southern agricultural states. By 1820, most of the northern states, whose economy was based more on industry than agriculture, had abolished slavery. By the late 1790s, Southern plantation owners using slaves to produce rice and tobacco found those crops no longer profitable, so the demand for slaves began to decline considerably. But that was to change dramatically by 1810, when the cotton gin, invented by Eli Whitney of Connecticut, became popular in the South. Up until then, removing seeds from cotton fibers was slow, labor-intensive, costly work, which made cotton a not very profitable crop. Whitney's invention changed all that. His cotton gin was able to remove seeds from 55 pounds of cotton per day—ten times the output of hand labor.

There was enormous demand for cotton in Europe, with its huge textile mills. Cotton could readily be shipped long distances, unlike other agricultural products, which would spoil over time. As a result, states in the deep south switched to cotton as their main crop and soon that crop made up more than half of all U.S. exports. The amount of cotton exported from the South increased one hundred-fold from 1810 to 1860. The renewed profitability of a crop that used slave labor resulted in the growth of the slave population to nearly four million out of a total U.S. population of 32 million, according to the 1860 census. Nearly one out of every four families in the Southern slave states owned slaves.

The abolitionist movement began to grow in ever-increasing numbers in the Northern free states. Its leaders included Quakers, who believed that all men were created by God and therefore equal; Unitarian ministers, Presbyterian ministers and educators, like John Rankin of Ohio. He wrote letters that became a widely-circulated anti-slavery book, and assisted hundreds of slaves in their escape to freedom—the legendary underground railway. Northern sentiment against slavery was aroused by the publication in 1852 of Harriet Beecher Stowe's novel, "Uncle Tom's Cabin", which showed the horrific effects of slavery on individuals. In its first year, more than 300,000 copies of the book were sold.

In 1857, a southerner whose parents were slave owners, Hinton R. Helper, published "The Impending Crisis of the South". In it, Helper wrote that seventy-five percent of the southerners did not own slaves and that they were being used by the wealthy plantation slave-owners to support slavery. As a result, the South remained an agricultural area that was being left behind by the rapid industrialization of the North. He advocated the abandonment of slavery for economic, not moral, reasons. Unfortunately, most southerners condemned his ideas. When war finally came, the great manufacturing capabilities of the North, which mass-produced armaments, cannons, materials and equipment, was one of the main reasons for the South's ultimate defeat, along with the fact that the population of the North outnumbered that of the South by more than two to one.

In November of 1860, when Abraham Lincoln was elected president, the south saw this event as a threat not only to slavery, but to its agriculture ["king cotton"] and its way of life. On December 20, South Carolina declared that it was seceding from the Union. On January 9, 1861, southern guns prevented a Union supply ship from reinforcing

Fort Sumter in Charleston Harbor. During the next three weeks, Mississippi, Florida, Alabama, Georgia, Louisiana and Texas seceded from the Union. On February 9, Jefferson Davis was elected President of the Confederacy.

On March 4, 1861, Lincoln was inaugurated as President of the U.S. On April 12, the Confederate Army fired upon Fort Sumter, which surrendered the following day, marking the beginning of the Civil War. A couple of days later, Lincoln called for the state militias to provide 75,000 troops. Within the next six weeks, four more states: Virginia, Arkansas, North Carolina and Tennessee, seceded from the Union. Over the next three months, Confederate troops scored a series of victories in battles against the Union forces: at Big Bethel, Virginia, on June 10, 1861; at the First Battle of Bull Run in Virginia, on July 21; and at the Battle of Wilson's Creek in Missouri on August 10, in which Union General Lyon was killed. The next twelve months were marked by seesaw victories by each side.

Henry Freeman not only had strong religious beliefs against slavery like his parents, but also was patriotic with immense pride in our nation which espoused freedom for all and had obtained its independence from England seventy-five years earlier. In mid-September of 1862, after news of Confederate General Stonewall Jackson's victory at Harpers Ferry, West Virginia, in which he captured more than 12,500 Union soldiers, Henry discussed with his fiancée, Elizabeth, joining the Union Army.

"Oh no, dear, please don't. You know that, as a Quaker, I abhor slavery and pray to God that the Union is victorious. But you are in your first year of medical school. One year more and you will get your degree and be a doctor. You will be able to devote your life to helping people, curing the sick and injured. Please don't leave medical school to fight in the war and risk your life and limbs. Your services would be worth much more to the North as a doctor than as an armed soldier."

"Alright dear Liz. But if things get worse.... I may change my mind."

CHAPTER 4:

HENRY LEAVES MEDICAL SCHOOL TO JOIN THE UNION ARMY

Henry was pleased that he had decided to attend medical school rather than receive medical training from his father. Cleveland College of Medicine was one of the few medical schools in the nation that had lab classes once a month where students dissected corpses. That gave them knowledge of the interconnected parts of the human body as well as hands-on training in surgical techniques. The professors at the medical school attempted to keep abreast of new methods, standards and improvements in the prevention and treatment of disease. They taught new surgical techniques, including the use of ether or chloroform as anesthetics, recommended in articles published by Dr. Oliver Holmes, who learned of it from a Boston dentist. One of Henry's instructors at the medical school, Charles Ashley, made certain that his students became familiar with Dr. Holmes' article on lack of sanitary conditions during birth surgery being a cause of puerperal fever. He stated:

"While we do not yet know what organism causes that or other diseases, we are now fairly certain that such diseases can be spread from doctor to patient by unsanitary conditions during surgery. In 1843, Dr. Holmes recommended using antiseptic to sanitize scalpels and other medical instruments and that surgeons wash their hands and wear clean clothing prior to surgery. We now believe that his recommendation should apply to all types of surgery. Unfortunately, most doctors have ignored these recommendations. Dr. Meigs' claim that such procedures are not necessary because 'surgeons are gentlemen and gentlemen's hands are clean', is preposterous and has led to the death of numerous mothers after giving birth."

Henry thought: "My father should have attended this lecture. His stubborn resistance to Dr. Holmes' conclusions has undoubtedly led to the death of some of his patients."

Henry listened intently to each lecture and spent many hours reading every medical journal available in the school's library. He told Elizabeth:

"I want to become the best doctor that my abilities will allow. I hope I never become set in my ways and resistant to improvement like my dad. Helping those in need is my goal."

But, in late December of 1862, as he neared the completion of his first year of medical school, Henry's lofty goals were about to change. News reached Ohio that Confederate troops under General Lee defeated Union General Burnside's forces in the battle of Fredericksburg, Virginia, killing or wounding 12,500 Union soldiers.

"My God", Henry said to Elizabeth, "I cannot stand idly by, going to school as if nothing bad was happening, while thousands of our nation's troops are being killed or wounded. Our Union is threatened by evil men who want to maintain the immoral system of slavery, treating blacks as property with no rights or freedom. It is my duty to our country to join the army and fight to preserve our democracy and end the abominable enslavement of blacks. When the current term ends in late January, I will enlist in the 30th Ohio Infantry Regiment."

"My dearest Henry, I realize your patriotic attitude and desire to serve your country in its time of need. But wouldn't it be better if you finished medical…."

"Please forgive me for interrupting you, Liz. I've made up my mind. I wrote a letter to Colonel Hugh Ewing, the regiment's commander, telling him I will be joining the 30th Regiment on February 1. He replied, thanking me for my patriotism and saying he looks forward to my enlisting in the regiment."

"All right, Henry. I won't try to discourage you. But what about us…our relationship…. our engagement to wed?"

"I've given a lot of thought to that, also. I love you and have promised to marry you. I know we planned to wait one more year, until I completed medical school. But now, I thought, if you'll agree, maybe we could get married right after my final exams for the first year are over, on January 20."

"Yes dearest. That's a wonderful idea. I'll tell my parents. We can have a small church wedding and then spend eleven wonderful days as husband and wife until you join the regiment on February 1."

Henry embraced Elizabeth, holding her close for a minute and then gently kissing her lips.

On January 21, 1863, Henry and Elizabeth were wed in the Congregational Church attended by Henry's family. The bride and groom's parents and about a dozen of their closest friends were in attendance. After the ceremony, the young couple drove away in a horse and buggy to spend five days honeymooning in a small cabin that Liz's parents owned on the shore of Lake Erie.

CHAPTER 5:

HENRY JOINS THE INFANTRY

T he sun rose early in the morning of February 1, 1863, to welcome an unseasonably mild winter's day. Horace made one last-ditch attempt to dissuade Henry from leaving medical school to join the military.

"You know, son, there's word that Congress is about to pass a Military Draft Act, and that it will exempt those who pay three hundred dollars. I'd gladly pay that so that you could complete your medical education."

"No, dad. I understand your concern, but I am not going to evade my duty to my country while less fortunate young men go off to war. Besides, I already told Colonel Ewing that I will be reporting for duty today and I intend to keep my word."

"Well, son, at least let me drive you in our horse and buggy to the train station in Cleveland." [That is where Henry was to board the train to Columbus, the location of the 30th Ohio Regiment's headquarters.]

"Alright, dad. But first I want to say goodbye to mother and Liz."

Henry's wife had been staying with him at the Freeman house since they returned from their honeymoon. She and Henry's mother entered the living room and walked up to the young man. Both women's eyes seemed full of tears.

"Don't be sad. The war will be over soon and I'll be back home within a few months."

Both women knew that was not likely to happen, but they forced a smile on their countenances so as to reassure Henry. Then the young man leaned towards his mother and kissed her on the cheek. Turning to his wife, he embraced her, pressing his lips against hers for what seemed like an eternity although it was only a couple of minutes.

"Take care, my love. I will pray for your safe return."

"I will miss you, Elizabeth. At least once each week, I'll write you a letter—that is, as long as I'm in a place where I can mail it to you. I spoke to mother and dad, and they said they would love to have you stay with them until I return. Goodbye for now."

Henry turned, walked out of the house with his father. They got into the buggy and drove to the Cleveland train depot. When they arrived, Henry hugged his father, said goodbye, alighted from the buggy, walked into the station and waited for the train. A few minutes later, the train arrived and he boarded it. A few hours later, the conductor called out:

"Next stop is Columbus. We'll arrive in ten minutes."
At the station, Henry noticed a man in military uniform standing nearby, Henry walked up to him and asked:

"Excuse me sir, but do you know how to get to the 30th Ohio Regiment's headquarters from here? I'm supposed to enlist there today."

"It's about two miles down that road over there, son. If you can wait a couple of hours, I'll be going back there and can take you in my buggy."

"No, that's alright. I can walk there. Thanks, anyway."
Henry started walking down the dirt road to the military camp. A half hour later, he arrived at the entrance to the regiment's headquarters. He entered a wooden building bearing a placard stating: "REGIMENTAL COMMANDER'S OFFICE". A soldier in a captain's uniform was seated at a desk outside Colonel Ewing's office.

"Sir, I'm here to see Colonel Ewing. My name is Henry Freeman. I told the colonel that I would be here today to enlist in the 30th Ohio Regiment."

"The Colonel has been away in Washington since mid-January for a meeting with General Joseph Hooker. He's expected to return in a couple of days. But I can sign you up for duty in his absence. Take a seat over there and fill out these papers." [He pointed to a nearby table and chair and handed Henry a background questionnaire].

The papers included questions about Henry's home, marital status, health, education and highest school grade completed. Henry wrote, in answer to the latter question: "Completed first year at Cleveland Medical College." He handed the papers to the Captain, who then asked him to raise his right hand and repeat after him the oath of enlistment.

"Congratulations, young man. You are now a recruit in the 30th Ohio Infantry. You'll have three weeks of basic training at this camp, and then be assigned for duty at wherever the Union Army needs the 30th Ohio. Now, go over to the Quartermaster building next door, where they'll issue you your uniform, musket, canteen and supplies, and assign you to a barracks or tent."

Henry and the officer saluted each other and the new recruit walked to the large wooden warehouse-like building to get his military issue.

At five feet eight inches and one hundred sixty pounds, Henry was average size for a man his age in the mid-1800s. He had been in top physical shape, with daily chores requiring lots of physical labor on the family farm. But, during the past year, most of his time was spent sitting in classes or in the library reading medical literature, so he had lost some of his muscle tone and put on about ten extra pounds. After loading him down with a uniform, boots, a .58 caliber rifle-musket, bayonet, backpack, canteen and blanket, the sergeant at the quartermaster building directed Henry to a wooden barracks about thirty yards away. Entering the barracks, he was greeted by a corporal, who assigned Henry to one of the forty bunks and told him to get into his uniform and, in a half hour, line up outside with the other recruits as they will be going on an eight-mile march.

"Be sure to bring your musket with bayonet attached, and your backpack with all your supplies." As Henry donned his uniform, he thought:

"March eight miles? I've done so little exercise this past year that I'm out of shape. I am not sure that I have the stamina for such a long march, especially after having just walked a couple of miles to get here from the train station."

His musket with bayonet attached weighed more than ten pounds, and his backpack, loaded with his blanket, tin eating utensils and other gear, weighed at least 30 pounds. Each of the heavy black leather boots he had been issued seemed to weigh more than one pound.

"I am gonna have one hell of a time walking even one mile with all of this, let alone eight," he murmured to himself.

One half hour later, at 1:30 p.m., Henry lined up outside the barracks, along with thirty-nine other recruits. A sergeant strode to several feet in front of the group and yelled in a booming voice: "Attenhut! All of you are new recruits. None have ever served in the military before. The army appreciates your patriotism, your willingness

to fight to preserve the Union, its democracy and freedom. But understand this: you are no longer civilians, and the rights and freedom you had in civilian life, DO NOT EXIST IN THE MILITARY."
The recruits became wide-eyed with the realization of the truth of the sergeant's words. They had enlisted so as to preserve the union and democracy. But in joining the army, they had given up their freedom.

"During the next three weeks, we will be training you to prepare for battle. You will learn to do as you are told, without question. Success in battle depends on each soldier following orders. It also depends upon each infantryman being in top physical shape, knowing how to use weapons of war and doing so to the best of his ability. So, get ready for three weeks of grueling physical and mental challenges. We are going to start today with an eight-mile march on the dirt path through that forest over there [pointing to thick woods about one hundred feet distant]. You all should have your canteens filled with water. Take a few sips whenever you need. But once the water is gone, it's gone. There is no place—and no permission—to refill it along the way. One other thing. No supper will be served until you return from the march, no matter how long it takes. So, the sooner you complete the march, the quicker you will eat. Do you understand?"

"Yes sir, sergeant," the recruits responded in unison.

"Alright. Fall in single file behind me and start marching. Hep, one two three four…"

The forty recruits began marching single file behind the sergeant, who led them in counting their steps in a sing/song manner:

"Listen to us, traitor Jefferson Davis and your General Lee, We Yankees are gonna defeat you and the Rebel army. Sound off one, two, three, four…"

Halfway through the march, Henry's feet hurt, his legs felt weak, and he stepped out of the line of march to momentarily rest and regain his strength. Seeing this, a corporal who had been walking alongside the marching soldiers, watching out for stragglers, strode towards him.

"What's the matter, soldier? What's your name and why did you step out of the line?"

"My name is Henry Freeman, sir. I'm not used to such strenuous physical exercise. I guess I've gotten out of shape, going to medical school and mostly sitting during the past year. My feet and legs are killing me."

"That's a damned shame, son," the corporal mockingly replied. Some nearby recruits chuckled as the corporal glared at Henry and angrily said: "You're in the army now. You were told you've gotta obey orders. So, I'm ordering you now to get the fuck back in line, stop your whimpering, weak excuses. Start marching now, or you'll regret what's in store for you."

Henry felt the hair on the back of his neck rise up as he momentarily was overcome with fear. He called on every ounce of will power, saying to himself: "Come on, you can do it. Move." He got back in the line of march. Despite the cool weather with temperatures in the 45-degree range, he began to sweat profusely. At about 5:00 p.m. the line of soldiers returned to the 30th Regiment's headquarters, having completed the march. The sergeant told them they had forty-five minutes to wash up and report to the mess hall for chow. About 5:45 p.m., when Henry arrived at the dining hall, there was a long line of recruits, picking up tin trays and then proceeding through the food line while servers loaded the compartments of their trays with carrots, corn, beans, a slice of ham, a piece of hard tack bread with butter, and a cup of coffee. The famished soldiers ate every bit of the food as if it had been cooked by a gourmet chef.

Before they left the dining hall, the sergeant announced that, since it was their first day, he was going to let them off early. But tomorrow would be a full day of training in the use of their muskets and bayonets. Henry returned to his barracks, lay down on his bunk, exhausted, and soon fell sound asleep.

CHAPTER 6:

HENRY REALIZES HE'S NOT CUT OUT FOR THE INFANTRY

At 6:30 a.m., a half hour before sunrise, Henry was awakened by the sound of a bugler playing reveille. He had been asleep, lying in his uniform on his bunk since about 6 p.m. yesterday. The sergeant opened the barracks' door and shouted:

"Wake up, recruits. Get up, put on your uniforms, and line up outside in a half hour."

Henry thought:

"No problem. I've already got my uniform on," as he was the first soldier from his barracks to walk outside. When they all stood in line, the sergeant walked to his place about six feet distant from the center of the line and addressed the troops.

"Now hear this, men. Each of you will have to do ten pushups and then five chin-ups on the bar in front of the entrance to the mess hall, before eating breakfast. If you fail to do that, no chow. Understand?"

"Yes Sir, sergeant."

"Don't dilly-dally eating, men. One hour from now you are to line up here with your muskets, bayonets, and canteens filled with water. We are going to spend most of the day at the range, doing target practice."

The recruits ate what was to be the standard breakfast: an egg, hard tack, couple of slices of bacon, milk, coffee and an apple. At 8 a.m., they marched about a mile to a large open field. On the ground on one side was a row of forty 2 by 4s, and about fifty yards in front of them were forty round targets, each three feet in diameter and raised two feet off the ground. The sergeant demonstrated how to use the rifle-muskets.

"You lie down on your stomach, facing the target, with your left hand holding the rifle up about a foot beyond the trigger, with the butt of the weapon resting against your right shoulder, near your cheek, as you look down the sight and aim at the target."

"Sarge, what do you do if you're a lefty, like me?" one recruit called out.

"Do like I said, but with the butt of the rifle resting against your left shoulder and holding the rifle up with your right hand and the index finger of your left hand on the trigger," replied the instructor. "When you pull the trigger, the hammer strikes a small metal cap inside of which is some mercury, which explodes, igniting the gunpowder in the barrel. That drives the cone-shaped lead minnie ball down the spiral-grooved barrel towards the target. It's very accurate shooting at an object up to 50 yards away." He pulled the trigger and hit the bulls-eye on a target.

"Now I'll show you the steps you have to take to reload and fire the musket each time after you've shot a bullet. With practice, if you do it correctly, you should be able to load and fire a Minnie-ball in less than one minute."

The recruits spent the next three hours practicing loading and firing the muskets from the lying position, and then another hour from a standing position. At first, most of the recruits missed the targets or just hit the outer of four circles. After a half hour, most began to hit one of the two inner circles, and about five of the soldiers frequently hit the bulls-eye.

"You guys are sharpshooters", the sergeant told the five. "The army really needs more like you. You guys will have special assignments and privileges."

Horace did not like to hunt. He never taught his son how to use a rifle. So, Henry was at a disadvantage when compared to most of the recruits, who for years had hunted for sport and food. In target practice, he could not seem to do any better than hitting the outer edge of the second circle from the bulls-eye. To the amusement of some of the recruits, the sergeant tried to motivate him to do better, shouting:

"C'mon, Freeman. What are you, blind? Do as I told ya and you'll get closer to the bulls-eye. If you don't learn to do better than that, your life won't be worth shit on the front lines."

That just served to embarrass Henry, not inspire him. The more the instructor taunted him, the more difficult target practice seemed to Henry. Nearly three hours after the start of practice, his right arm was painful and he noticed he had bruises from his wrist to the top of his elbow.

"The recoil's injured my right arm. It hurts like hell."

"Don't be a cry-baby, Freeman. Most of the troops have the same problem."

"Yeh? Well the barrel of my musket is hot as Hades."

"That's normal, soldier, when you've fired 50 or more shots in a couple of hours. Get used to it. But if it gets too hot, it could misfire. If that happens during battle, you look around to see if there is a fallen comrade nearby, and get his rifle and use it. If not, the only alternative is to take a break and let it cool down. But that could cost you your life in a battle."

Henry thought, "Jeez, maybe I made a mistake joining the infantry. I'm really not cut out for this."

The sergeant said: "Colonel Ewing's back from Washington. I'm gonna take you to see him this afternoon, after we return to camp. Your performance is about the worst of these recruits. He'll have to see what can be done about that."

Late that afternoon, the sergeant accompanied Henry to Colonel Ewing's office. The recruit saluted the colonel and sat down at a chair in front of his desk.

"The sergeant tells me you're having difficulty keeping up with your fellow recruits, Freeman…"

"I'm sorry, Colonel. You see, unlike the others, my dad never taught me how to use a rifle. He doesn't hunt…"

"What does he do, son?"

"He's a doctor—a surgeon."

"Has he taught you anything about medicine?"

"Well, he did, for about a half year, a couple of years ago. I assisted him in several surgeries. Then I enrolled in the Cleveland College of Medicine and completed my first year, right before I joined the 30th Regiment."

"I was reading that in the papers you filled out when you signed up. When I was in Washington, General Hooker told me that Dr. Letterman, the Medical Director of the Army, established an Ambulance Corps which would provide each regiment with two wagons—one with medical supplies and the other for transporting wounded soldiers. Up to three Medical Corpsmen would be assigned to each regiment, as well as a doctor with the rank of Surgeon Major and another as his assistant. Division level hospitals with tents to accommodate up to one hundred wounded, staffed by several doctors, nurses and cooks, are also being established. And in times of battle, small tents close by with several bunks and an operating table will be set up. One or two doctors, a hospital steward, and possibly a nurse, will be assigned to those regimental hospitals. All of this has increased dramatically the need for doctors and other medical personnel. Hooker requested that I advise him if the 30th had any such people available."

A smile began to appear on Henry's face as he thought: "I hope this means what I think it means," as Ewing continued.

"When your sergeant told me of the problems you are experiencing in basic training, and your background and education, the first thing that came to my mind was that you'd be an asset to the army in the Medical Corps instead of being a liability in the infantry. So, I am transferring you to the Medical Corps."

"Thank you, Colonel. I agree that I'd be far more valuable to the Army Medical Corps than I could ever be to the infantry."

"You understand that you will still have to complete infantry basic training. It's not unusual for regiment hospitals, and even sometimes division hospitals, to be overrun by enemy forces during battle. For your own safety, as well as for your regiment, it's advisable that you complete basic training."

"I understand, sir."

"Well, do your best for the rest of the three weeks you are here. I will notify Hooker that, as soon as you have completed basic training, I will send you wherever he deems you are needed most, to serve in the Medical corps."

Elated, Henry saluted the colonel, turned and walked out of the office and back to his barracks. He promptly took a pen and paper, sat down on the edge of his bunk, and wrote a letter to his wife.

"Dear Liz,
Army life has proved a lot harder than I ever anticipated.
Yesterday, we had to walk at a fast pace, eight miles through the woods. What made it most difficult was that we wore our uniforms, including heavy leather boots, our backpack loaded with about thirty pounds of supplies, and carried our musket and bayonet, which weighed another twelve pounds.

After a year of sedentary life at Medical College and studying, I realize I was in poor physical shape for such strenuous exercise.

I had difficulty keeping up with the rest of the troops, and the sergeant and his assistant singled me out, ridiculing my lack of stamina in a nearly failed attempt to inspire me to try harder. I finally did complete the march and fell asleep, exhausted. Today, we learned how to fire our muskets and spent several hours at the target range. Unlike most of my fellow recruits, I never learned how to use a rifle. After an hour or so, I began to get the hang of it and finally started hitting the target. But my accuracy left a lot to be desired. While most of the recruits generally hit the inner two circles or bullseye, at best I could only hit the outer two circles and occasionally missed the target altogether. Once more, the sergeant tried to motivate me by ridicule and warnings about the dangers I'd face in battle. All that did was to discourage me, make me feel inadequate, and question why I ever joined the army.

But things all turned out fine. Late today, Colonel Ewing, who just returned from Washington, said General Hooker told him the Army had a desperate need for more doctors and medical personnel. Considering my training under my dad, and my one year of medical school, he thought I'd fit the bill. So, after I complete my three weeks of basic training, he's going to re-assign me to the Medical Corps. I'll not only be able to serve my country in the best capacity for my abilities and education, but also gain lots of experience in my chosen field.

I hope everyone is well back home. How are you and mother spending the days? If you have some free time, the soldiers would love to get baked goods or fresh fruit and vegetables— apples, pears, carrots, potatoes, etc.—from home. Anything that wouldn't spoil in a two-week trip to us soldiers. Army food is kind of bland, tasteless. We almost never get cookies, cake, fresh fruit or vegetables. Anyway, it's just a thought. Maybe you and mother could get together with some of the women and send a few boxes of baked goods, fruit and vegetables to some soldiers.

*I miss you and love you. Please give my love to mom and dad.
Your loving husband,
Henry."*

The time seemed to go very fast during the rest of Henry's basic training. He did his best, but was no longer upset by his poor performance. He looked forward to joining the Medical Corps. Neither the sergeant nor his fellow recruits heckled him anymore. They all realized that, in his new position, he would be likely to save the lives of servicemen like them in times of battle.

CHAPTER 7:

ASSIGNED TO THE MEDICAL CORPS IN VIRGINIA

It was early in the morning of February 24, 1863. Henry's company of 100 men had just completed their basic training and were awaiting orders of assignment to one of the Union corps opposing the Confederate Army. The sergeant entered the barracks and shouted:

"Private Henry Freeman, report immediately to Colonel Ewing's office to receive your orders of assignment."
Henry, who had been sitting on the edge of his bunk, arose and walked out of the barracks to Regimental Headquarters. Standing at attention in front of Colonel Ewings' desk, he saluted:

"Private Freeman reporting to receive my orders, sir."

"At ease, private. You have been assigned as a medical corpsman at the divisional hospital attached to the XI Army Corps at its winter quarters in Stafford, Virginia. You will be under the command of the Surgeon-in-Chief. The XI Corps is part of the Army of the Potomac, commanded by General Joseph Hooker. Say, do you happen to speak German?"

"No. Why?"

"It's really not that important. Forget I asked. Well, here's your train tickets to Washington. It's about an eleven-day trip to D.C. From there you'll have an officer escort you to the divisional hospital. Good luck."

Twelve days later, on March 8, Henry and his escort, a corporal, dismounted from their horses in front of a huge tent in Stafford, Virginia.

"This is it—the divisional hospital."

They walked inside. Henry had never seen a tent so large. It had about a hundred bunks, but only twenty-five had patients lying in them. There was a dirt floor. Two nurses were tending to the patients. The corporal asked one of the nurses:

"Ma'm, can you tell me where I can find the Surgeon-in-Chief of this hospital?"

"That would be Doctor Adams. His office is over there "[pointing to a wood enclosure at a far end of the tent].

"I'm going to leave now," the corporal said, as Henry entered the small office, saluted, and then spoke to the middle-aged gentleman seated behind a desk:

"Doctor Adams, my name is Henry Freeman and I have been assigned as a medical corpsman to work under your command. Here are my orders."

Adams inquired about Henry's education and training. "Seems like you are qualified to take care of minor medical problems, as well as assist the surgeons during operations. Let me show you around the hospital and the tent where your sleeping quarters are. Tomorrow morning at 0630 you are to report to Surgeon Major Harris, who you will assist."

Henry had a look of satisfaction on his face. He finally was going to get a chance to put his education and skills to work.

At 5:30 a.m. the following morning, the shrill sound of the bugle playing reveille awakened Henry from a deep sleep. After putting on his uniform, he walked outside his small tent. It stood in a row of a couple of hundred white tents, the outlines of which were barely visible in the dim light of the full moon. Patches of snow still remained on the ground, giving the land a quilt-like black and white appearance. Henry turned up the collar of his jacket to shelter his neck from the cold wind that made the ambient temperature seem even lower than forty degrees. He walked about one hundred yards to the mess hall, entered and had his breakfast. He then walked about another hundred yards to the divisional hospital tent. Entering the small office of Surgeon Major Harris, he saluted and said:

"Private Freeman reporting for duty, sir."

"No need to be so formal, private. You are in the Medical Corps now. Leave the formality to the infantry. You can call me Major Harris and, if it's alright with you, I'll refer to you as Henry."

Encouraged by the friendliness and informality of his commanding officer, Henry replied: "That is fine with me, sir."

"Fortunately, we are in our temporary winter quarters with no military action going on now. So, we have only twenty-five patients and no surgeries scheduled today. That will probably change within a month or so when the army starts its spring offensive."

"What do you want me to do now, Major Harris?"

Harris handed the private a couple of pencils and some blank papers entitled "Examination of_____", and said:

"Make the rounds of all twenty-five patients. At the foot of each bunk is an envelope containing daily entries of the diagnosis and treatment of each. Talk to the patient, ask how he is feeling, any complaints or pain, and stuff like that. Then examine him and add your findings and recommendations to the examination sheet, which you are to initial and date. If you think anyone needs immediate care or treatment, report back to me."

"Are there any other things I need to know before starting my rounds, Major Harris?"

"Oh, yes. I forgot to mention. At about 8 o'clock two nurses will be reporting for work. Actually, only one is a nurse. She had no formal education in nursing. There's only one nursing school in the entire country. But she did have on-the-job training for several years in the office of a well-known doctor, Randall Smith, in Philadelphia. Doctor Smith is a prominent graduate of the University of Pennsylvania Medical School, the first medical school in our country, where I also received my medical degree. Her name is Alice Hunter. She is extremely competent and hard-working. The other so-called "nurse", Gertie Steinmeyer, has no education or training in nursing. In fact, she was a milkmaid on her parents' farm just outside of Stafford, until three weeks ago, when she volunteered her services caring for the sick and wounded. Her parents are German immigrants and she speaks their native language fluently. She is young—only 18—and has little medical knowledge or experience. But most of our patients, about half of whom are of German descent, adore her. She is very pretty, gregarious, and what she lacks in medical training she more than makes up for in caring for the patients and cheering them up. She probably will need some guidance from you in caring for the sick and wounded."

"I'll keep an eye on her, Major, and help train her in the proper care of her patients."

Henry turned and walked into the main ward of the hospital to begin checking on the patients.

CHAPTER 8:

AT THE DIVISIONAL HOSPITAL IN STAFFORD, VIRGINIA

There were fifty bunks in a row on each side of the huge tent. Only twenty-five, all on the left side, were occupied. As the Medical Corps private approached the first bunk, he noticed that the occupant appeared to be asleep. Henry opened the envelope at the foot of the bunk and began reading the examination sheets. The patient was Corporal Diepold Friedland, age 28, who had been admitted to the hospital three days earlier after complaining to his company commander of stomach pains, mild nausea and diarrhea. The diagnosis was dysentery and Dr. Harris had recommended bed rest, one pint of liquid [coffee, tea, water or apple juice] every waking hour and small amounts of food every couple of hours so long as the patient was able to tolerate it without vomiting. Subsequent entries showed slight improvement in his condition [less frequent bowel movements, less nausea]. As Henry reached out and touched the man's forehead to see if he had a fever, the corporal suddenly woke up and exclaimed with a slight German accent:

"Who in Hell are you and what are you doing?"

"I am Private Henry Freeman of the Medical Corps, and I was just attempting to see if you had a fever. I am under orders to examine you and write my findings on the examination sheet."

"What happened to the nurse? Her mother is German, she speaks the language and is prettier than you. I prefer her doing the medical exam. Do you sprechen ze Deutsch?"

"If you are asking if I speak German, the answer is 'No'. But I have medical training. I have assisted my father, a surgeon, in operations, and I have completed one year of medical school. I interrupted my education—I was just one year away from getting my M.D. degree—to join the army. So, let me conduct my examination cause I have a very busy day with twenty four other patients to examine. Now, what complaints or symptoms do you have today?"

"For the first time in days, I don't feel like I'm going to vomit. In fact, I am kind of hungry and thirsty now."

"What would you like to drink?"

"Some coffee."

"When the nurse shows up, I will tell her to get you some coffee and a light breakfast. Any other complaints?"

"Yeh. Two. First, when I joined the XI Corps of General McClellan's Army of the Potomac, it was part of the Grand Division under Major General Franz Sigel. About half of the Corps were German immigrants or, like me, sons of immigrants. Sigel was of German stock, spoke German, and was popular with the troops. We used to say with pride: 'We fights mit Sigel.' But a lot of the rest of the Corps were prejudiced—called us 'Dumb Dutch' or 'Dutch cowards'. They held Germans in contempt. After Hooker replaced McClellan, he disbanded the Grand Division, pushed Sigel into retirement, and put the arrogant, strict discipline, prejudiced teetotaler, born-again Christian Major General Oliver Howard in command of the XI Corps. That dumb ass wasted our time making us clean up our bunks, polishing our shoes, and cleaning our uniforms for frequent inspections instead of practicing shooting at the target range."

"A word of caution, soldier. You're in the army. You don't have the freedom you had in civilian life. You gotta respect and obey your superiors, not criticize them. Especially a General—you could face severe punishment."

"Listen, that jackass sent one of his Captains to lecture us on the evils of alcohol. He called good German beer 'the devil's brew'."

Upon hearing the corporal's remarks, Henry understood why Colonel Ewing had asked if he spoke German. He cautioned Friedland:

"Maybe so, but I think you would be wise to keep your opinions to yourself. Anyway, when I asked if you had any complaints, I didn't mean those kinds of complaints."

"Yeh? Well it felt good to get it off my chest. I have another complaint. I heard that, about a week ago, Congress passed a Draft Law with a provision that a draftee can get a substitute to serve in his place or pay the government three hundred dollars so as not to be drafted. If that had been in effect when I joined about ten months ago, I could have offered to join in place of some rich guy and gotten a few hundred dollars from him—more than a half of a year's pay—for doing that. As it is, the army is about three weeks behind in paying us our thirteen bucks weekly salary."

"I am sorry to hear that. But I'm not the one for you to make the complaint to. And if I were you, I would not complain about that to your commanding officer. Sometimes, life is just unfair. But I have good news. You're doing well. You've almost got the disease licked. I'm going to make an entry on your records that if your diarrhea seems gone tomorrow, you can be released and return to your regiment."

"Great," thought the recovering patient. "Instead of returning to my regiment, I'll desert, go home, and offer my services to some wealthy coward who is subject to the draft, as a substitute enlistee in return for two hundred seventy dollars." [In fact, after Congress passed the draft law, many thousands of men received pay from wealthy men who were about to be drafted, for substituting in their place, deserted the army at the first opportunity and then offered their services as a substitute enlistee to some other wealthy individual. It became so common that the army authorized the shooting of any soldier caught attempting to desert.]

Henry made notations on the medical records about his examination of Corporal Friedland, placed them in the envelope at the foot of the bunk, and moved on to the next patient, who also was nearly recovered from a bout with dysentery. Before he moved on to examine another patient, the two nurses arrived. They approached Henry, introduced themselves, and asked if there was anything he needed them to do before they commenced their usual daily routine.

"No, thanks", Henry said. "I'll let you know if I need your assistance."

The two women proceeded to perform their usual duties, starting with gathering the bedpans and urinals that had been placed on the ground at the side of each bed, emptying them in pails, and then carrying the pails outside to empty their contents in the "sinks" [large ditches under the latrines located near the stream at the far south end of the encampment].

"Phew. Thank heaven those stinkin' things are gone. Cool fresh outside air is blowing in through the vents," Henry thought. [The vents were large flaps running horizontally across most of the length of two sides of the tent. They could be raised by pulling on strings at each end, so as to provide ventilation.]

He was to diagnose seven more patients with dysentery in various stages. The last two of them had high fevers, severe dehydration, extreme nausea, tenderness and swelling of the intestinal area, and foul-smelling bloody stools. Their medical records indicated that, for the past several days they had been given a dose of opium at night to reduce intestinal contractions, and daily doses of Calomel [a sweet-tasting mixture of honey, chalk and mercury]. In the mid-1800s, doctors were unaware of the poisonous effects of mercury, and they commonly used Calomel as a remedy for a number of diseases. Henry noted on the medical records that those two patients complained that most of their hair and teeth had fallen out. He attributed that to their extreme cases of dysentery, unaware that those were really symptoms of mercury poisoning. He reported his findings to Major Harris, who agreed with Henry's prognosis that the two were likely to die within a week. Of the rest of the patients, Henry concluded that ten had a common cold, but that he believed two of those had developed into pneumonia; and three had symptoms of typhoid, which in those days resulted in death in one out of every three cases.

The remaining three patients had been placed in bunks at the far end of the row of beds, to isolate them from the other patients. According to their medical records, the person who examined them was uncertain of their illness, but presumed it to be either measles or smallpox, and had placed the initials "GS" on the medical records. Henry had measles as a child and his father had vaccinated him against smallpox, which preventive measure had been available since its discovery by Dr. Jenner more than a half century earlier. Henry therefore was certain he had lifetime immunity from both diseases, so he conducted a thorough examination of each patient. They said they had fever, headache, fatigue, back pain and nausea for several days before being sent to the hospital. Within a few days after their admission, red spots appeared on their face, hands and forearms. The following day, the spots turned into blisters filled with clear fluid. Henry observed that scabs were forming on the blisters. He concluded that the patients had obvious symptoms of smallpox and that whoever had made the diagnosis that they might be suffering from measles was dead wrong and his mistake had undoubtedly resulted in a lack of proper treatment.

"What a stupid and potentially deadly mistake for a doctor to make," Henry thought. "I'm going to report that Doctor G. S.to Major Harris, before he really screws up and causes permanent injury or the death of a patient." Just then, it occurred to him, "Wait a minute. 'GS'. Could that be the so-called nurse, Gertie Steinmeyer? She may be pretty, but she's a milkmaid, not a nurse. She has no business tending to sick and wounded soldiers. They deserve better care than that."

There was another reason Henry was irritated. He had completed one year of medical school and had some training in surgery. More than half of the doctors in the nation never even went to medical school. They were only trained by another doctor for as little as one month to a couple of years before holding themselves out as doctors. A majority of the Army surgeons fell into that category. They all were given the rank of commissioned officers. But Henry, despite his superior education and training, was only a Private in the Medical Corps. Now, a milkmaid was called a nurse and given some work that should have been reserved for medical doctors. This irritated Henry no end.

Henry grasped the medical record with the erroneous diagnoses and briskly walked to the other end of the hospital and stood at the foot of the bunk where the young nurse was tending to a patient.

"Miss Steinmeyer, could you come here for a moment?"

She walked towards Henry, saying, "Yes, Dr. Freeman. What do you want?"

Henry showed her the medical record, placing his index finger next to the diagnoses with the initials "GS".

"Did you make this entry? Are those your initials?"

She replied, "Yes, Dr. Freeman."

Henry's voice grew louder, as he angrily said: "First of all, I am not a doctor—yet. I have had training in surgery and have completed my first year of medical school, and have but one year left before I get my degree. But, as I have been informed, you have no medical training or education. You were just a milkmaid until less than one month ago. You have no business diagnosing a patient's illness, which could result in improper treatment. If you make any entries in his medical records, it should be limited to what a patient tells you or what a doctor instructs you to enter. Do you understand?"

The young woman's face began to blush with embarrassment, her hands began to tremble, tears welled up in her eyes, as she exclaimed:

"I'm sorry, Dr. Freeman. There was no doctor on duty that day. Major Harris told me to talk to each patient, ask his symptoms, and record them and my observations in the records."

"I am sure the Major never intended for you to make a diagnosis of what ails any patient. As far as I'm concerned, you don't belong here. You're attractive, pleasant, but incompetent as a nurse. You should be home, getting married to some young man, cooking, cleaning and raising children."

Appearing distraught, the young woman ran down the aisle towards Major Harris' office. Having witnessed the scolding Henry gave Gertie, the patient to whom she had been attending shouted out:

"You didn't need to get Gertie so upset, Doc. She's a nice young woman, trying to do her best for us soldiers. I hope she doesn't quit because of your crappy treatment of her. In the old country we call men like you 'schveinhunts'."

Henry didn't understand the language but figured that meant something like 'pig-dog.'

Ten minutes later, Gertie returned, walked up to Henry, and said: "Major Harris says he wants to see you immediately, Dr. Freeman."

Still irritated, Henry turned and walked to Harris' office.

"Sit down Freeman and tell me what started this brouhaha." Henry related the incident, emphasizing that the young woman had no education or training in medicine, was not really a nurse, had no business diagnosing a patient's illness and entering it in the medical records.

"I see, Freeman. What would you have us call the woman?

Maybe a servant or maid. Would that make you less angry? I should mention that we have a shortage of doctors as well as nurses. On the day in question, the doctor who you replaced had just been reassigned to another unit. So, I told the young woman to make the rounds and make entries in the records."
Henry began to regret the incident.

"Your chastising her almost caused her to quit her volunteer work. Let me emphasize the word 'volunteer'. She does NOT get paid. She works hard and does work that I'm sure you would never do, like gathering the patients' putrid waste and emptying it in the latrines. Well, let me assure you that, if she quits, I will order you to do that task until I can find a replacement, is that clear?"
Reluctantly, Henry said: "Yes sir."

The Major continued: "She brings food and water to the ill and wounded, makes their beds, reads to them, writes letters for them, cheers them up. They love her, and I dare say her effect on their recovery is at least as important as our medicine, some of which I suspect does patients more harm than good. Yet you seem to want to get rid of the woman?"

The Major's angry words struck Henry like a bolt of lightning. He realized that he would never willingly do a lot of the dirty work performed by Gertie, like gathering and emptying human waste. The Army was fortunate to have young women like her who volunteered to take on such jobs with no pay and tend to and cheer up the ill and wounded soldiers. Embarrassed at ever having caused the incident, Henry said:

"Oh, no sir. I overreacted. Forgive me. I will apologize to Gertie."

"Glad to hear that, Henry. Now return to your work and remember that we are all here to work together to help the Union defeat the Confederacy and restore our nation."

Henry promptly walked over to where Gertie was tending to a patient, apologized, and assured her that he was pleased with her tireless efforts on behalf of the ill soldiers.

Later that day, a tall man who appeared to be in his forties, with long grey hair down to his neck, a receding hairline, large sideburns, beard and a thick mustache that nearly hid his mouth, approached Henry. His right hand was grasping a notebook.

"Are you Private Freeman?" he asked.

"Yes, what do you want?"

"Major Harris told me you might be able to help me. I'm looking for my older brother. I read in the newspaper that he was wounded in a clash with Confederate troops in northern Virginia. I've been visiting several of the army hospitals trying to locate him. His name is George, and here's a picture of him," he said, opening up the notebook he was carrying.

"No, sorry, I haven't seen any soldier who looks like him. Besides, right now we have no wounded soldiers here—only sick ones. But I've only been stationed here for a short time. Maybe that nurse over there [pointing]—Alice Hunter—might have seen him".

"Thanks. Here's my name and address in Washington. [The man handed Henry a paper.] I'd appreciate you sending me a message if you do see him. "

Henry looked at the paper and saw the man's name.

"I'll let you know if I see or hear of your brother George, Mr. Whitman. Hope you find him soon."

It wasn't until a couple of weeks later, when Henry mentioned the incident to Major Harris, that he learned Walt Whitman was a famous poet.

Returning to his tent that evening, Henry lit a couple of candles and wrote a letter to his wife, but not mentioning his altercation with the young nurse.

"Dearest Liz,

Today I spent nearly eleven hours doing purported medical work at the divisional hospital. In fact, much of it was just making notations on the records of the complaints of each patient, their symptoms, and general information they gave me, which was mostly about army life and their observations and opinions of their superiors [which I did not include in my notations]. I spent an average of about a half hour with each patient, and less than ten minutes of that was doing what I consider to be a doctor's work, namely examining, diagnosing and making recommendations or prognosis. I felt that much of my education and training is being wasted, as most of my time was spent writing entries in the records—a task that could have been performed by a nurse or secretary. If things keep on like that, in a few weeks I will talk to Major Harris about it.

It's been cold but sunny here. The patches of snow on the ground are melting and it looks like spring will soon arrive. I've been told that, when that happens, we'll move out of our winter quarters and the army will begin an offensive against Confederate General Lee's army. Several of the patients I interviewed today complained about General Howard, who is commander of the XI Army corps. They say he is an evangelical Christian, teetotaler, morality enforcer, and a strict disciplinarian, more interested in making sure his men have clean uniforms, polished boots and shoes, than training in weaponry and battle tactics. I don't understand how he can get along with his superior, General Hooker, who seems the direct opposite of Howard. General Hooker's nickname is 'fighting Joe'. He has the reputation of being a battle-hardened soldier and a hard-drinking man who throws parties with camp-follower women. It's rumored that that is why some journalists refer to prostitutes as 'hookers'.

How is everything at home? Are you and mother doing anything to help the war effort? The men here miss good home-baked apple pie and cookies. The army doesn't feed us any desserts. The only vegetables we get are corn, beans, and an occasional potato. If you and mom could send me a box of cookies, cake and maybe an apple pie, and some vegetables like carrots or turnips, I'd really appreciate it. Even better, if you could organize a group of ladies to do that and send boxes of that stuff to me, I'd distribute it among the troops.
Give my love to mom and dad. I miss you very much.
With all my love,
Henry"

CHAPTER 9:

HENRY REQUESTS TO BE ASSIGNED TO A FIELD HOSPITAL NEAR A BATTLE

By March 17, 1863, more than one week after Henry had begun working at the divisional hospital, he had become tired of the daily routine of entering notations in the medical records of each patient. Henry didn't mind examining and diagnosing each patient, but spending several hours each day making entries in their medical records seemed like a waste of time. Those clerical tasks should be left to nurses—even so-called nurses like Gertie. A doctor's time was just too valuable for menial tasks like that. He resolved to discuss the matter with Major Harris that morning, before making his rounds.

"You still have one more year of medical school before you become a doctor, Henry, but you think you're too good to do such 'menial work.' I know, probably half of the doctors in the army never even went to medical school. They just had on-the-job training from other doctors. But you see, shortly after the war began, the Surgeon General determined that we should keep accurate records of the illnesses and disease contracted by our soldiers, the wounds sustained in battle, the treatment provided, and those who recovered and those who died. Among the important things that taught us was that more than twice the number of deaths resulted from disease than from wounds sustained in battle; that large numbers of illness and death from smallpox resulted from troops that had never been vaccinated."

"Why, since smallpox vaccine has been available for over half a century?"

"Good question. Because some groups spread rumors of ill-effects or even coming down with the disease due to vaccinations, so many states exempted people objecting to the requirement of vaccination. And many army commanders ignored the orders for vaccinations."

"Well, what does that have to do with the record-keeping requirement, Major?"

"Reviews of the records is how we found out those things. You should not merely make the records I have ordered. You should also review them, make comparisons, and draw conclusions.
Several months ago, the U.S. Sanitary Commission sent a surgeon to our winter encampment to ascertain why so many troops came down with dysentery. He found several latrines had been built upstream from the camp, that the ditches beneath them were not being covered daily with a layer of earth. He concluded that, during heavy rains, the human waste runoff entered the stream that provides drinking water for the troops. He advised relocating each regiment's latrine downstream from the camp."

"If that's true and the advice was correct, why do we still have so many cases of dysentery?"

"Because some colonels ignored the orders, others didn't want to make their soldiers walk a mile or more to relieve themselves. The medical records show a considerable decline in the number of soldiers suffering from dysentery in those regiments that followed the Sanitary Commission doctor's advice."

Henry realized that he had been wrong in complaining about having to spend so much time making entries in the medical records. He resolved to review the records of each patient, compare them with those of others suffering similar illnesses, and see if they might indicate better methods of treatment, better or worse medications, and foods that might provide better nutrition. In so doing, Henry was taking a first step through the door to modern medicine and scientific experiment.

As he examined each patient that day, Henry not only made entries in the records, but also compared the records with those of other patients with similar illnesses. He noticed a difference in treatment and results among those with dysentery whose cases were mild or recovering, from the two who were now on the verge of death. The condition of the latter was not only rapidly deteriorating, but their faces were painfully distorted and they had lost all of their hair and teeth. The one difference in treatment was that they had been receiving daily doses of Calomel. Henry, like all doctors of that time, was unaware of the poisonous effects of mercury, but made a notation in the records that

Calomel was no longer to be administered to patients suffering from dysentery."

He reported his findings to Major Harris, who agreed with him. It was too late to save the lives of the two patients, but undoubtedly saved the lives of many future patients ill with dysentery in the divisional hospital.

As springtime drew near, word spread through the camp that General Hooker's army would soon be relocating to Falmouth, Virginia, a couple of miles north of the heavily fortified Confederate city of Fredericksburg, to do battle with General Lee's Army of the Confederacy. Wanting to hone his skills in surgery, Henry asked Major Harris if he could get him reassigned to a regimental hospital near the proposed site of battle. Harris had seen the horrors of war while serving as a surgeon at a regimental hospital in December, 1862, at the first Battle of Fredericksburg, where 12,000 Union soldiers were casualties in a Confederate victory. He wanted to spare the young doctor from living through such Hell. But Henry was so persistent that the Major finally said:

"All right. I'll do as you wish. But I will ask General Hooker to promote you to the rank of Captain. You'll need that to make certain that soldiers of lower rank will follow your orders and requests during battle. With the current shortage of doctors, I'm certain Hooker will grant my request."

A few days later, the General's order promoting Henry was received. Major Harris sent him to the quartermaster's building to pick up his Captain's uniform, his Military Surgery Manual by Dr. Gress, and his surgeon's kit. Harris reviewed the contents of the kit with Henry: the surgical set containing bullet forceps; extractors including forceps with an expanding wire tip to grab mini ball bullets; a ceramic tip locator to find the mini ball by feel and mark the location; a scoop tip to remove a bullet; a saw for cutting bone; a needle and thread; tweezers; and a tourniquet used to apply pressure on an artery to stop or reduce bleeding. The instruments came in a black leather bag on which was engraved the name: "Captain Henry Freeman, U.S. Army Medical Corps." The Major explained to Henry how to use each instrument. He also gave Henry the standard West Point book on treatment of various illnesses and how to conduct surgeries [most notably, amputations].

Henry thanked Major Harris, saluted, and left the Major's office. Harris thought:

"Poor bastard. He doesn't realize the Hell he's getting himself into. I still have nightmares from my experience at Fredericksburg."

CHAPTER 10:

IS THERE NO ONE WHO CAN LEAD THE ARMY TO VICTORY?

George B. McClellan was a major general in the Union Army who had organized the Army of the Potomac, which protected Washington D.C. and operated in northern Virginia. His careful planning, preparation and attention to details resulted in a well-trained and organized army. But he lacked the aggressiveness and daring that was characteristic of Confederate General Robert E. Lee and constantly speculated that the Confederates had far more troops than the Union Army. Out of an abundance of caution fueled by such speculation, he repeatedly hesitated to attack Lee's Army of Northern Virginia and demanded reinforcements, despite the Union forces outnumbering Lee's by more than two to one [134,000 to 61,000]. When he finally did move cautiously against the Confederate Army and came within several miles of Richmond, the Confederate capital, in late July, 1862, General Lee's Army routed the much larger Army of the Potomac.

In September of 1862, Lee and 38,000 of his troops invaded Maryland. Major General McClellan with 75,500 men commenced a three-pronged attack against the right and left flanks and center of Lee's army near Antietam Creek on September 17. The Union forces broke through the center of the Rebel lines, but McClellan cautiously kept about 38,000 of his men in reserve, away from the battle, and failed to take advantage of the breakthrough. Finally, Confederate General Hill's division arrived, counter-attacked, driving back the Union Army, and the battle ended. Lee withdrew his army back into Virginia. The two armies suffered a total of nearly 23,000 dead and wounded [the Union forces lost 2,000 more than the Confederates]. Even today, Antietam stands as the bloodiest one-day battle in U.S. history.

McClellan's overly cautious behavior, constantly overestimating the number of opposing forces and using that as an excuse not to attack, infuriated Lincoln and his cabinet. The last straw was his failure to pursue Lee's Army when it retreated into Virginia after Antietam. Lincoln removed him from the command of the Army of the Potomac.

Most of the generals in the Union and Confederate Armies, especially those who had attended West Point, followed the Napoleonic era military tactics and rules of combat taught at the Military Academy as set forth in the West Point Manuals, such as Hardee's Infantry Tactics [used by Confederate generals], McClellan's Bayonet Exercise, and Casey's Infantry Tactic. As prescribed in those manuals and Military Academy classes, the troops would march towards the enemy in close formation. When they reached about one hundred yards from the enemy's position, the front row would fire its muskets and then kneel down to reload, as the next row would fire its weapons, and so on, while continuing to move forward. Then, when close to the opposing force, they would attack with fixed bayonets. But such tactics had become obsolete and suicidal with the introduction of new weapons: the rifled musket with Minnie-ball, which were made standard issue to the U.S. infantry by order of Secretary of War Jefferson Davis in 1855 [yes, a little over five years later he was to become President of the Confederacy]; and the Springfield and similar rifles, which were far more accurate and had a much further range [500 yards] than the musket [50 yards].

Unfortunately, it took generals on both sides a long time—and huge casualties—to realize this. In the battle of Antietam, McClellan ordered Burnside to make several attempts to cross a narrow bridge as Rebel sharpshooters on the hills above decimated the advancing Union troops. A couple of months later, on November 7, 1862, Lincoln placed General Burnside in command of the Army of the Potomac. A little over a month later, Lincoln's hopes for a victorious Union battle were once more dashed. With an army of more than 114,000, Burnside attacked the 72,000-man army of Confederate General Lee in and around Fredericksburg. West of the city, rising up 50 feet above the open field, were several hills known as Marye's Heights. Near the top was a road protected by a stone wall that was four feet high, behind which were 2,000 Confederate riflemen. Concealed at the top of the hill were another 7,000 Rebel infantry, behind which were some cannons with coverage of most of the open fields below. A Confederate officer told General

Longstreet that "…a chicken could not survive on that field once we start firing." Apparently still not realizing that Napoleonic tactics had become obsolete, General Burnside ordered commanders of his seven divisions to attack Marye's Heights one brigade at a time. After several failed attempts during which the Union troops were mowed down and never came closer than 40 yards from the wall, General Hooker pleaded in vain for Burnside to abandon the siege of the wall. By late afternoon, fourteen failed assaults had been made, the Union had sustained 8,000 casualties to less than 1,200 for the Confederates, and Burnside asked General Lee for a truce so that he could remove and administer to the wounded, to which Lee agreed. The following day, December 14, Burnside ordered his army to retreat.

General Lee was said to express sympathy for the Union troops who suffered such huge losses in the attempt to capture Marye's Heights. Amazingly, though, he apparently did not realize that the former tactics were obsolete and suicidal with the introduction of new weapons. At the Battle of Gettysburg Lee ordered General Pickett's 12,500 infantry troops to cross an open field to make repeated assaults against Union Army defenders that were behind a low stone wall. The Union soldiers repulsed the Rebels, inflicting casualties on more than half of the attacking Rebs.

On January 26, 1863, a discouraged Burnside offered to resign. Lincoln promptly accepted the offer, replacing him with 'Fighting Joe' Hooker, who had a reputation for aggressive tactics. Hooker molded the Army of the Potomac into what he believed to be an invincible fighting force, proclaiming:

"I have the finest army on the planet; the finest army the sun ever shone on. If the enemy does not run, God help them. May God have mercy on General Lee, for I will have none."

Lincoln was encouraged. Maybe he had finally found a tough and capable general who would lead the North to victory. If only Hooker's resolve and deeds matched his words, the bloody war might have ended much sooner.

CHAPTER 11:

ASSIGNMENT TO A BATTLE AREA

T he meeting with Major Harris spurred Henry to approach his duties at the hospital with new zeal. He was elated by his promotion to the rank of Captain, assignment as an assistant surgeon in a regimental hospital when the Union Army renews its attack on the Confederate forces, and the opportunity to gain experience in surgery. For the next several weeks he diligently conducted examinations of each patient, made the required entries in the medical records, and studied and compared those entries in an attempt to ascertain if changes might be advisable in the treatment or medications provided to the patients. To furnish an additional source of clean water, he obtained from the Quartermaster four large empty barrels, which he placed outside the hospital to collect rainwater. Henry also got Major Harris to authorize hiring of a civilian man to assist the nurses emptying the bed pans each morning and evening—twice a day—so as to improve air quality in the hospital.

On April 24, Henry received written orders that he was to pack all of his clothing, personal items, medical instruments and supplies, and be ready to move with the XI Corps in two days at 0830 to the winter headquarters camp of the Army of the Potomac in Falmouth, Virginia. A covered wagon containing a regimental hospital tent, operating table, medical supplies, chloroform and antiseptics, driven by an ambulance driver, would be provided for the thirteen- mile trip. Surgeon Major Thomas Sedgwick, hospital steward John Massey, and nurse Alice Hunter would be accompanying him in the wagon. Major Harris told Henry that Sedgwick was an experienced battlefield surgeon and a cousin of General John Sedgwick, one of General Hooker's most trusted aides and a competent military commander. The Orders also contained an admonition that he was not to tell any civilian, including his family in letters, of his location or the army's movements.

On the morning of April 26, Henry rose early and packed his clothing, personal items, black leather bag containing medical instruments, supplies and Military Surgery Manual into a large duffel bag. As he carried them outside his tent, he observed that most of the tents in the camp had already been dismantled and were being loaded onto a row of covered wagons that seemed to stretch for over a mile and a half. The approximately 12,000 soldiers of the XI Corps were in the process of loading their belongings and armaments onto the wagons, climbing into the wagons and readying for departure. Hundreds of cavalrymen on horseback were riding into formation. Henry walked over to the Quartermaster building, in front of which was a four-wheeled covered wagon. On top of the front of it, attached to a thin, one-foot long pole, was a triangular shaped green flag, which both armies used to identify a medical ambulance or field hospital tent. For the most part, both armies would respect that ID, not aim canon or rifle fire at it, and not capture the Medical Corps soldiers. Unfortunately, occasionally Medical Corps personnel were unintentionally wounded or killed by shrapnel or an errant cannonball or bullet.

"Am I supposed to dismantle my tent and load it onto the wagon?" Henry inquired of a sergeant standing nearby, who was giving instructions to soldiers in front of a nearby wagon about what to put in their wagon.

"If you want a place to sleep where we're going, you better do that, Captain," the sergeant replied. Then he turned to a private standing next to him and said: "Private, go with the Captain and help him dismantle his tent and load it on his wagon."

The soldier hurried with Henry to his tent, assisted him in dismantling it, and placing it in the wagon. Henry also loaded his duffel bag onto the wagon and climbed inside. It had already been filled haphazardly with three other small tents, canvas and poles for a field hospital tent, a barn door and two wooden barrels that Henry was told would be the operating table, a couple of chairs, a stretcher, bottles of alcohol and whisky, two fold-away cots, tins with chloroform, antiseptics, iodine, and rolls of cotton bandages, a couple of boxes of hardtack, and tins containing rations—mostly beans, peas, corn, bacon and preserved meat in a creamy sauce [in modern times the latter known as 'creamed chipped beef', which, when served on hardtack, soldiers affectionately referred to as 'shit on a shingle']. All of this clutter left only about eight square feet of space for the medical personnel to occupy. Henry introduced himself to Surgeon Major Thomas Sedgwick and hospital steward John Massey, and greeted nurse Alice Hunter. As Henry sat down on the floor of the wagon next to Sedgwick, the mile-long row of wagons and cavalry men on horseback began to move. Henry's ambulance driver called out to his horse to start moving the wagon:

"Giddyap, you fuckin' lazy beast," he shouted as he cracked his whip a couple of times on the horse's rear end.
Upset by what appeared to be the driver's cruel treatment of the animal, Alice Hunter shouted:

"You don't have to whip the poor horse, and mind your language, there's a lady present."

Irritated at the admonition, the driver turned towards her and yelled:

"Fuck you sister. You ain't the boss of me, so shut up or get off my wagon."

As the nurse's face blushed red with embarrassment and anger, Major Sedgwick tried to calm her and said:

"Don't let the foul-mouthed bastard upset you, Alice. Our driver is a formerly often-unemployed laborer with unsanitary habits, a filthy mouth and an alcohol problem. His breath already smells of whisky and it's still early in the morning. The Army scraped the bottom of the barrel when it hired ambulance drivers. It's gonna be a bumpy thirteen-mile ride on a mostly dirt road full of potholes and rocks, so just try to relax and ignore the driver. I just hope we make it safely in one piece to our destination."

The occupants were to learn the truth of Sedgwick's comments by the time they arrived at their destination. Their rear ends felt as though they had sustained half a dozen strikes with a wood paddle. They already felt pity for the wounded soldiers the driver would transport from the battlefield.

During the two-hour ride, the passengers conversed with each other, mostly about their backgrounds and experiences. Sedgwick revealed that he had never gone to medical school. He apprenticed for two years under the supervision of an experienced surgeon and then started his own medical practice. Five years later, when the Civil War began, his cousin, Colonel [now General] John Sedgwick, urged him to join the military. He enlisted in March, 1862 and served as assistant surgeon with Surgeon Major Harris at the Battle of Fredericksburg, Virginia, on December 13, 1862, in which General Robert E. Lee's Army of the Confederacy defeated Union General Burnside's much larger Army, inflicting more than 12,000 casualties. The two surgeons were overwhelmed with wounded soldiers seeking treatment and desperately requiring surgery. Despite working feverishly for fourteen hours a day, operating [mostly amputations] on as many as six patients per hour, they were able to treat only a fraction of the hundreds of wounded brought to their small field hospital. Those with less serious wounds not requiring immediate surgery were sent by ambulance wagons on a long trip to the divisional hospital or permanent hospitals in Washington, D.C. Because many of the drivers hastily hired by the Medical Corps were bums, alcoholics, and uncaring individuals, who did not even stop for water or food for their passengers, a lot of the wounded became severely ill, died, or were even abandoned by the drivers before they reached their destination.

"Well, at least you got a helluva lot of experience doing so many surgeries," Henry said.

"I wasn't in it for the experience, Captain. I hoped I could save as many lives as possible of those brave young soldiers. Even today, I am haunted by the horrors I saw and my inability to save more lives. It also hurt to be called 'a butcher' by so many of those I tried to help."

"Why would the soldiers call you a butcher?"

"You'll see for yourself, once the battle begins," Sedgwick and nurse Hunter said, almost in unison. Hunter had worked as a nurse with Major Sedgwick in that battle.

As the long line of carriages, led by the cavalry, arrived at Falmouth, it stopped next to a General on horseback who had raised his left hand, signaling them to halt.

"That's Oliver Howard, the Major General in command of our XI Army Corps," said Major Sedgwick. "He's got a six-inch long dark beard and moustache and some flecks of grey in his thick head of hair, but don't let that fool you. He's only 32 years of age—the youngest Major General in the entire Union Army."

"Looks like he's missing most of his right arm," Henry commented.

"Yep, he was wounded by a lead mini-ball when he led his troops against the Rebs at Fair Oaks in June of '62. The surgeon had to cut off

his arm from a couple of inches above the elbow, leaving just a stub".
[Howard was later to receive the Medal of Honor for his bravery in that
battle.]

A moment later, a Brigadier General on horseback rode up to
where General Howard was located, at the front of the wagons. A
conversation between the two Generals ensued for the next five minutes.
Major Sedgwick turned toward the occupants of the wagon and said:

"That's General Charles Devens. He's a Massachusetts 'Blue-
Blood'—his father is a prominent resident of that state. A few days ago,
General Howard put him in command of the 1st Division of the XI Army
Corps, to which we've been assigned. A lot of the German soldiers in
our Division were upset about that. The 'Christian General' is probably
relaying to Devens Hooker's new plans for action and placement of our
Division so that his junior officers can advise the troops."
Moments later, General Devens rode his horse to a nearby tree under
which six Colonels had gathered on horseback. He told them of General
Hooker's change of plans and ordered them to inform the troops. It took
those officers one hour to notify the occupants of each wagon about the
General's new orders. When one of those colonels reached Henry's
wagon, he told Surgeon Major Sedgwick:

"There's been a change of plans. General Howard's V, XI and
XII Corps, which includes you, are to proceed northwest about 13 miles
along the north bank of the Rappahannock River, cross it and go
southwest to the Rapidan River, where you are to camp overnight.
Tomorrow morning you will cross the Rapidan at Ely's Ford and
proceed a couple of miles to the intersection of the Orange Turnpike and
Orange Plank Road, known as The Chancellorsville Crossroads. It's at
the eastern edge of the thick forest and bushes area called The
Wilderness. There you will await further orders from General Howard."
The long line of wagons made a 180 degree turn and proceeded
northwest in accordance with the new orders.

CHAPTER 12:

THE ROAD TO CHANCELLORSVILLE

E arly in April, 1863, Hooker's army was still at its winter quarters in Stafford and in Falmouth, Virginia, about two miles northwest of Lee's army of Northern Virginia, which was located at heavily fortified Fredericksburg. Hooker formulated a seemingly brilliant plan of attack. He would send General Stoneman and ten thousand cavalry several miles northwest to cross the Rappahannock River and go deep into the Confederate rear to attack supply depots along the railroad lines between Fredericksburg and the Confederate capital, Richmond. He would thus cut off Lee's supply lines and, Hooker thought, force Lee to retreat towards Richmond. Fighting Joe would then order the XI and XII Corps to attack Lee's retreating army. Unfortunately, as poet Robert Burns said, "The best laid plans of mice and men often go awry." The weather did not cooperate. When general Stoneman attempted to cross the Rappahannock, heavy rains made the crossing impossible.

Still confident in the superiority of his army and the sure-fire success of his strategy, in late April Hooker devised a second plan. He would again send Stoneman to attack the Rebels' supply lines. Simultaneously, General Oliver Howard's V, XI and XII Corps, totaling 42,000 soldiers, were to march northwest about thirteen miles along the north bank of the Rappahannock River, cross it, and then proceed southwest to the Rapidan River, which they were to cross at Ely's Ford. Howard's Corps would then proceed to the Chancellorsville crossroads [the intersection of the Orange Turnpike and Orange Plank Road]. There they would dig in, build earthworks barriers, from which they could attack Lee's Army from the west, or successfully defend any attack by the rebels. Hooker also planned for forty thousand men from General John Sedgwick's I and VI Corps to cross the Rappahannock about three miles south of Fredericksburg to attack General Stonewall Jackson's men on the right flank of the Confederate Army. Hooker felt certain that, by attacking the much smaller Rebel Army on its east and west flanks, Lee would be forced to retreat. However, Hooker had underestimated Lee's brilliance as a military tactician and his willingness to take chances to achieve a victory against far superior numbers.

Late in the afternoon of April 29, when Howard's XI and XII Corps arrived at Ely's Ford on the Rapidan River, they decided to camp for the night and cross the river into position at the village of Chancellorsville the following morning. When the army's covered wagons came to a halt, hospital steward John Massey said to his companions:

"Until we get to Chancellorsville tomorrow morning, the mess hall won't be set up. If you are as sick as I am of the lousy canned meat and hardtack we've been eating, I can take one of our rifles and get us a beve for dinner. We can roast it on a spit made from some of the thick bushes and brush in the Wilderness area."

"A what?", asked Henry. "What in hell is a beve?"

"You must be a city boy," John replied. "You don't know what a beve is? Ain't you ever lived by a river? I seen a dome-like lodge made of mud and branches in a pond near the river. They probably got as many as a dozen beves—beavers—living there."

"Ugh. You're going to shoot and roast a beaver?" Henry exclaimed.

"Don't knock it until you've tried it," Major Sedgwick interjected. "They have plenty of tasty meat and adults weigh fifty pounds or more."

Yup," John said. "After cutting off the head and tail, and skinning it, there's about thirty-five pounds of meat left. It smells great and is real tasty after it's roasted for two and a half to three hours. And the fur makes a great hat or warm jacket."

John took a rifle and walked over to a nearby pond formed by a dam the beavers had built in the river. He waited patiently for fifteen minutes until a beaver exited the dome-shaped nest. Henry heard a rifle shot and within minutes Massey returned, dragging a beaver. Massey beheaded, skinned and removed the tail of his prey. He then placed it on the spit and lit a fire under it. Three hours later, the hungry group began salivating as the sweet smell of roasted meat wafted over to their wagon. Massey took some tin plates and, using a large knife, sliced off about a pound of meat for each occupant of the wagon. Somewhat reluctantly,

Henry placed a piece of the roast beve in his mouth and, with a look of satisfaction like a fox that has just caught a chicken, said:

"Mmm. This is tasty and really tender. Thanks John."

About a dozen soldiers from nearby wagons came over and asked if they could share in the feast. Within an hour, there was nothing left of the beve except for the head, tail, skin and a pile of small bones. To show their gratitude, three of the soldiers who had just shared in the meal of fresh roasted meat for the first time in weeks, went to their wagons and returned with two banjos and a harmonica. Sitting around a campfire, they entertained Henry and the others with a medley of popular songs, ballads and hymns. They played the haunting music and soulful words of Stephen Foster's melancholy ballad written shortly after his wife and daughter separated from him: "I Dream of Jeannie With the Light Brown Hair." It brought tears to the eyes of the soldiers as they recalled the wives and sweethearts they had left behind, who they might never see again. Their spirits were lifted by the group's rendition of the patriotic composition, "The Army Hymn", by Oliver Wendell Holmes. The musicians/singers wound up their concert with the popular inspirational theme of the Union Army, "The Battle Hymn of the Republic."

As if in response, wafting in the crisp night air from a Rebel camp a couple of miles away, they heard the faint sound of the stirring ballad, "Dixie". It was now nearly ten p.m. The troops were tired from a long day of traveling. They had to get up early the next morning for the final march to Chancellorsville, where they would have to construct earthwork defenses in preparation for the anticipated Rebel assault. So, everybody retired for the night under a blanket of twinkling stars and a crescent moon.

CHAPTER 13:

CONFEDERATE GENERAL STONEWALL JACKSON'S SURPRISE ATTACK

On the morning of April 30, 1863, the three corps of the Army of the Potomac under General Oliver Howard reached the Chancellorsville Crossroads. The Crossroads was located at the intersection of the Orange Turnpike and the Orange Plank Road. It was an area of low-lying brush and weeds. A couple of hundred feet west was an area known as the Spotsylvania Wilderness. It consisted of thick forests stretching for about three and one-half miles north to south and about three and one-half miles east to west, for a total of more than ten square miles. The Union Army commanders assumed the Wilderness was impenetrable by an army due to the thick woods and lack of any road or wide path through the forest. That made the Union generals certain that the Rebels would not attack from the west. So, they positioned their troops and most of their artillery [except for two cannons] facing southeast.

Neither Generals Howard nor Hooker had much faith in the capabilities of the XI Corp as a fighting unit. The reason they distrusted that Corps was partly prejudice, because the majority of them were German immigrants who spoke little or no English, and were derogatorily referred to as "dumb Dutch" by the rest of the Army. Also, most of them had been untested or losers in battles. Hooker reasoned that the likelihood of the Rebels attacking the northernmost flank of the Union Army was remote, but the fact that more than forty thousand Union soldiers were positioned there might add to Lee's concerns that he was vastly outnumbered and cause him to retreat to Richmond, which Hooker believed to be Lee's only reasonable course of action. He ordered the XI Corps to dig in along the easterly border of the Crossroads, facing southeast, at the extreme northern flank of the Army of the Potomac. There they were to construct earthworks [raised wall-like mounds of earth as a protective barrier in battle] and lumber and rock barriers on the southerly side of their positions, in anticipation of a Rebel attack from the southeast. What Hooker failed to realize was that Lee was not a typical military commander. When faced with seemingly overwhelming opposition forces, he was willing to take risks, to abandon conventional military strategy for a chance at victory.

The execution of Hooker's grand plan to defeat the Confederate Army began on April 27, when General Stoneman began attacking the Rebel's supply lines between Fredericksburg and Richmond. The attacks proved ineffective. Undaunted, Hooker ordered General Sedgwick to attack Confederate positions in and around Fredericksburg, creating a pincer-like attack on the south and north flanks of Lee's forces. Lee decided to go against conventional military wisdom. He ordered about 40,000 soldiers from his army in and around Fredericksburg to march north towards Chancellorsville to engage Hooker's army in battle. That left only 11,000 men behind to defend against the anticipated attack against Fredericksburg by Union General Sedgwick's 40,000-man Corps. Fortunately for Lee, heavy fog along the Rappahannock River concealed much of the Rebel Army's northwestward movement. At 11:20 a.m. on May 1, the two armies met and the battle began, with the Rebels first gaining some ground and then a Union counter-attack repulsing them and gaining back the area. This back and forth movement continued for several hours, but with the Union gaining the upper hand. It was then that Hooker made a decision that irritated his general staff. He ordered the Union Army to halt the offensive and withdraw back to its fortified defensive positions around Chancellorsville, forcing Lee to attack the Union's much larger army or retreat. Hooker's decision was influenced by his recollection of last December 13th's Union Army attack on Fredericksburg, when the army was soundly defeated by a much smaller Confederate Army entrenched in and around the city.

"This time, let the Rebs take the offensive and suffer defeat with huge casualties", he thought.

So, the Army of the Potomac withdrew from the battle and took up its positions in and around Chancellorsville, with General Howard's XI Corps in place facing south for about a mile and a half along the Orange Turnpike. Shortly after dawn on May 2, General Hooker arrived on horseback at the XI Corps' position for a meeting with General Howard and to inspect the earthworks. He told Howard that he was not satisfied with the earthwork defenses constructed and ordered Howard to construct defenses on the north side also, to prepare for an attack from the Wilderness area to the north. Howard ignored that order, telling an aide that no army could march through the Wilderness, so there's no need to have the men build such defenses.

Meanwhile, General Lee and his most trusted and capable general, Stonewall Jackson, whose very name struck fear in the hearts of many enemy soldiers, devised a daring plan. A local resident, Charles Wellford, who was sympathetic to the Confederate cause and familiar with the Wilderness, told them that, within the past couple of years an abandoned furnace in the area was restored so as to produce iron for the Confederacy; that he owned the furnace, and that a road had been constructed through the Wilderness to enable shipment of the product. It was a narrow road, only wide enough for a four-man wide column, but could not be seen from the nearby Turnpike or Plank Road because of the thick woods and bushes. They devised a plan for Jackson to lead his Corps of 28,000 men on a circuitous 13-mile route to avoid tipping off Union scouts of the Rebs' intentions, and to make it appear as a retreat. They would enter the Wilderness and march along Furnace Road until they reached the northern flank of General Howard's Corps. There they would wait until all 28,000 had massed, and then commence a surprise attack from the rear on the unsuspecting XI Corps. Jackson informed his army of the plan and at 7 a.m. they began the march.

Jackson's Corps was in poor physical condition. During the recently ended winter months, they had done so little exercise that their limbs had become stiff and weak. Their winter rations lacked fruit and vegetables, resulting in nearly one quarter of the men suffering from scurvy, with its symptoms of weakness and hemorrhages on the legs. Men who less than six months earlier were noted for their ability to march long distances at a rapid pace, now struggled to keep up. Many fell exhausted by the wayside until they could recover their stamina, and a few even died. Once they arrived at three miles long Furnace Road in the Wilderness, they marched on in a two-mile long column of four soldiers wide. At one point there was a narrow opening between some trees and some Union Pickets spotted the line of Rebels marching through the forest. They reported their observations to Generals Hooker, Howard and Devens. The generals confidently said it was obvious that Lee was retreating. Hooker, who had been relaxing with his aides and generals, told them to be ready to start a pursuit of the retreating Rebel Army early the following morning.

One XI Corps colonel, Robert Reilly, realizing that Generals Howard and Devens had foolishly dismissed as unimportant the reports of Confederate troop movements through the Wilderness, addressed the troops of the 75th Ohio Regiment, which he commanded.

"Men, some of us will never see another sunrise. If there are any of you not ready to die for your country, come forward now and I will give you a pass to the rear. I want no half-hearted, unwilling soldiers or cowards in the ranks. We need every man to fight the enemy. Keep your guns close by."

Stonewall Jackson and the first contingent of his troops arrived near the edge of the woods about one hundred fifty feet from the rear of Howard's XI Corps' positions at shortly after 3 p.m. His officers began organizing and placing his soldiers in position for the attack. Stonewall waited patiently for a couple of hours until nearly all of his 28,000 soldiers had arrived. As if in response to the general's waving a magic wand, at about 5:30 p.m., when Jackson gave the signal to attack, his men felt a burst of strength. They admired their charismatic and daring leader, wanted to do their best, and were willing to die for him.

Many hundreds of the XI Corps were in the huge tent that served as a mess hall, sitting down to eat dinner. Most had placed their rifle-muskets in neat piles just outside the entrance. The rest of the Corps were either resting inside their tents, sitting on the ground outside, chatting, playing card games, roasting beves on spits by their tents, writing letters to loved ones, or waiting until some soldiers would leave the mess hall so that they could enter the dining area. Henry and his Medical Corps group were in the field hospital tent located about a mile north, near the river. Suddenly, from the woods about one hundred fifty feet across the open field, burst forth hundreds of rabbits, squirrels, foxes, deer and other wild animals, as well as various kinds of birds.

"Will ya look at that", shouted one soldier seated on the ground near the mess hall. "I ain't never seen anything like it. What in heck could be scarin' those critters?"

He got the answer in less than thirty seconds. There was a blood-curdling yell by the 28,000 men of Jackson's Corps, as they burst out of the woods and raced towards Howard's surprised troops. Most of the Union soldiers had never heard the "Rebel Yell" before. After the battle, many admitted they were frightened, some even saying that they peed in their pants. Most—especially those who were in the dining hall-- got up and ran away in a northeasterly direction towards Hooker's headquarters at Chancellorsville Mansion as fast as their legs could take them, with the Rebs in hot pursuit, shooting, wounding, killing or capturing many. The Union soldiers fled in fear and disarray, like a flock of sheep pursued by a pack of hungry wolves. The Rebel soldiers only stopped their pursuit momentarily to grab some of the food the Union troops had been eating, including parts of some beavers roasting on spits near the tents. A few Union soldiers managed to get ahold of their rifles and fire a few rounds at the Rebs until their positions were overrun by the Confederates.

At the first sound of fighting, Colonel Reilly ordered the men of the 75th Ohio Regiment to turn around and face west, the direction from which the Confederate onslaught was coming. Before they could complete this maneuver, the Union soldiers from the XI Corps who were fleeing to the rear ran through their lines, accompanied by their horses, wagons and ambulances, with the Rebs in hot pursuit. The Ohio regiment sustained heavy enemy fire that caused 150 casualties, including Colonel Reilly, who was shot in the leg and fell off his horse. The Ohio Regiment retreated, leaving its wounded colonel lying on the ground. Generals Howard and Devens watched helplessly as their XI Corps disintegrated. Some of the fleeing Union soldiers reached Dowdall's Tavern, where 5,000 men of the Army of the Potomac were entrenched in a last line of defense, but could not stop Stonewall Jackson's advance. It was the arrival of darkness at 7:30 p.m. that finally halted the Rebel's attack and enabled the survivors of the XI Corps to escape to the vicinity of Chancellorsville Mansion.

In the field hospital tent, located about a mile north of the scene of battle, near the Rappahannock River, Surgeon Major Sedgwick and his group had been busy setting up their tent in preparation for treatment of the anticipated wounded soldiers. The previous day, May 1, the fighting had occurred several miles south, so Henry's tent had very little to do. But the evening of May 2 was very different. The unexpected surprise attack had resulted in more than a thousand casualties [dead and wounded] within a couple of hours. Some of the Medical Corpsmen had fled when the attack first began. But, the majority of them—stretcher bearers, ambulance drivers, and the like—remained, rushing to bring the wounded to the nearest regimental field hospital tent. Henry was about to get the medical experience he had craved. He was also to experience the horrors of war.

CHAPTER 14:

THE FIELD HOSPITAL PREPARES TO TREAT THE WOUNDED

On May 1, 1863, the field hospital tent was set up about fifty feet south of the Rappahannock River. The tent, intended to hold six patients, was about 12 feet wide and 24 feet long, with a large fabric flap entrance. About one foot inside the entrance, so as to take advantage of the outside light during daytime, was a 7 foot by 4 foot barn door resting on two wooden barrels, to be used as an operating table. Nearby was a cabinet containing tins of alcohol, chloroform, iodine, various surgical instruments, aprons, and cardboard boxes filled with lint and bandages. On the edge of the operating table was a kerosene lamp, and in each of the four corners of the tent were one-foot tall candelabras, each holding a large candle. This was the only lighting in the field hospital. On a small table was Dr. Sam Gress' Military Surgery Manual, which provided instructions on proper procedure for various types of surgery, especially amputations.   In a corner, a couple of feet from the operating table, was a wheelbarrow. When Henry asked Major Sedgwick why the wheelbarrow was inside the tent, the Major responded with a wry smile, "You'll see soon enough, son."

The persons who would be working in and in connection with the field hospital gathered at a meeting called by Major Sedgwick. There was the ambulance driver and two soldiers who had been assigned to assist him as stretcher bearers. He told them that, once the battle starts, they are to drive the ambulance to the scene of the fighting, load six of the wounded onto the ambulance wagon, and bring them back to the hospital, place them on the ground by the tent, and then immediately return to the place of battle to gather more wounded. John Massey, the hospital steward, was a strapping, muscular man. He was ordered to assist Sedgwick by placing the wounded on the operating table and holding them down while nurse Alice Hunter administered the anesthetic, usually chloroform, which she would drip onto a cotton cloth that she would hold over the patient's nose and mouth for as long as necessary so that he would not feel pain. He ordered Henry to examine the wounded lying on the ground outside the tent.

"Henry, you are to determine which soldiers appear to have mortal wounds, such as serious bleeding chest or head wounds, which we cannot treat. Simply stuff lint in the wound to reduce the flow of blood, cover the wound with a bandage, and administer some opium to ease the pain. Leave the soldier in place on the ground, until an ambulance can carry him and other hopelessly wounded to the nearest Division Hospital in Stafford."

"But, Major, shouldn't I at least try to remove the minie-ball or shrapnel that caused the wound?"

"No, Henry! That will waste time treating a hopeless case. We'll, have more work than we can handle as it is. Those wounded who you believe can be saved—such as soldiers with bullet wounds that did not shatter bones, or with simple flesh wounds—you should use your various forceps instruments to locate and remove the bullet, pour some fresh water on the wound to flush out any dirt, swab the area at the edge of the wound with iodine, and sew up the skin on the wound. As for those wounds to legs or arms where the bullet has shattered bone, do not waste time trying to locate and remove the bullet. Just call out to Massey that the soldier is next in line for surgery."

"What kind of surgery, sir?"

"Amputation, of course."

"Shouldn't I try to remove the bullet? Maybe his limb could be saved."

"No, Henry. All that would do is lead to gangrene and death, and a huge waste of time that would be better spent on the overwhelming number of patients we're going to have. I'm sure we'll have far more patients than we can handle. We'll be working 'round the clock. Every six hours, you can take a one-hour break to rest and have something to eat. That goes for all of you. Do you understand?"

In unison, the soldiers, Medical Corps personnel, Massey and nurse Hunter, said: "Yes, Sir."

CHAPTER 15:

THE YOUNG DOCTOR IS INTRODUCED TO THE HORRORS OF WAR

Henry awakened and walked to the entrance to his tent a few minutes after 6 a.m. on May 2, 1863. The sky appeared as if bright streaks of red paint had been splashed across it, as the sun gradually arose above the horizon. A little over a mile away slightly to the northeast was General Hooker's headquarters, the Chancellorsville mansion. In between were mostly barren farmland and open space with low-lying bushes and weeds. The Rebel Army was positioned about a mile to the south and east. Behind Henry's tent, a few hundred feet to the west, were the dense trees and thick vegetation of the Spotsylvania Wilderness. The temperature was a cool 55 degrees, but under the springtime sun it would rise to the high 70s within a couple of hours.

Henry donned his uniform and walked to the mess hall to have a breakfast of bacon, stale hardtack [from which he picked off a couple of weevils and hurled them on the earth floor of the dining tent] and coffee. Then he walked a mile north to the field hospital tent, arriving about 6:45 a.m. John Massey had already filled a barrel outside the tent with fresh water which he had carried in three trips from the Rappahannock River, in two five-gallon pails. The ambulance wagon was parked near the tent, and its driver and two stretcher bearers were seated on the ground nearby, playing a game of cards. Alice Hunter, Massey and Major Sedgwick were seated on a bench in the tent. The Major said:

"Come over here, Captain, and sit down. There's room for one more on this bench. You'll be standing on your feet for hours at a time, once the action starts."

As Henry sat down, he replied:

"I'm looking forward to that. It got kinda boring yesterday, just waiting around for hours."

A couple of hours passed with no activity in the tent. Not even a soldier with a wood splinter or a small accidental cut from whittling a piece of wood with a knife. Massey got up from the bench and said:

"I gotta stretch my legs. They're getting cramped. I'm gonna take a rifle and go down to the pond near the river and shoot us another beve. We can roast 'im for lunch."

Less than a half hour later, he returned dragging a beaver by the tail. He took a scalpel from the cabinet, removed his prey's head and tail and skinned it. Then he placed it on a spit and lit a fire under it, to roast it. No wounded soldiers had come to the tent by three hours later, although they heard the faint sound of gunfire and cannons coming from the direction of Fredericksburg, about 8 miles to the southeast. The sweet smell of roasted meat wafted through the air, as Massey took the scalpel and carved off about a pound of meat for each member of the group. They enjoyed their feast, washed it down with cups of fresh water from the barrel, and then sat down, with the driver and stretcher bearers resuming their card game. About 5:20 o'clock in the afternoon, Henry took a pen and paper and started writing a letter to his wife. As he did so, he said to Major Sedgwick:

"I'm gonna tell Liz how we've just been sitting around twiddling our thumbs for two days. I got more experience helping my dad do one operation a few years ago."
He began writing:

"Dearest Elizabeth,
We expected to be busy all day treating wounded and ill soldiers.
But it's turned out to be a repeat of yesterday. We can hear the
sounds of battle several miles away, but the XI Corps near us has
been peaceful, with no action. I'm getting real bored and
disappointed at not getting any experience treating wounded
soldiers....."

As Henry wrote, Sedgwick said, "let me assure you, Henry. If you stay in the Army long enough, you'll get more experience treating the wounded and ill than you could ever get in a hundred years of medical practice as a civilian. In fact, you'll pray for a break from..."

The sudden noise of hundreds of frightened wild animals bursting out of the Wilderness woods, followed by the Rebel Yells of 28,000 Confederate troops led by General Stonewall Jackson caused the Major to cut short his statement to Henry. The Captain dropped his pen and paper. He felt the hair on the back of his neck rise up like a resting soldier whose sergeant had just yelled: "Attention." Henry had never been anywhere near an actual battle before. For a moment, he was caught in the grip of fear. Within a few seconds, he recovered his composure, retrieved his surgeon's kit, some lint, iodine, opium, carbolic acid, a pint of whiskey, bandages, needle and thread from the cabinet, and stood outside the tent as Sedgwick ordered:

"Get ready everybody. We're about to get an onslaught of wounded soldiers. Prepare to be up all night caring for them."

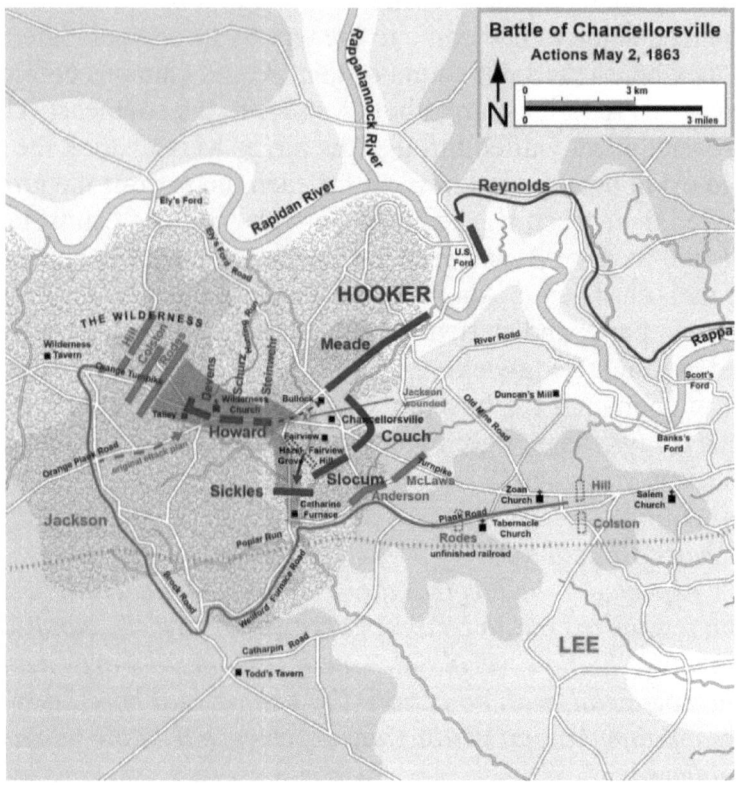

The group stood in dismay as they observed thousands of men of General Howard's Corps turn and run in a state of fear and disarray, pursued relentlessly by Stonewall's men, like leaves being blown forward by a hurricane wind. A few Union soldiers who had their rifles nearby valiantly put up some resistance until they were shot, overrun or captured by the Rebels. Hundreds of that Corps of the once proud Army of the Potomac fell to the ground, killed or wounded by the Rebs.

The Major commanded the ambulance driver and two stretcher bearers:

"Drive the wagon to the scene of battle and pick up at least six of the wounded and bring them back here as soon as possible. Then go back and get at least six more. Keep doing that until all the wounded have been removed from the battle grounds. If any Rebs try to stop you, make sure you tell them you're with the Medical Corps and point to the green flag flying on the ambulance. They should let you do your work without interference. Get going men, and Godspeed."

In less than a half hour, the ambulance returned, loaded with ten wounded soldiers, who they placed in two rows on the ground near the entrance. Henry was saddened by their moans and cries for help:

"Help me O Lord. I can't stand the pain. Blood is flowing from my stomach," cried one.

Henry called to Massey to help carry the wounded soldier to the operating table. But Massey and the Major took one look at the helpless man and Sedgwick took Henry aside and said:

"Don't waste valuable time with that soldier. Just put some lint in his wound to slow down the loss of blood, put a bandage on it, give him some opium to ease the pain, and leave him alone."

"But, sir. He'll die if I do that."

The Major angrily ordered:

"He's going to die no matter what we do. We can't waste time operating on him while there are other wounded that we might be able to save if we treat them as soon as possible. So, do as I say."

Reluctantly, Henry did as his superior ordered. The next soldier was crying out:

"Please help me. My right arm hurts like hell. I think the minie-ball shattered the bone. I'm bleeding. Please, save my arm. I gotta be able to plow the field when I return home to my wife and kids."

Henry took a tourniquet and applied it to the man's upper arm above the wound to stop the bleeding and then probed the wound with a ceramic tipped locator to find the ball, which he began to try to remove with a bullet forceps. The Major, waiting impatiently for him to release one of the wounded for surgery, hurried over to Henry and angrily said:

"What the hell is taking so much time, Captain?"

"I'm trying to remove the bullet and some of the shattered pieces of bone, so we can save this poor man's arm."

"You're wasting precious time again. Didn't you listen yesterday when I gave you orders? There's no way to save this man's arm when the bone has been shattered and pierced the skin. And that tourniquet you wasted time putting on will lead to gangrene of his arm below the elbow. Just give him some opium or whiskey to lessen the pain and have Massey place him on the operating table so we can amputate…"

"Please don't amputate my arm, Major. I'm a farmer. I can't plow the fields if I only have one arm."

"I'm sorry, son. If I don't operate, you'll have gangrene or blood poisoning and die. I never heard of dead men plowing a field." Turning to Henry, Sedgwick continued: "Now stop wasting time, give this man some opium and help Massey place him on the operating table, or so help me, I'll have you court-martialed for disobeying orders."

Henry had never seen Sedgwick so angry before this. He promptly did as he was told, but the cacophony of cries from the wounded, begging not to have their limbs amputated, praying to God for mercy and to save them, calling for their wives and mothers, was almost too much for Henry to bear. Tears welled up in his eyes as he packed lint in the wounds of several of the men who had been shot in the neck, head, chest or stomach, and then applied a bandage and administered opium to put them in a state of delirium and to relieve the pain. He set them aside on the ground to slowly die. Only one soldier had a flesh wound in the leg from a minie-ball, which Henry removed with forceps, then rinsed the area with fresh water, applied iodine to the edge of the wound, and sewed together the skin to cover it. About twenty minutes later, just as he and Massey were placing on the operating table the sixth man whose limb was to be amputated, the ambulance arrived with another ten wounded soldiers. The Major ordered Henry to remain near the operating table for a few minutes so he could observe the proper operating procedure. Although the patient was under the influence of chloroform and opium, his arms and legs were flailing around as he repeatedly cried out:

"Don't cut off my arm, you butchers. You're devils. You bastards belong in Hell."

Massey, standing at one side of the operating table, was forcefully pinning down the patient by grabbing the soldier's good arm in a firm grip and pressing down on his chest to keep him still. Nurse Hunter held a foot square cloth over the soldier's nose and mouth, on which she dripped chloroform to sedate the patient so that he would not feel much pain. Surgeon Sedgwick used a scalpel to cut the skin and flesh down to the bone, in an upward angular manner just above the elbow, leaving some flaps of skin to close over the bone after the amputation. Then Sedgwick grabbed the handle of a saw that had an eighteen- inch long steel blade stained with blood and proceeded to rapidly cut through the bone slightly above the elbow, immediately below which was a gaping three square inch wound with shattered pieces of bone and skin hanging from it. Nurse Hunter then threaded a ligature needle, handed it to the Major, who used it to pass the thread through the muscle and around an artery, and then closed the flaps over the stump of remaining bone and sewed them closed. The whole procedure took only about six minutes and, as Massey removed the patient from the operating table to place him on the ground outside, the Major took the forearm and

hand that he had just separated and hurled them into the wheelbarrow, where it landed on top of the pile of rotting, putrid severed limbs. For the first time, Henry realized the purpose of the wheelbarrow. He observed hundreds of flies swarming around the rotting flesh. Maggots and beetles were swarming over it, feeding on the severed limbs. The

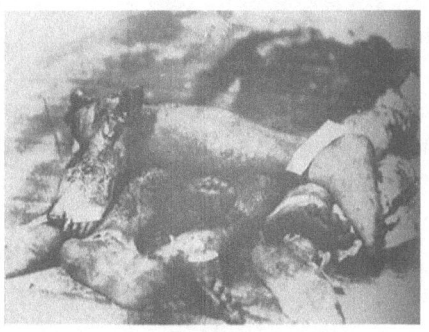

stench was unbearable. Henry suddenly felt queasy and sick to his stomach. He turned towards the entrance and rushed outside the tent. Bending over a thick bush about ten feet from the entrance, the Captain began vomiting uncontrollably. He felt like he was puking his guts out and felt a pain in his stomach. Wiping his mouth with a cloth rag, he walked back inside the tent.

"Sorry, Major," Henry said sheepishly. The horrible odor and all that vermin-infested rotting flesh made me feel real sick."

"Don't worry about it, Captain. That happened to all of us the first time we experienced such a sight and smell," Sedgwick said. He turned to Massey and ordered: "John, take that wheelbarrow outside to at least twenty feet from here, dig a small trench, dump the rotting flesh and bones in it, cover it up with dirt, and return here to help me operate."

"I'll do it right away, sir. Be back in less than a half hour."

The Major turned to Henry and said:

"Alright, Captain. Now that you've seen how the surgery is done, you can go outside and return to your pre-op preparation"

For the next couple of hours, at least twenty wounded men per hour were brought to the hospital tent. Twelve inoperable patients were lying in a row about fifteen feet from the side of the tent, sedated with opium, crying out to their mothers, wives, or God for salvation. Thirty-six others who had their limbs amputated were lying on the ground on the other side of the tent, cursing the surgeon for treating them like butchers cutting up a cow. All were waiting for an ambulance to deliver them to the Division Hospital in Stafford. The remaining two were on the ground by the entrance to the tent, where Henry was administering the pre-operation treatment. About ten minutes before eight p.m., the sun had just set and the shroud of darkness swept over the area. Massey brought a kerosene lamp outside the tent and placed it on the ground near Henry.

"Major Sedgwick says this'll give ya some light to finish up your work on the two-remaining wounded. After that, it's so hard to see inside the tent that he says we may have to shut down operations until the morning sunrise. We still gotta find two or three ambulances or wagons to transport the ones we operated on, and the poor souls we couldn't operate on, to the Division Hospital. Can't leave 'em lying out here on the ground tonight."

Just then, Henry approached one of the two remaining soldiers waiting for surgery, a corporal with a badly shattered and bloody left forearm from a bullet wound. The corporal, who had been cursing the surgeon while waiting for surgery, screamed at Henry as he was about to bend down to administer some opium:

"You mugging [scoundrel]. You ain't gonna touch my arm. If that butcher in thar even tries to cut off my arm, I'll kill the bastard with this here Arkansas toothpick. And that goes for you, too."

Henry observed that, as the soldier shouted out his warning, his right hand pulled out from its sheath a bayonet, waving it in a threatening manner at the Captain. Henry called to Massey and Sedgwick for help. They came running outside the tent. The Major tried to calm the soldier, telling him that amputation was the only way his life could be saved, and the alternative was gangrene, blood poisoning and certain slow and painful death. The corporal momentarily seemed to calm down, but as Sedgwick bent down and reached with his right hand to take away the bayonet, the soldier made a slashing motion, resulting in a deep cut in the middle of Sedgwick's forearm.

"You stupid bastard. I ought to let you rot and die right here. How am I gonna keep operating this evening after you sliced up my arm? Henry, John, stop the bleeding, clean my wound, swab the edges with iodine, sew it up and bandage it. Henry, you'll have to finish up the amputations for tonight. Just do like I showed you. If this miserable corporal doesn't want you to operate, leave him alone to die right here."

When Henry and Massey finished treating Sedgwick's wound, Massey turned to the corporal and said:

"Alright, hard case [tough guy], do you want us to put you on the operating table and amputate to save your worthless life, or should we just leave you here to die and become food for the ants, flies and rats? It's your call."

"Please, I'm sorry. Operate."

Massey carried the soldier to the operating table, where Henry administered some opium and nurse Hunter placed over the soldier's nose and mouth a cloth onto which she dripped chloroform. Henry put on a clean apron, wiped off the blood-stained scalpel with a rag dipped in carbolic acid, and, at first with shaky hands, until he regained his composure a few minutes later, began to cut away the flesh above the elbow. Then he took the saw and cut through the bone, folding flaps of skin over the stump, which nurse Alice sewed up. Henry and Massey went outside to carry in the last soldier there needing surgery.

"We're gonna have to find a couple of wagons to take these wounded soldiers to the Divisional hospital at Stafford," Massey said.

"Yeh, John. Well about half a dozen of those poor souls look like they won't need a ride. All they'll need is a hole a couple of feet deep, three feet wide and six feet long."

"Don't get upset about it, Captain. We all done our best," John said as he and Henry carried the wounded soldier to the operating table. John walked outside to look for a wagon.

Just then, they heard the sound of six horses rapidly approaching. Massey, still outside the tent, looked up as the men on horseback pulled up a few feet from him and dismounted. Massey said to Henry:

"Uh, oh. They's wearin' grey uniforms. Looks like they're Rebs and a couple of 'em got their pistols aimed right at us."
Henry strode outside the tent and started to walk slowly towards the intruders, saying:

"Hey, Johnnies, you can't see it in the dark, but there's a green hospital flag up on top of the entrance to our tent. I'm a doctor and this man here is my assistant." He held up high the kerosene lamp so the Rebs could see the flag.

"Don't y'all get worried, Captain. And don't anyone make any fast moves or reach for a gun, 'cause we ain't gonna hesitate to use our weapons. I just want to look inside the tent to make sure you fellas are tellin' the truth."

He strode up to the entrance, looked inside, saw nurse Hunter holding the cloth over the patient's nose and mouth while dripping chloroform on it, and the Major, with a blood-stained apron, standing nearby, waiting for Henry to pick up his scalpel and start cutting away flesh and skin of the patient's leg.

"Please leave us alone. We're all in the Medical Corps, trying to save the lives of badly wounded patients. Honor the rules of war and let us continue with our work. We're no threat to you," the Major said.
The Confederate who appeared to be the officer in charge said smiling:

"Just checking, Doc. We is leavin'. Y'all keep up the good work. We'll do our best to keep woundin' lots of Yanks so y'all will have plenty of business."

He turned and left the tent, and the Rebs mounted their horses and galloped away.

Henry resumed operating. About six minutes later, the surgery complete, the Captain took off his blood-stained apron, folded it and placed it on top of the cabinet. Then the four of them walked outside, with Massey holding the kerosene lantern. He hailed a couple of wagons about a hundred feet distant, and loaded all but seven of the soldiers, who were near death, onto the wagons for transport to the Divisional Hospital. They placed the remaining seven inside the tent, to shield them from the elements.

Just then, their ambulance pulled up to the front of the tent. "How many more wounded do you have for us?" asked the major.

We ain't got any," replied the ambulance driver.

"Yep," said one of the two stretcher-bearers. "They's mebbe over a thousand soldiers lyin' all over the place. Lots o' them's cryin' out for help, for their sweethearts, mothers, Jesus and who knows what. But it's too dark to tell how badly they's wounded, or if they could be saved, or are near death. And it's hard to tell if they's wearin' a grey uniform or a dark blue one, it's so dark and this here kerosene lamp doesn't give much light and is almost out. We got 'fraid that if we hung around too long, some Reb troops might shoot or capture us, tho we think they mostly were a mile or so south, chasin' after the fleein' men of the XI Corps. So, we come back here without any wounded."

"That's alright, soldier," said the Major. "It's too dark here now to fix their wounds or operate. Why don't we all get on the wagon and you can drive us over to the Mess Hall. Maybe it's still open and running, if the Rebs have all gone. If not, there must be food in the kitchen that we could eat," he said to the ambulance driver.

They all got up on the wagon and proceeded to the Mess Hall tent. Nobody was there but, as they walked into the kitchen, they found food left on the tables, including dried meat, beans, carrots, hardtack and coffee. The kitchen help, cooks and soldiers had fled in a hurry when the Rebel attack occurred, leaving all the food behind. The medical group gathered some food, sat down at a table, and ate their fill. Then Major Sedgwick said:

"We better return to the field hospital tent. We got to look after the seven dying soldiers we left inside the tent, give them water when they need it, and care for them. We don't want to go searching at night for the remainder of General Howard's Corps. We're not sure where they are and don't want to chance running into a bunch of Rebs. We can sleep in the wagon tonight."

They returned to the field hospital, disembarked from the wagon, gave some food and water to the dying men who asked for it. Then the group got up into the wagon and fell asleep.

CHAPTER 16:

WHEN RELATIVES ARE THE ENEMY

B y the time darkness had set in on May 2, 1863, Jackson's two
divisions had driven Howard's XI Corps from its positions on the
Orange Plank Road and Orange Turnpike and routed General
Howard from his headquarters at Dowdall's Tavern. The fleeing Union
soldiers joined the rest of the Army of the Potomac, regrouping in a
somewhat horseshoe shaped line several miles long, stretching from the
hilltop of Hazel Grove northward to each side of U S Ford on the
Rappahannock River. The Union soldiers began to dig earthworks and
place lumber in front of their lines to protect from an anticipated post-
dawn assault by the Confederates, who had begun massing troops on the
west and southeast, a couple of hundred yards from Hooker's army.

About 9 p.m., General Jackson and several of his officers rode
their horses in a southwesterly direction along Plank Road to assess the
damage his troops had inflicted on the Union Army and to determine if
the Rebs might be able to attack Hooker's troops that night, before they
were able to regroup in defensive positions. When Stonewall's party
turned their horses to head back to camp, some Rebel soldiers fired
several volleys at them, mistakenly believing they were Union troops.
Three bullets struck Jackson. One below his left shoulder severed an
artery and broke the bone. His men helped the General down from his
horse, applied a tourniquet to stop the bleeding, and put him on a
stretcher. An ambulance took him several miles south to a field hospital,
where a surgeon amputated his arm and then transported Stonewall thirty
miles further south, away from the battle, to a safe place within
Confederate territory, where it was hoped he would recover.

As dawn broke on the morning of May 3rd, Henry and his
medical team awoke and stepped off the ambulance wagon that was still
located by the field hospital tent, a hundred feet south of the pontoon

bridge Hooker's engineers had placed at U.S. Ford on the Rappahannock River. As they gazed in a southerly direction, they could see the nearly 100,000 Union Army troops in place behind barriers in a several miles long defensive position. Those at the far center of the Union lines, including artillery emplacements atop the hill at Hazel Grove with the Orange Turnpike and Chancellorsville within easy range, were under the command of General Sickles. They were awaiting attack from the west by 25,000 Rebs under General Stuart, who had taken over command of Jackson's Corps. But shortly after dawn, General Hooker visited Hazel Grove and, in a strategic blunder, possibly due to timidity resulting from Jackson's onslaught of the previous day and Hooker's determination to fight a defensive action, ordered Sickles to abandon Hazel Grove and relocate his men closer to Chancellorsville. Confederate General J.E.B. Stuart promptly took advantage of Hooker's tactical mistake and moved more than thirty cannons to the abandoned hilltop of Hazel Grove. His artillery then began a devastating barrage of cannon fire against the southernmost center of the Union line. A cannonball struck a pillar on the front porch of the Chancellorsville mansion where Hooker was standing, shattering it and knocking him unconscious. An hour later, when he awoke, the dazed commander refused the entreaties of his generals to relinquish his command. Instead, about 9:30 a.m., although the Army of the Potomac was putting up strong resistance to the Rebs' attack, 'Fighting Joe' ordered his army to pull back about a half mile to a line north of Chancellorsville, forming a horseshoe-shaped line near the pontoon bridge at U.S. Ford on the Rappahannock. It seemed as though Hooker had begun to lose his nerve and wanted an escape route to be close by. Lee's army promptly occupied the Orange Turnpike and Chancellorsville.

Meanwhile, the field hospital team was kept busy all day. The fighting was the most intense and costly of the Chancellorsville Battle. Both sides sustained thousands of casualties that day. Major Sedgwick was still unable to fully use his right arm, so Henry had the duty of performing all the surgeries. The ambulance driver and two stretcher bearers worked feverishly throughout the day, making at least two trips per hour to the scene of battle and returning with ten or more wounded soldiers each time. They said it was difficult—and depressing—to try to move on the battlefield littered with dead and wounded. Cries of pain, desperation, and for help filled the air. They had to carefully step over bodies, some lifeless and others with wounds ranging from serious to hopeless, but all of the wounded reaching out to grab the trousers of the stretcher bearers, desperately begging for help. The medics had to make heart-wrenching choices about who to load onto the wagon and who to leave behind to die. The scene was to cause them restless sleep and nightmares for years to come.

The ambulance brought to the field hospital tent about forty wounded soldiers per hour. The stretcher bearers placed them on the ground outside the tent, in rows of ten. Major Sedgwick then examined each one, placed lint in their wounds, brushed the outside circumference of the wound with iodine, placed a bandage on it and administered opium to the soldiers to ease the pain. Then he left in place on the ground those he deemed inoperable and dying, leaving them to end their lives in a state of delirium. He called out to John Massey to place on the operating table those he believed might be saved by surgery. All the while, he tried to calm the patients and ignore their cries and cursing of him and Henry as monsters and butchers. Inside the tent, John Massey would hold each patient down on the operating table, as their arms flailed wildly in all directions, while nurse Hunter dripped chloroform on a cloth that she held over the nose and mouth of the patient. Henry, wearing a badly soiled apron with ever-increasing spatters of blood, pus and tiny pieces of bone and flesh, worked feverishly cutting skin and flesh and sawing bones, as he amputated the limbs of as many as ten patients per hour. He also tried to ignore the curses and name-calling ["butchers; bastards; monsters"] of the wounded soldiers, although the words of hatred spewing rapidly, like heavy rains during a storm, from the mouths of those he was desperately trying to help, were to haunt him for years. As he finished each surgery, Captain Freeman hurled the dismembered body part into the wheelbarrow, wiped off the blade of his scalpel with a cloth dipped in carbolic acid, poured a cup of water over his hands to wash off the soil, blood and guts, and then began another operation.

About 1 p.m., his eyes becoming blurry and his hands weak from the intense stress of continuous surgeries, Henry said to Massey, Hunter and Sedgwick:

"Let's take a half-hour break to rest and have something to eat and drink."

The exhausted crew agreed. They opened up a can of beans, which they placed on their tin plates along with some canned dried beef and stale hardtack, threw on the ground the weevils crawling on the hard cracker-like bread, which they made more palatable by pouring a quarter cup of water over it to soften its texture.

"Too bad we don't have the time to catch and roast us a beve," Massey commented wistfully.

"You're making my mouth water, just thinking about it," Henry said.

In less than a half hour after taking their break, the crew returned to work. The Captain looked at the wheelbarrow overflowing with dismembered body parts with bacteria-infested wounds, pus and blood, covered with beetles, maggots and flies. Putrefaction had already commenced, exuding a gut-sickening putrid odor. Henry asked Massey to take the wheelbarrow outside the tent and dump its contents by the river, and cover it with a layer of a foot of dirt. Twenty minutes later, Massey returned to assist Freeman with the surgeries.

Early that afternoon, as Sedgwick was administering to one of the wounded soldiers that the ambulance had just brought from the battlefield, the Major noticed a tall, heavy-set man with a thick grey beard and long greyish white hair, dressed in a wide-brimmed hat, brown leather jacket and khaki-colored trousers approaching him on horseback.

"Is that you, John?" the rider called out.

"Walt, what in hell are you doing here? There's a fierce battle going on, and it looks like our side may be getting the worst of it."

"A New York paper requested that I write a report about the conditions at field hospitals, so I interrupted my work as a nurse at a hospital in Washington to ride down here to get the facts for the story. I see you are still devoting your talents to trying to save the lives of our valiant soldiers, like you did the last time I saw you in Fredericksburg. Say, what's the matter with your right arm?"

"A Union Army corporal called me a butcher when we attempted to move him to the operating table for amputation of his badly wounded arm and sliced my forearm with his bayonet."

"That dumb bastard. Didn't he realize you were trying to save his life?"

"Not at that moment. But I finally got him to calm down and explained to him that it was his choice: amputation or a slow, painful death from blood-poisoning and gangrene. Luckily, my assistant, Captain Henry Freeman, was able to take over the surgeries for me. He's been upset at being called a monster and a butcher by most of the wounded he's trying to help. Maybe you could go inside the tent and talk to him. You know, reassure him that he's doing something worthwhile, saving lives, and that the wounded that are calling him names are just scared of losing a limb; that someday they'll realize he saved their lives and be thankful."

"Sure, John. Be glad to do that." The bearded man stepped inside the tent and approached Henry, who had just completed another surgery. "Captain Freeman," he said to Henry, "My name is Walt; I'm a friend of Major Sedgwick. I'm here as a journalist to write a story about the Battle of Chancellorsville and the treatment of our wounded soldiers. John tells me that you're upset cause so many of those you're trying to help are calling you a butcher."

"You are darn right about that," Henry said. "It's kinda depressing, being accused by so many I'm working long hours under almost unbearable conditions, trying to help. You know, I was anxious to get experience in surgery when I joined the Medical Corps. Was I ever naïve? I didn't realize what I was getting myself into. War is a living—and dying—Hell on earth. I have performed more amputations this day than the average civilian surgeon ever performs in a lifetime. And I get no thanks from the patients. They mostly call me names like 'butcher'."

"Don't let that get you upset. They are just afraid. Frightened of what their loved ones will think when they see them. They are scared because they think they may never be able to earn a living or support their families in their crippled state. Just keep in mind, you and hundreds of doctors like you, are really heroes. Under nearly intolerable conditions, you are working long hours to save lives. You deserve praise, not contempt. And in my article that will be published in several newspapers, I'll make sure the public is aware of that."

"Thanks, Walt. Say, you look familiar. Didn't you come to the Divisional Hospital at Stafford weeks ago, looking for your brother?"

"That's right. You've got a good memory. I finally found him. Well, I've got to be going now. Keep up the good work. You and those like you are saints, not butchers."

After he departed, Henry asked the Major what the journalist's full name was. Sedgwick replied:

"Oh, didn't he tell you? That was Walt Whitman. He's a famous poet. Our President, Abe Lincoln, keeps a book of his poetry, 'Leaves of Grass', in his bedroom at the White House."

Uplifted by the praise of the famous literary figure, Henry returned to his surgical work. The group was to endure one more day of nonstop surgeries from dawn until a couple of hours after dusk, in a desperate attempt to save lives. Meanwhile, the battlefield became littered with an ever-increasing number of dead, dying, and maimed bodies of soldiers from both sides.

The utter savagery and horror of the War hit home a couple of hours after Whitman left the area, when Henry was about to operate on a private from Ohio who had sustained a deep wound with shattered bone in his left leg. Noticing that the soldier's insignia indicated he was from the 25th Ohio Regiment, Henry said: "I'm from Ohio, too, soldier. I miss the place. I'll be glad to return when the War is over."

"I'm not sure I ever want to return. I'm kind of ashamed of what I done. You see, I was lying behind an earthworks and lumber barrier as some Rebs approached. I got up, aiming my rifle at one of the advancing Johnnies and shot him in the stomach. As he collapsed onto the ground, he called my name, saying he was my cousin, Jeb Longworth. I stood in a state of shock for a moment, and one of his fellow soldiers discharged a round that struck me in my leg. I hadn't seen my uncle Bill's son since nearly five years ago, when my dad sent me to his brother's house in Georgia to spend a few weeks vacationing there. They were real nice to me, and Jeb and I spent loads of time together, fishing, hiking, swimming in a local stream. My dad and uncle are gonna hate me when they learn I maybe killed my cousin."

Henry tried to comfort the distraught soldier with reassuring words before operating. But in his heart, Henry painfully realized that this war that pitted brother against brother, relative against relative, countryman against countryman, was of the devil's making, a living Hell. Shortly before sunset, Major Sedgwick commandeered two wagons, ordering the drivers to take all but the hopelessly dying and those who had already passed on into the hereafter, to a Divisional hospital in Stafford or Washington. Then, about 9 p.m., the exhausted medical group climbed into the wagon and fell asleep.

CHAPTER 17:

A DEFEATED UNION ARMY RETREATS

As the bright yellow sun arose in the east on the morning of May 4, the fierce battle began again. There were heavy casualties on both sides. Only a few of the badly wounded lying on the ground outside the field hospital tent survived the night. Massey, Henry and the stretcher bearers dug shallow graves near the bank of the Rappahannock River and buried the dead, covering them over with a one-foot layer of dirt. They then resumed their feverish pace of transporting wounded from the field of battle to the hospital tent, treating and operating on them.

Confederate General Lee observed Hooker's soldiers strengthening their defensive fortifications. He concluded that Hooker had lost his nerve. Despite the Union Army vastly outnumbering the Rebels, Fighting Joe' had no intention of taking any aggressive action; he would only fight a defensive battle. So, Lee ordered General Stuart and his 25,000 men to remain in the Chancellorsville area and to continue attacking the perimeter of Hooker's line of defense. He then marched 21,000 of his men about twelve miles in a southeasterly direction to battle Union General Sedgwick's 19,000-man Division that was forming defensive positions on the south side of the Rappahannock, where Union engineers were hastily constructing a pontoon bridge as an escape route. Lee hoped to add the decimation of Sedgwick's Division to his thus far victorious battle. Arriving at the location of Sedgwick's army late in the afternoon, the Confederates began the attack. But by that time, Sedgwick's men had constructed strong earthworks defenses. Despite being outnumbered by the Rebels for the first time during the Chancellorsville Battle, the Union soldiers gave up no ground and inflicted as many casualties on the Confederates as they received. A few hours after the fighting died down due to darkness, Sedgwick's Army stealthily crossed the river at Scott's Ford and removed the pontoon bridge after reaching the safety of the north side. Disappointed at losing the opportunity to crush Sedgwick's Army, Lee and his troops marched back to Chancellorsville to join Stuart in the attack against Hooker's troops.

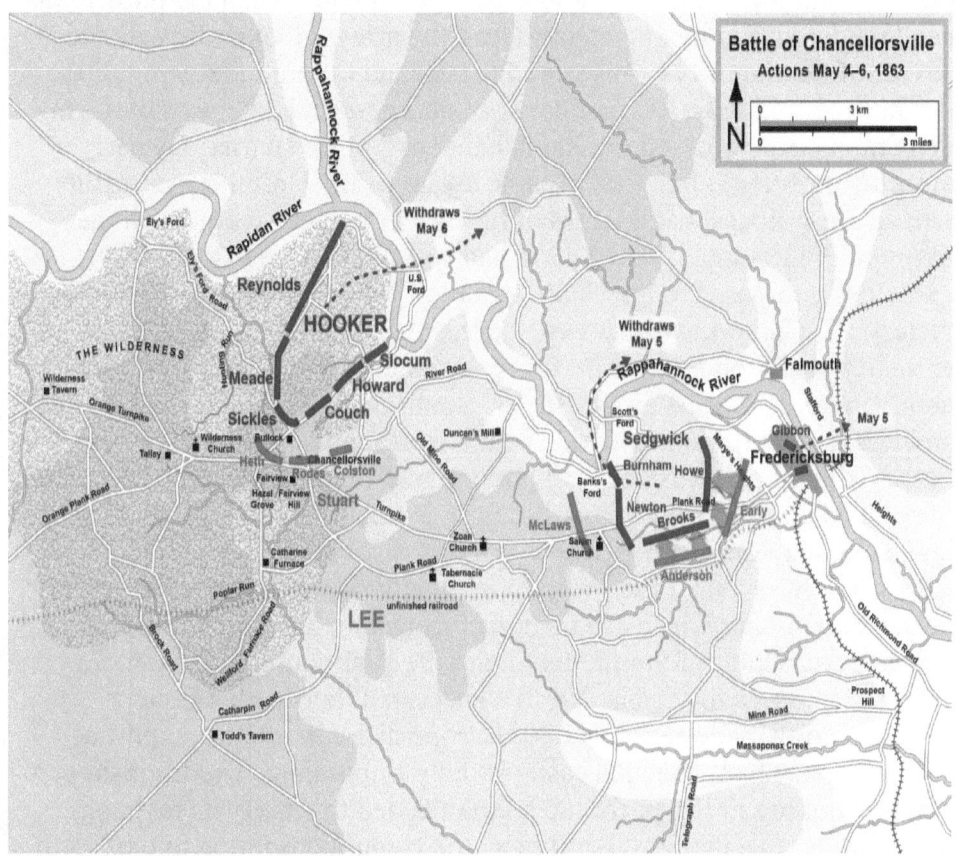

By the afternoon of May 5, the Union's defensive fortifications were so strong that the Rebels were unable to penetrate the Union lines. Despite his success in repulsing the enemy's assaults that day, shortly before midnight Hooker called his generals to a meeting to determine whether to fight on or retreat. 'Fighting Joe' had still not recovered from the blow to his head. Most of his generals distrusted his reasoning. The majority of them recognized that the Union Army had substantial numerical superiority to the Rebs, and voted to continue the battle. But Hooker had lost his nerve, lost confidence in the ability of most of his generals to wage a successful battle. In that, he was justified in blaming Howard, who had disobeyed his orders to build earthworks defenses in preparation for a possible invasion from the west, resulting in Jackson's spectacular crushing of the XI and XII Corps. But as for the other generals, Hooker was attempting to shift the blame from his own tactical mistakes, timidity, and failure to give up command when the blow to his head rendered him incompetent to lead the army. Hooker disregarded the advice of the majority of his general staff, and ordered the Army of the Potomac to withdraw. Under cover of darkness and a heavy rainstorm, the Union Army crossed the Rappahannock before sunrise. By early morning on May 6, Lee first became aware of the Union's successful retreat. He was upset at the loss of his chance to decisively crush the Army of the Potomac. The Union had sustained more than 17,000 casualties compared to the Confederate's 13,000. But it was a Pyrrhic victory. The Union, with its vast superiority in numbers, and huge civilian population to draw on for replacements, could afford to lose about one-eighth of its army. But the South, with its much smaller army and less than half the population of the North, plus its advocacy of 'states' rights' and weak federal government that left most of the drafting of soldiers and control of the militias up to each state, could ill afford to lose more than one-fifth of Lee's Army in a single battle.

Lee was aware that, with more than twice the population of the South and vast superiority in manufacturing capabilities over the primarily agricultural South, the longer the War continued, the more likely a Union victory. The North's successful barricade of major southern ports made supplies from Europe difficult and the export of cotton to raise badly needed cash virtually impossible. The English were already looking to Egypt for the cotton needed to supply its ravenous textile mills. Lee thought that if he could bring the fighting to the North's own territory and win a decisive battle, its leaders might be pressured to 'throw in the towel' and seek a settlement to this costly War. He began to plan an attack at Gettysburg.

When a victorious General Robert E. Lee rode into Chancellorsville on his white horse, Traveler, for about five minutes the Confederate troops gave him a rousing welcome, cheering and shouting "Hurrah", as the band played "Dixie". Lee felt an apotheosis similar to Caesar, victorious in the Gallic Wars, upon entering Rome with his army, after crossing the Rubicon. Lee truly believed that, under his leadership, the Confederate Army of Northern Virginia was invincible.

Meanwhile, General Jackson, who seemed to be recovering, complained of pains in his chest. The doctors examined him, but could find nothing wrong. The stethoscope, which had been commonly used by doctors in Europe for some time, had not yet been introduced in America. A couple of days later, on May 10, Jackson died from previously undiagnosed pneumonia. Southern soldiers and civilians wept at the passing of their daring, brilliant and charismatic hero. General Lee commented that he felt as if he had lost his right arm.

As for the site of the Chancellorsville Battle, both armies had abandoned the area. They left it up to the civilians who moved back into the area and to hundreds of volunteers to clean up the remnants of battle: thousands of dead and dying soldiers and horses from both armies; huge amounts of human waste that, together with the dead and dying, filled the air with noxious odors; wrecked and abandoned artillery, wagons and supplies. It would be weeks before the once peaceful wilderness and farmland would be restored to anything like its previous condition.

Captain Freeman was promoted to Surgeon Major and given a four week leave to return home to visit his wife and family before being reassigned to a hospital in Washington. Nurse Hunter and hospital steward John Massey were given three weeks leave to return to their homes before also being assigned to the same hospital. Major Sedgwick received an honorable discharge from the Medical Corps due to his injured right forearm, which would take almost a year to fully heal.

Disappointed at Hooker's lack of aggressiveness and failure in battle, President Lincoln once more raised the question: "Is there no one who can lead our army to victory?"

CHAPTER 18:

HOME ON LEAVE, HENRY SPENDS PRECIOUS MOMENTS WITH HIS YOUNG BRIDE

On the morning of May 9, 1863, the wagon carrying Henry arrived at the B & O train station in Washington, D.C. He boarded the train that would start him on the journey to his home in Cleveland, Ohio. There was no through train to his destination. It would be a boring ten-day journey with several changes of trains and three overnight stops between trains. On those nights, he would stay at a hotel near the depot, which would give him the opportunity to have a good hot dinner and breakfast, have a bath and change into clean clothes. On the other nights, if the train had a sleeping car, he would pay the extra fare for one of the cramped bunks that was convertible into a chair for daytime use. The luxurious and comfortable Pullman sleeping cars did not come into general use until after the Civil War. A couple of nights during his journey, the train had no sleeping car, so he would have to fall asleep sitting up on a hard wood seat.

Henry happily tolerated these discomforts, although he was irritated at the fact that the long train ride to and from Cleveland would leave him with only ten days to visit his wife and parents. It had been several months since he last saw them. He missed his beautiful wife and longed to hold her in his arms once more. On some nights, he would dream of her, only to have the image of her fade away as visions of the horrors he saw during the Chancellorsville Battle rushed in, with wounded soldiers calling him a butcher, a monster. Henry wished those nightmares would stop. He also became determined to have a photograph taken of his wife while he was home on leave. He would carry it with him when he returned to duty. Looking at it would provide him with solace and hope for the future during lonely nights at the hospital or during battles.

On May 17, two days before the train was to arrive at Cleveland, it stopped for an hour at a depot that was near a Western Union office. Henry went to the telegraph office and sent a telegram to his wife and parents telling them of the time the train was scheduled to arrive at Cleveland, and asking one of them to meet him there with a horse and buggy. At about 1:00 p.m. on May 19, the conductor announced:

"Next stop is Cleveland. We should arrive there in about a half hour. If that's your destination, gather up all your belongings and get ready to disembark from the train."

Henry's face flushed with excitement. As soon as the train stopped, he rose from his seat, grabbed his duffel bag, and quickly exited the train. Looking towards the depot about fifty yards away, he saw his wife, Elizabeth, seated in a buggy. He yelled her name as he ran towards her. She turned to look at him, jumped out of the carriage and ran towards him. Seeing her golden tresses glistening in the sunlight, framing her pretty face with a bright glow, Henry thought:

"I almost forgot how beautiful my wife is."

Within a minute, they were locked in an embrace. Tears rolled down her cheeks as she said:

"Oh, dearest. I missed you so. I longed to have you hold me in your arms. "

Henry felt warm all over.

"I missed you terribly, Liz. Seeing you and holding you in my arms again makes all the horrible events of the past few months worthwhile. I love you so much."

The two lovers remained locked in an embrace for several minutes. Then Elizabeth said:

"We should go home now. Our parents are anxiously awaiting your return."

They hopped onto the waiting buggy and drove to Henry's parents' home.

As the horse and buggy stopped in front of Henry's home, the couple's parents rushed outside to greet the returning soldier. With tears of joy rolling down her cheeks, his mother hugged and kissed her son, telling him how glad she was that he returned unscathed from the War. Liz's mother hugged him and gave him a kiss on his cheek. Their fathers shook his hand and expressed how glad they were to see him.

Henry said, "I haven't taken a bath or changed my clothes in two days. I have one set of clean underwear and socks left in my duffel bag. I feel real grimy after sitting in that hot, dirty, dusty rail car for the last couple of days. Would you mind if I take a bath right now and put on some clean clothes?"

"I'll go to the well and get some pails of fresh water, heat them on the stove, and pour them into the bathtub. You get settled in your and Liz's bedroom, and in less than fifteen minutes, your bath will be ready, son," his dad said.

Henry spent nearly a half hour in the bathtub. He found the warm water soothing and relaxing after spending so many hours on the train during the last ten days. He got dressed and entered the living room, where his and Liz's parents were eagerly waiting for him. His father said:

"Come outside with me to my office—you know, the converted barn. I want to show you something."

The major accompanied his father to the former barn, located about fifty feet away from the house. He noticed that it had a fresh coat of white paint and a couple of large windows had been installed on each side of the building. On the front door was a sign that stated: "THE CLEVELAND MEDICAL CLINIC

Resident Physicians/Surgeons Horace Freeman, M.D. and Henry Freeman, M.D."

Inside, there was a large reception/waiting room with eight chairs and, on each side of the hallway were four patient examination rooms with examination tables, a couple of chairs, and a cabinet containing medical supplies. At the far end of the hallway was an operating room with a table and a cabinet with scalpels and other surgical tools, alcohol, chloroform, bandages and various medications. Horace said:

"The design and equipment are all state of the art, the best available. Once you leave the military, you can work here as my full partner. There's no need for you to return to medical school to complete your second year. I'm sure the experience and training you are receiving in the Medical Corps has made further schooling unnecessary."

"Thanks, dad. It gives me something to look forward to—joining your medical practice. But for now, none of us know how much longer this War is going to last, and I intend to stay in the Medical Corps until it's over."

As they walked back to the house, Horace showed Henry an article that recently appeared in the Cleveland newspaper. A reporter had learned of Henry's achievements at the Divisional Hospital in Stafford and at the field hospital during the Battle of Chancellorsville. It said that Henry had proved to be a skilled surgeon, performing dozens of surgeries that saved the lives of wounded soldiers, and that he was promoted to the rank of Surgeon Major in recognition of his skill and courage. His father, beaming with pride, asked his son to relate some of his experiences.

"I'd rather not, dad. You see, I operated on more than one hundred wounded young servicemen during the few days of battle—mostly amputations. Fearing a future as a cripple, they cursed me, calling me a monster or butcher, or worse. I had to choose those whose wounds were, in my opinion, inoperable, and sedate them with opium and leave them to pass on alone into the next world. I had to order the stretcher bearers to leave to die slowly on the battlefield those soldiers with wounds to the head, chest or stomach. They followed my directions, but told me of their agony as they walked on the battlefield littered with thousands of dead as well as wounded and dying who would reach for and tug at their trouser legs, begging for help. One soldier I operated on even told me that he had shot his cousin, a member of the Rebel Army, and did not want to go home for fear of his father's reaction if he was to learn that his son had killed his nephew. War is horrible. I still have nightmares about it. I'd like to forget my experiences, at least while I'm home on leave."

Horace felt somewhat embarrassed at his son's reaction to his inquiry about Henry's wartime experiences. Never having actually been a soldier in wartime battles, Horace had only contemplated it in the abstract. But his son had witnessed and experienced the horrors of war, which caused him to wish to forget those events, at least for a while. Henry said:

"You know, dad, I think Liz's parents' religion, the Quakers, have the right idea about war. Practice pacifism. Know that all men and women, regardless of race or ethnicity, are creatures of God, contain goodness and truth, and should be treated as equals. The only question I cannot resolve involves their pacifism. I mean, how can you turn the other cheek if an enemy chooses evil over good and is intent on killing you?"

"I don't know the answer to that one, son. But I'm sorry for asking you to recall and relate some of the awful things you saw."

"That's all right, dad. You never experienced an actual battle. You just didn't realize......"

Henry then accompanied his father into the dining room where his mother had set out on the table a lavish spread, including roast turkey, potatoes, corn, peas, home-baked bread, butter, and apple cider. Henry hardly spoke as he was so busy consuming the delicious repast, finishing it off with a slice of his wife's apple pie. With a blissful look of satisfaction on his face, he exclaimed: "This is the best meal I've had in months. Thanks mom and Liz."

The group then retreated to the living room, where Henry and Liz cuddled together on the sofa. For the next several hours, they engaged in small talk, with Henry catching up on the events that had occurred in the lives of his family and friends while he was away in the Army Medical Corps.

When he was asked to relate some of his wartime experiences, he politely declined, giving a similar reason to that he had told Horace earlier. About 9 p.m. Henry said he was exhausted after his long journey home, and he and his wife retired to their bedroom.

Liz lit the kerosene lamp on the end table near their bed. She walked to the closet, removed her dress, placed it on a hanger, took off her shoes and underclothing, then walked over to the large dresser and removed a nightgown from a drawer. As she turned around, facing Henry who was standing naked by the bed, he approached her and said:

"Please wait there for a minute, darling, before putting on your gown."

Gently pulling her close to him, he embraced her, kissed her full red lips, and whispered:

"It's been so long. I forgot how beautiful you are. I love the feel of your body close to mine."

He bent down. Lifting her into his arms and carried her over to the bed, once more kissing her lips and then her ample breasts, which began heaving in excitement and pleasure. He lay on top of her, she sighed, and for the next couple of hours they engaged in amorous love. Henry forgot about the horrors of the War, and they both felt as if they had been lifted up to heaven. Finally, at about 11 p.m., the couple fell asleep, exhausted.

Henry and Liz spent most of the next nine days together, rekindling their romance. One morning they went to a studio in the city, where a photographer took several photos of Henry's wife. He developed them, and Henry had one four by six inches photo that he would put in the coat pocket of his uniform and carry with him during the War. They spent two days together at Liz's parents' cabin on Lake Erie, where they had gone on their honeymoon. Their time together seemed to fly by, and all too soon it was May 29 and Henry had to leave the comforts of his home and the love of his wife and family, to return to Washington. He embraced and kissed Liz, vowing to return as soon as the War ended, and boarded the train for the long, lonely and uncomfortable ride back to Campbell Hospital in Washington, D.C.

CHAPTER 19:

HENRY SERVES AS A SURGEON MAJOR AT CAMPBELL HOSPITAL IN WASHINGTON

At 10 a.m. on June 6, 1863, at the Baltimore depot, Henry boarded the B & O railroad train for the last leg of his journey back to his new post as Surgeon Major at Campbell hospital in Washington, D.C. He felt sad that he once more had to leave his beloved wife and parents back home in Ohio for an indefinite period of time. Of his thirty days' leave, he had spent eleven days traveling home and ten days traveling back to Washington. That gave him only nine days to spend with his wife and parents. But at least this time he was assigned not to a battlefield, but to a recently constructed army hospital in Washington. He looked forward to a more normal medical practice: helping ill and wounded soldiers recuperate; no more stressful, seemingly endless hours of amputations in rapid succession.

Henry was one of the first passengers to board the train, which was not scheduled to depart for a half hour. About five minutes after he and a few other passengers sat down on the wood bench-like seats, he looked out the window and saw hundreds of soldiers marching in an orderly fashion towards the train. He asked a nearby conductor:

"Are all those troops going to board this train?"

"Yes sir, Captain" [Henry was wearing his Captain's uniform].

"The B & O is the only company that serves the Capital. Thousands of soldiers ride it every day. You are lucky you got here early and got a seat. There will be standing room only in a few minutes."

By the time the train departed the station, each of its ten passenger cars was filled with about one hundred soldiers, packed so close together that they could hardly move. It was a hot June day and the temperature inside the cars was elevated about ten degrees above the ambient outside atmosphere. As the mass of bodies began to perspire, the humidity in each car rose, making everyone more uncomfortable. Henry thought:

"The ride to Chancellorsville in that wagon was a pleasure compared to this."

About one and a half hours later, the conductor called out:

"Next stop in five minutes is Washington D.C. That's as far as this train goes. Gather up all your belongings and be ready to depart. To take you wherever you're going in D.C., there are the horse-drawn streetcars that run from M and Wisconsin Streets in Georgetown, along Pennsylvania Avenue past the Capitol Building, and then south on 8th Street to the Navy Yard by the Potomac. They are usually crowded— carry millions of passengers a year—but after riding on this train, you should be used to that. Anyway, the fare is only four cents. For those of you who can afford better transportation, there usually are horses and buggies in front of the station, but a ride with them cost fifty cents to a couple of dollars, depending on where you want to go. Oh, those of you who need to relieve yourselves, there are ladies and gentlemen's saloons off the great hall of the depot."

As the train pulled to a stop, most of the passengers pushed and shoved their way to the front and rear exits, like a herd of stampeding cattle. Henry and a few others remained in their seats until most of the crowd had disembarked before departing from the passenger car. Carrying his duffel bag, he walked through the great hall of the depot to the exit. Despite being the largest room Henry had ever seen, it was crowded with people. As many as four hundred freight cars and one hundred passenger trains arrived at the B & O station each day, carrying soldiers, businessmen, politicians and visitors to the bustling and rapidly growing city. He stepped outside and turned around to look at the building. It was an impressive Italian-style structure with a one-hundred-foot high-clock tower on its left. Coming from the small city of Cleveland, Henry had never before seen such a magnificent building.

About ten feet away, parked by the curb, was a row of six horses and buggies. The driver of one noticed Henry holding onto his duffel bag while gazing at the building. He thought:

"That there soldier's actin' like a dumb hick. If I can get him to hire my cab, I bet I can separate him from his money quicker'n lightnin'."

The cabbie yelled to Henry: "Hey Cap'n. Need a ride? I'll give ya the best deal."

Henry walked over to the horse and buggy.

"I have to be at Campbell Hospital by 5 p.m.—three and a half hours from now. How much will you charge to drive me there?"

"Well sir, it'll cost ya only fifty cents, but if ya got over three hours, for an additional three bucks I can give you a tour of Washington—that is if ya ain't ever been here and would like to see the sights."

"That's kind of a steep price, but I only came to Washington once before, for less than an hour, on my way to General Hooker's Army of the Potomac, and I didn't get to see much. So, I'll take you up on the offer, just so long as you get me to Campbell before 5 p.m."

The cabbie said he wanted the $3.50 paid in advance, which Henry did.

"Hop on board, Cap'n, and we'll get movin'. Oh, yeh. My name is Charles Seavey. But them what knows me calls me 'Chuck'. What's your name, Cap'n?"

"Henry….Henry Freeman."

A couple of blocks from the depot, Chuck stopped the carriage and said:

"This here building is the Capitol. You can get out and look around for a little while."

Henry stood in awe of the magnificent structure. He had never before seen such a massive building. Looking up the numerous stone steps he noticed the tall columns in front of the entrance. Behind and above it was a two-level rotunda, on top of which was a large crane.

"Why is that crane there, Chuck."

"It's cuz the building ain't finished. They are gonna be placin' a huge metal dome on top, but construction's slow due to the War."

Over the next three hours, the cabbie took Henry to the President's House [now known as 'The White House'], just south of which was a canal and swamps, the apparent breeding ground for the mosquitos that were abundant in many areas of the city. Chuck momentarily stopped the cab in front of many of the sights, including: the Smithsonian Institution with its Italian Fortress appearance; the marble/granite Treasury building; the family mansion of Confederate General Robert E. Lee on the edge of Arlington, where, sitting on the front steps by the huge columns was a group of Union soldiers; a couple

92

of the more than 68 forts surrounding D.C. that were constructed for its defense at the outset of the War, which made Washington the most fortified city in the world; and the docks at the Potomac River, where the U.S. Hospital steamboat 'Red Rover' had just unloaded two hundred ill and wounded soldiers to be transported to one of the more than a couple of dozen hospitals in Washington.

Earlier that day, as they came to the 1300 block of E Street NW, Chuck pointed to a two-story red building with a light green awning in the front, saying:

"That's Shoemaker's Restaurant. They say you can get a real good lunch for just 75 cents."

Henry was hungry. He hadn't eaten anything since he had breakfast at a hotel near the station in Baltimore. He said:

"Stop here and wait while I get some lunch."

"If I do that, it'll cost ya another buck and a half, cuz it'll add to the time I gotta spend showin' ya around town."

Henry became irritated at the cabbie's demand for more money, but felt somewhat uncertain whether he could trust Chuck to wait for him to finish his meal. He decided it would be cheaper--and safer—if he offered to pay for the cabbie's lunch instead. The two of them entered the restaurant and each ate a meal that exceeded their expectations, and then continued on their tour.

At 4:30 p.m., the horse and buggy pulled up midway on a circular driveway by a flagpole, in front of a cluster of long, narrow wooden buildings.

"Why are we stopping here? What is this place?" Henry asked.

"This is Campbell Hospital."

Henry looked southward and saw the clock tower of the B & O Depot less than a mile away, and the Capitol Building a couple of blocks beyond that.

"You son of a bitch, Chuck. You could have brought me here from the depot in less than fifteen minutes. You bull-shitted me when you said the hospital was at the other end of town."

Chuck laughed, called Henry a 'dumb ass' and, cracking a whip on the horse's rear, quickly drove off.

CHAPTER 20:

HENRY SUGGESTS IMPROVEMENTS IN SANITATION

Henry entered the building located at a right angle to the flagpole at the center of the driveway. A sign indicated it was the 'Administration Building'. On a desk located a few steps from the entrance was a nameplate identifying the soldier seated behind the desk as 'Sergeant Richard Monroe, Information Officer". Henry saluted, identified himself, and said he had orders to report to Surgeon Colonel Samuel Corcoran for duty.

"His office is two doors down on the right."

"Thanks, Sergeant," Henry said, as he proceeded down the hall. Officer Freeman knocked on the door and entered, saluting and stating:

"Surgeon Major Henry Freeman reporting for duty, Colonel. I'm a little early—my orders say to be here tomorrow morning. Oh, and I went on thirty days leave right after being notified of my promotion, so I still am wearing my Captain's uniform."
Henry handed his orders to the colonel.

Corcoran walked over to a nearby closet, took out a jacket with a major's insignia on it and handed it to Freeman.

"We've been expecting you, so I had the quartermaster deliver this to my office. I also have something else I'm sure you'll be pleased to receive—your pay for the month of May."

The colonel unlocked a drawer on his desk and handed $115.50 to Henry.

"Due to your promotion to major, your pay for this month will be $53.50 more. Now, I'll show you around the hospital and tell you about the ward where you'll be assigned, the nurses and others who will assist you. The work here will be a lot different from that in a battlefield hospital: few if any amputations, mostly treating illnesses and minor surgeries, less stress."

"Thank God for that. I was performing about ten amputations per hour on screaming, frightened, badly wounded young soldiers, hurling their detached and bloody limbs into a wheelbarrow where flies, beetles and larvae gathered. Every few hours or so, we'd empty the wheelbarrow, dig a shallow hole, dump the contents of the 'barrow in it, and cover them with a layer of dirt. Really depressing work for a young doctor."

"I think you'll find your work here more pleasant and uplifting. Most of the time you'll be able to see the beneficial results of your work: the recovery of the wounded and ill soldiers. They and their families will often express their gratitude. And you may even meet our president. He and his wife Mary occasionally visit the wounded, bringing flowers, fruit and vegetables."

The colonel then showed Henry around the hospital. He said that at first, the army expected the War to be of short duration, so it took over some buildings as temporary hospitals. But by late 1861, when it became clear that each battle brought unexpectedly large numbers of casualties, and that the war was going to take years, the army constructed more than twenty hospitals capable of handling a total of more than 21,000 patients. Steamboats were converted into hospital ships that daily transported many hundreds of wounded along the Potomac River from the battlefields of Virginia to the docks at Washington, D.C., where horse-drawn ambulances transported them to the hospitals. By early 1862, the thirteen long single-story wood army barracks at Boundary Ave. and 7th Street had been converted into Campbell Hospital. Eleven of those buildings were wards, each with a row of 25 beds located against each of the longest side walls, with a large window after every third bed. There was a wide aisle in the center of each ward, between the two rows of beds. At the far end of each ward, hanging from the ceiling on each side, was an American flag bearing a total of thirteen red and white stripes and, in its upper left corner, 34 stars. One-half of the wards contained a bathroom, with a constant flow of water piped in from the Potomac River to the sinks and latrines, with the waste water flowing into drains that led to sewers. Each ward was staffed by one doctor, an orderly, two nurses [many of whom were Sisters of Mercy—Catholic nuns trained and experienced in the care of the ill and wounded]. Four of the wards located behind the administration building enclosed a quadrangle, in the center of which was the building that served as a dining hall and kitchen. To the right of those buildings were the nurses' quarters, the supply building, and the doctors' quarters.   At the far left of the hospital buildings were fifty tents, each with six beds. The hospital complex could thus accommodate about nine hundred patients.

As they walked through one of the wards, Corcoran said:

"We have cross ventilation with the windows open on each side. Unfortunately, that brings in loads of those pesky mosquitos that breed in the city's many swamps and canals. Despite that, very few of the patients use netting to keep the mosquitos away from them, because they claim it increases the heat."

It would not be until many years later that doctors discovered that the saliva of mosquitos transmitted to humans bitten by the pests, contained a protozoan that caused malaria. So, during warm weather months, more than one million soldiers came down with malaria. Thanks to the work of an apothecary who was a Jesuit priest in Peru, Father Salumbrino, in the early 1600s, the bark of the cinchona tree was found to successfully treat [but not cure] malaria. In 1820, quinine was isolated from the bark and ever since has been used to treat that illness. As a result, of the more than one million soldiers who contracted the disease, there were only 10,000 deaths.

Henry found the atmosphere in the wards to be almost sickening, heavy with the odor of urine and feces. He said:

"I've noticed that there are loaded bedpans at the foot of most beds. Doesn't anyone collect and dispose of them? That would substantially reduce the horrible odor. Even with the windows open, these wards smell as bad as latrines."

"The two nurses assigned to each ward are busy caring for the fifty patients. They work very hard for long hours at a time. They empty bedpans when they have the time, but just cannot be expected to empty all of them. The orderly picks up the bedpans about an hour before the end of his shift, brings them to the latrine, where he empties them. He has so many duties during the day—bringing each patient's food from the kitchen; taking dirty bedding and clothes to the laundry to be washed by the five Sisters of Mercy who operate the facility; getting medicines and supplies from the supply building when requested by doctors and nurses; and making the patients' beds—that he often does not even have the time to empty the bedpans at the end of his shift. As for the odor, it's harmless and after a while, everybody gets acclimatized to it."

"I'm not so sure it's harmless or that nobody notices the odor, colonel. You know, in Stafford, Virginia, at our winter quarters, the doctor from the Sanitary Commission who inspected the camp ordered us to move the latrines from their location by the river at the northernmost part of the base, southward to a place by the river just beyond the camp. He said that would prevent overflow of human waste from contaminating the river upstream, which was our only source of water. He was right. As a result of following his instructions, the number and frequency of illnesses like dysentery were greatly reduced. I realize that the patients and others in the wards are not ingesting the contents of the bedpans, only breathing in their odor. But I believe that it is unhealthy for man to live among his own waste, and that cleanliness of surroundings would speed patients' recovery."

"I see, major. And what would you have us do? Hire a second orderly at each ward whose duty it would be to constantly empty the bedpans?"

"Precisely sir," Henry said, as he stepped over one of the hundreds of dirty bandages that littered the floor. "And also, he could periodically clean up these bandages stained with blood, medication and pus that the doctors and nurses have apparently thrown on the floor."

"Major, once a day, those are also picked up and thrown into a rubbish barrel outside. Let me remind you, also, that the pus is laudable pus—harmless and an indication that the patient's wounds are healing." [At that time, medical practice was totally unaware of the existence of bacteria or that they were the cause of many diseases.]

"I'm not so sure, colonel. But the Sanitary Commission's inspector made it clear that cleanliness of the surroundings was essential to the health and recovery of patients in the divisional hospital in Stafford."

"Even if that were true, Campbell Hospital cannot afford the expense of hiring an additional orderly for each ward. The appropriation we receive from the government is barely enough to cover our current expenses."

Henry was upset at the filthy conditions he saw. He believed his recommendations would have a beneficial effect on patients' recovery as well as make their stay in the hospital more tolerable. Out of frustration, he blurted out:

"Sir, these poor souls have given their limbs, their health, in the service of our country. The least we can do for them is give them a pleasant environment in which to recover. You said I'll be getting fifty dollars more a month in pay. Well, take twenty dollars of that and use it to hire an additional orderly for the ward to which I am assigned. That should be more than enough to cover his wages for cleaning up the ward. After all, it's nearly twice the monthly salary of the soldiers who sacrificed their lives and limbs fighting this ungodly war."

"I'll give you this much credit, Major. You obviously put the welfare of your patients first. You are not just talk. You are willing to pay for what you believe to be right. Consider it done, Henry. I'll hire somebody immediately."

Feeling pleased at the outcome of his discussion with the colonel, Henry accompanied him to the dining hall, where they consumed a supper that was a vast improvement over the meals he had eaten at Chancellorsville. Thereafter, Corcoran showed him to his room at the doctor's quarters. A couple of hours later, an exhausted Henry fell asleep.

CHAPTER 21:

EVEN A WOUNDED ENEMY DESERVES MEDICAL CARE

The following morning, Henry awoke at 6 a.m., got dressed, and walked to the dining hall for breakfast. At 7 a.m. he reported to Colonel Corcoran's office for assignment to his ward.

"I'm assigning you to ward E, Henry. It's been without a doctor for nearly a week, ever since the doctor assigned there came down with typhoid fever. With the constant flow of ill and wounded soldiers coming into Washington, D.C., there's an acute shortage of qualified medical personnel. About the same time, we fired the orderly. With no doctor to advise him, he overdosed with opium and laudanum a wounded soldier who was in considerable pain, and the patient died."

"An orderly with no medical education or training? He should never have been allowed to give medication to a patient without a doctor's supervision."

"I know, Henry. But those kinds of things happen when we're short of doctors. Anyway, I replaced him with someone that I understand worked with you in Chancellorsville: John Massey."

"Great. He's a good and capable medical assistant."

"Another person who worked with you, nurse Alice Hunter, is also in ward E, as well as Sister Mary Healy, one of the best-trained and experienced of the Sisters of Mercy, who cares deeply for her patients, who seem to adore her."

"Sounds like I'll have some capable help. But what about the additional orderly to clean up the bedpans and stuff?"

"We contacted one of several civilians who recently signed a waiting list for jobs, and he is due to report to you at 8 a.m. in ward E. If he works out satisfactorily, maybe I will be able to convince the Army to allot more funds to pay for an additional orderly in each ward."

Henry proceeded to ward E where he greeted his friends Massey and Hunter. Family and friends of the patients were given free access to visit the wounded at all times. Reporters, evangelical ministers, politicians and even the curious also had unlimited access. As a result, the main aisle and the spaces between the beds were often crowded with people who stepped on and scattered the used bandages and occasionally tipped over bedpans, unknowingly spreading disease-causing bacteria. But by noon that day, the additional orderly had disposed of the contents of most of the bedpans and removed and dumped in outside barrels the used bandages and other trash that had littered the floors. As a light breeze on that balmy warm June day brought fresh outside air into the ward through the open windows, many of the visitors as well as the medical personnel commented on how improved the atmosphere in ward E had become. Henry was pleased and told the visitors to be sure to advise Colonel Corcoran of how clean and odor-free the ward was. The colonel relayed those comments to the Army, and within a couple of weeks Corcoran was given a supplemental monthly allotment sufficient to hire an additional orderly for each ward.

Henry had nurse Alice Hunter accompany him as he made the rounds to each patient, to make entries of his examination and evaluation on the medical record at the foot of each bed. He noticed that she wore a black dress with long sleeves and a skirt that came down to the bottom of her ankles, and a black hat that covered most of her hair. Half in jest, he asked: "Are you trying to compete with the nurse from the Sisters of Mercy for the ugliest costume, Alice?"

"Not by choice, Major. Dorothea Dix, the Army's Superintendent of Nurses, insists that all the nurses dress like this. She also fired those who were not between the ages of 30 and 50 years. Miss Dix said she does not want any of us to appear very attractive to the patients. I guess the prudish old maid wants to make sure no hanky-panky goes on. Personally, I believe the bright, smiling face of a nurse dressed in a pretty uniform would cheer up some of the unfortunate souls in our care. But then, what do I know? She also made me attend a three-day training course on nursing. As if she knows more about nursing than me!"

By about 10 a.m., most of the patients that were able arose from their beds, got dressed in their uniform, and were sitting on the edge of their beds. About a dozen were too ill to do so, so they remained lying down in their bunks. Several sat in wheelchairs in the aisle. About half of the patients had visitors—friends, members of their family, and ministers seeking converts—crowding in the aisles and spaces between the beds, making the movement of Henry and Alice from patient to patient more difficult. Most of the ill and wounded complained of the food: cornmeal and hardtack fried in smelly lard, and a lack of fruit or fresh vegetables. Henry thought that diet was inadequate and might prolong patients' recovery. He assured them that he would speak to Colonel Corcoran about it. Many told the major how much they enjoyed the nightly entertainment at the hospital's theater, which was open to all ambulatory patients. Henry thought that was beneficial because it cheered them up, or at least helped them forget their disability for a while.

About halfway through his rounds, Henry noticed that the next patient was wearing a Confederate uniform, sitting on the edge of his bed with the left sleeve of his jacket hanging down, empty. He appeared to be crying, with a look of despair.

"What's that Reb doing here, Alice?"

"Oh, he was captured in Chancellorsville and brought back here. His arm had a shrapnel wound that became badly infected and had to be amputated. Everyone—nurses, most doctors, and all the visitors-- ignore him, turn their backs on him. I felt sorry for him, so I look after him whenever I have the time. He said he has a wife and 2-year old child back home in Virginia. He misses them badly. Once he's recovered, he hopes he will be exchanged for a Union prisoner. There are a number of Rebs like him in each ward. "

As Henry and Alice tried to make their way to the Reb's side, a few visitors intentionally tried to block their way.

"You ain't gonna treat that no-count Reb, are you, Major? Fellas like him is the ones that shot and wounded our brother, Will, in the next bed."

"It's our duty to treat every patient in this ward, so please move out of our way."

Reluctantly, the visitors moved out of the way. One of them commented to the others in a whisper:

"Guess that doc is a Copperhead Reb ass-kisser."

A few minutes later, there was a commotion at the other end of the aisle, as a short, rather heavy set middle aged woman, accompanied by a soldier carrying a large basket, entered the ward and said she wanted to see the surgeon major in charge. John Massey directed them to where

Henry and Alice were standing, by the bed of the Confederate soldier. As they approached the major, the sergeant carrying the basket said:

"Major, this here is Mrs. Mary Todd Lincoln, wife of our president. She's got this basket of lemons that she wants to distribute to all the patients in this ward."

One of the visitors who had blocked Henry's way, said:

"Give some to all but that there Reb. He don't deserve nothing."

Mrs. Lincoln turned to the man and angrily responded to his remark.

"Who do you think you are? This man fought for what he believed in, wrong though that may be. Looks like he gave his left arm for that cause. He's a human being in need and deserves our help. I wouldn't want the Confederate doctors to do any less for our wounded boys. And just for your information, my brother is a surgeon for the Rebs and my brother-in-law is a General in the Confederate Army. This unfortunate war has pitted relative against relative and friend against friend. Hopefully it will soon end and we all will be partners once more in this great nation."

With an embarrassed look on their faces, the three visitors turned and walked away. Henry thanked the first lady for the fruit, saying it was sorely needed to prevent scurvy. The countenance of the wounded Reb lit up as he smiled and expressed his thanks to Mary Todd Lincoln. That evening, after returning to his quarters, Henry took a pen and paper and wrote a letter to his wife.

> *"My dearest Elizabeth,*
> *After ten boring days on the dirty and often overcrowded train, I finally arrived in Washington, D.C. two days ago. It's a big city with over seventy-five thousand permanent residents plus twenty-one thousand wounded and ill soldiers in more than twenty army hospitals. Thousands of soldiers arrive by train every week. Some assigned to one of the more than sixty forts surrounding the city, others just passing through on their way to join divisions, front lines or battles in other areas of our nation or the Confederate territories.*
>
> *Right in front of the train station was a row of carriages waiting to take people to their destination. I got tricked by a muggins [scoundrel] into going on a three-hour tour of the city for about*

four dollars plus lunch at a huge high-class restaurant. This place has some of the biggest buildings I ever saw. They haven't finished putting the dome on the Capitol building, and the Washington monument is only half completed—but really tall. The President's House is a huge white mansion. Unfortunately, a short distance away there's a large swamp that breeds swarms of mosquitos and flies, as well as putrid odors. Actually, all over the city there are swamps, dirty canals, some open sewers, many unpaved dirt roads. And on the edge of many of the streets, garbage has piled up because the city has grown so fast that it doesn't have enough workers to collect it on a regular basis. As a result, rather unpleasant odors and swarms of mosquitos, flies and other vermin abound in many parts of the city.

My work is interesting, more like that of a civilian doctor, with far less surgeries and stress than in the field hospital. John Massey and nurse Alice Hunter are assigned to my ward, along with a nun who is a trained and experienced nurse. Oh, I had a big surprise today. Hunter and I were scorned by three visitors who attempted to block our way to examine and treat a wounded Confederate soldier who had been captured and brought here for treatment. Moments later, in walks a woman with gifts of fruit for the patients. It was Mary Todd Lincoln, Abe's wife. She chastises the three visitors, tells them she has relatives in the rebel army— a doctor and a general—and that she hopes the War will be over soon so that the Johnnies can rejoin the Union and be friends again. The bad-mouth visitors turned tail and left.

I miss you, dearest Liz. I think of you often each day and dream of you at night. I long to hold you in my arms again. Until then, I'll write you as often as I can. Please write and let me know how things are at home.

With all my love,
Henry "

CHAPTER 22:

THE CONFEDERATE ARMY MARCHES TO BATTLE IN GETTYSBURG

During the next couple of weeks, Henry appreciated the slower pace, shorter hours, less stress and better patient prognoses of hospital work. The lack of knowledge of the cause of disease did result in some frustration and disappointments for the Major. Doctors were unaware that malaria was transmitted to humans by the bites of female mosquitos, so Henry and his peers considered the two-winged bloodsucking insects simply as annoying pests. They did not insist that all patients use the readily available mosquito nets above their beds. In the short time Henry was at Campbell Hospital, several patients in Ward E contracted malaria, which Henry looked upon as an unavoidable consequence of hospital life during summer months. It never occurred to him why the nurses, who wore long gowns and caps that covered most of their bodies except for hands and face, almost never contracted the disease. Fortunately, quinine was recognized as the proper treatment for malaria, so all of the patients in Ward E that had malaria eventually recovered.

The Major's reputation for successfully performing more than one hundred amputations during the Chancellorsville Battle spread throughout Campbell Hospital. A few times, when amputation of a limb of patients in other wards became necessary, the assigned surgeon asked Henry to assist him in the surgery. During one such operation, the Major was shocked to see the surgeon pick up a dirty scalpel and sharpen its blade by scraping it against the filthy sole of his boot. Grabbing the arm holding the instrument, Henry removed the scalpel from the surgeon's grasp, wiped it clean with a piece of cloth soaked in carbolic acid, while explaining to him that noted doctor Oliver Wendell Holmes, Sr. espoused cleanliness as a means of avoiding post-surgery disease.

Meanwhile, in Fredericksburg, Virginia, Confederate General Robert E. Lee, still savoring his seeming miraculous victory in Chancellorsville against the much larger Army of the Potomac, began to form a plan to attack the Yankees on their own soil. He hoped thereby to reduce the threat of Union attacks on Confederate lands in Virginia, as well as increase the demands of Union residents to seek a peaceful settlement of the War. Aided by new recruits and shifting of regiments, his Army now numbered more than 72,000 men. Lee and most of his army proceeded northwards through Virginia, West Virginia and Maryland, while the 9,500-man cavalry division commanded by General J.E.B. Stuart moved northwards via a different route, several miles east of the main portion of the Reb Army.

On June 16, Lee's First Corps under command of Lt. General James Longstreet, arrived near the town of Sharpsburg, Maryland. One of its regiments, commanded by Captain Jeremy Johnson, had been ordered to locate and appropriate food, supplies and horses from Northern farmers and merchants. So as not to antagonize the northerners, Lee had ordered that his army pay them for any goods and livestock taken. Lee had obviously misjudged the resentment such actions would give rise to among the northern civilian population, since payment was to be made in Confederate currency, which was considered worthless in the North. He also ordered his men to round up and ship to the South into slavery any African Americans they encounter.

A few miles south of Sharpsburg, Captain Johnson and his regiment stopped at a large market in front of a farm that was about one hundred acres in size. A sign in front read, 'AMOS FAMILY MARKET'.

Entering the store with a couple of his men, he found on each wall shelves containing canvas bags of corn, beans, carrots and desiccated vegetables. On the floor were bins with flour, corn and apples. In one corner of the store were shelves containing more than one hundred pairs of adult shoes of various sizes. Eight black men were loading the bins and shelves with supplies, and two cashiers, a black man and an obviously pregnant black woman, stood behind the counter near the exit. All of the blacks looked surprised and somewhat fearful to see armed soldiers in grey uniforms enter the market.

The Rebel Captain said: "I am Captain Johnson of the Army of Northern Virginia. We are here to pick up food and supplies. Don't worry. We will pay for them. Just tell your master, this market's owner, that we want to talk to him."

"We ain't got no master, Cap'n. We's free men and women. This here is our store and farm."

"Oh, yeh? We Rebs don't recognize any free Negroes. You all are slaves or escaped fugitive slaves. And we ain't gonna pay for any food or supplies we take from slaves. [turning to the corporal standing on his left] Corporal Stuart, get three men and tie these blacks together—except for the woman with child. Then march them back to Richmond. If any try to escape, shoot 'em."

"Yes sir, Captain. Incidentally, I noticed an enclosure outside the barn with about a half-dozen horses."

"Have a couple of men round them up and take them with us. Also, about one in six men in the First Corps don't have shoes, so tell our men to come in here and load up the wagons with food and shoes before you depart for Richmond. [turning to the black cashier] We ain't gonna pay you for the stuff we take. As slaves, you ain't entitled to any money."

The black woman cashier tearfully begged:

"Please don't take my husband. We got two young uns in the farmhouse and I got one more on the way. They need their father."

"Shut up bitch, or I'll take you too."

The Rebs then proceeded to load the wagons with all the food and supplies from the market. Two Reb soldiers led the six horses to join their line of march in front of the store. The corporal and three men started marching their captive African Americans to the Confederate Capitol and into slavery. Their families and friends never heard from them again.

Incidents such as this and paying merchants and farmers with Confederate paper money for goods and supplies seized, antagonized northerners. General Lee had made a huge error in judgment.

About fifteen miles northwest of Fredericksburg near Culpeper, Virginia, Stuart's cavalry encountered a slightly larger force of Union cavalry and infantry, which the Rebs drove back in an inconclusive battle. The outcome did give the Union cavalry confidence that they were at least as good in battle as the Confederates. Stuart's men proceeded northwesterly, arriving at the outskirts of Washington, D.C. on June 28. From there, they proceeded north to Pennsylvania.

Early in June, Lincoln wanted Hooker and his 94,000-man Army of the Potomac to closely follow Lee's movements and make sure that the Reb Army did not attempt to invade Washington. Hooker at first insisted that his army should move southward and attack the Confederate Capitol of Richmond, but ultimately gave in to Lincoln's demands. In late June, in another dispute with Lincoln, who had been fed up for some time with Hooker's argumentative nature and failure to take aggressive action by attacking Lee on his march northwards, Hooker offered his resignation. On June 28, Lincoln promptly accepted the offer and appointed Major General George Meade as head of the Army of the Potomac.

That morning, at Campbell hospital, Colonel Corcoran ordered a sergeant to summon Major Freeman, nurse Alice Hunter and orderly John Massey to his office. Corcoran handed each of them written orders to immediately board an ambulance that was waiting outside the entrance to the hospital, to be transported to the town of Gettysburg, Pennsylvania, where two days earlier some Confederate troops had routed the Pennsylvania militia and were apparently awaiting the arrival of the rest of Lee's Army of northern Virginia to prepare for battle. Henry, who the prior evening had sent a letter to his wife saying how happy he was with his assignment to Campbell Hospital and hoped that he would never again serve at a field hospital during battle, was disappointed. But he and his two friends gathered their belongings from their quarters and climbed aboard the ambulance. It would be an arduous two-day journey over often unpaved dirt roads, watching out for and avoiding enemy troops, before the ambulance would arrive north of the town of Gettysburg and meet up with Union General Howard's XI Corps in the late afternoon of June 30.

On June 29, Lee ordered his troops to gather at the base of South Mountain, eight miles west of Gettysburg. Reb General Pettigrew proceeded to that town to seek supplies, including shoes that hundreds of the Confederate soldiers lacked. The following morning, while approaching the town, he observed Union cavalry coming near the town from the south. He reported his observation to division commander Major General Heth who, on the morning of July 1, ordered two brigades led by Generals Archer and Davis to advance towards Gettysburg. As they approached three ridges west of the town, the Rebs encountered dismounted Union cavalry troops under command of General Buford, who had set up defenses to conduct a delaying action against the superior

Confederate forces. Buford thus intended to give the Union infantry time to occupy strong defensive positions south of Gettysburg on the high ground of Cemetery Hill, Cemetery Ridge, and Culp's hill. At 7:30 a.m., at a location about three miles west of Gettysburg, Union soldier Lt. Marcellus Jones, fired the first shot commencing the Battle of Gettysburg. In less than three hours, the Rebs had forced the Yanks east more than a mile to a ridge about a kilometer outside of the town.

That morning, General Reynolds, commander of the Union I Corps, was shot and killed, and General Abner Doubleday [who legend erroneously claims invented the game of baseball] assumed command of that Corps. South of the Chambersburg Pike, the main road to town from the west, Confederate General Archer's brigade of the Third Corps attacked Union General Meredith's Iron Brigade, which captured several hundred Rebs, including General Archer. Despite that initial success, by late afternoon the Iron Brigade was forced back two miles into the streets of Gettysburg.

Union General Howard had positioned his XI Corps in a line about one mile north of the town, with one of its divisions led by General Barlow on the far-right flank, unprotected by any natural obstacle or other Union troops. This was a tactical error, as Barlow's men were thus easily subject to attack from the north and east. Within moments of Barlow ordering Henry's crew to drive their ambulance and a wagon loaded with supplies southward and to set up their field hospital tent about one hundred yards to the southwest of his troops, the division of the Confederate Second Corps led by General Jubal Early attacked the Union's right flank from the north. Barlow promptly rescinded his order to Henry, telling him:

"You better get the hell out of here as quick as possible and set up shop in the south of town, safely away from battle, Major."
Henry and his group hurriedly boarded the ambulance and drove a little over two miles south, setting up the field hospital tent by Cemetery Hill. Meanwhile, Early's Rebs crushed and overran General Howard's line, captured General Barlow, and Howard's XI Corps retreated two miles south of Gettysburg, where it regrouped on the high ground at Cemetery Hill, one hundred yards north of Henry's field hospital.

As of early afternoon, much of the Army of the Potomac had not yet arrived or set up positions at the scene of the battle. July 1 would be the only day of the three-day battle in which the number of Lee's army engaged in the fighting [27,000 soldiers] outnumbered those of the

Union [22,000 soldiers]. Lee was aware that the numbers would dramatically change in the Union's favor by the next day. He also was painfully aware that, if the Yanks continued to hold the high ground, once their defensive barriers were set up and their reinforcements arrive, it would be difficult, if not impossible, to dislodge them. Lee therefore ordered General Ewell, commander of the Rebs' Second Corps, to capture Cemetery Hill if feasible. Lee apparently assumed that Ewell, who had served under the recently departed Stonewall Jackson, would, as Jackson would have done, attack and capture that high ground. But Ewell was more cautious than, and lacked the fortitude and daring of, Jackson. In a huge blunder, he concluded it was not feasible to attack Cemetery hill.

Because the XI Corps had retreated a couple of miles, Henry's ambulance crew was unable to reach and bring to the hospital tent most of the wounded, who now lay helplessly on the battlefield behind enemy lines. Only the ambulatory wounded and the few who could be reached because they were not yet behind the advancing Rebs, totaling 25 wounded, were treated by Henry and his aides. Eighteen of the wounded required amputation of a limb, but whoever had loaded the wagon placed in it only one kerosene lamp and no candles or wheelbarrow. The crew thus had to place the operating table outside the tent, to the left of the entrance, where the daylight sun made artificial lighting unnecessary. And Henry was left with no alternative but to pile up the severed limbs on the ground on the other side of the entrance, where they gathered flies, larvae and other vermin, and began the process of putrefaction, eventually emitting noxious odors until John Massey dug a hole five-feet long and three feet deep, into which he placed the limbs and then covered them over with a layer of dirt. While the pace of the surgeries had eased, Henry became no less upset at the screams, cries and cursing of his patients, who were mostly young, formerly physically fit, men with loved ones, family and often children, fearful of what the future would hold for them in their severely disabled condition.

A couple of hours after sunset, the crew climbed aboard the wagon to go to sleep, after tending to the twenty-five wounded or dying who lay on the ground outside the tent. Henry, nurse Hunter, and John Massey all had difficulty for a couple of hours in erasing from their minds the scenes of horror, and in falling asleep.

CHAPTER 23:

HENRY'S FIELD HOSPITAL TENT IS IN AN AREA PROTECTED BY UNION TROOPS

By sunrise on July 2, all of the troops of both armies had reached Gettysburg and were deploying for battle, except for Reb General Stuart's cavalry, which did not arrive until after noon, thereby depriving Lee of his reconnaissance in preparing battle plans, and Confederate General Pickett's division, which arrived about 4 p.m. The Union forces had taken up positions south of town in what looked like a fishhook position. It ran three miles from General Slocum's XII Corps parallel to Rock Creek, north to Culp's Hill, then to the west, General Howard's XI Corps occupying Cemetery Hill, then southwesterly General Hancock's II Corps and General Sickles' III Corps along Cemetery Ridge. On his own, Sickles determined that a better position would be the higher ground one-half mile to the west, so he moved his troops there along Emmitsburg Road south for a half-mile and then east for another half mile to Devil's Den.

Lee had hoped that General Longstreet's First Corps would begin attacking Sickles' and Hancock's troops on the left flank of the Union army early that day. But Longstreet convinced him to postpone the attack until 4 p.m. which, fortuitously for the Union, gave Sickles time to reposition his troops. Once Longstreet began the attack, he overwhelmed the defending Union soldiers. Sickles' division suffered huge losses and his leg was shattered by a direct hit in a Reb artillery barrage and had to be amputated. His troops retreated one mile towards Cemetery Ridge. There, the Confederate advance was stopped by a reserve Pennsylvania division and beaten back by the Union's II Corps and a ferocious bayonet charge by a valiant Minnesota regiment. At sunset, Reb General Jubal Early's division attacked Union positions on Cemetery Hill, resulting in the defending Union brigade losing half of its men, but it held its position, causing Early's men to withdraw.

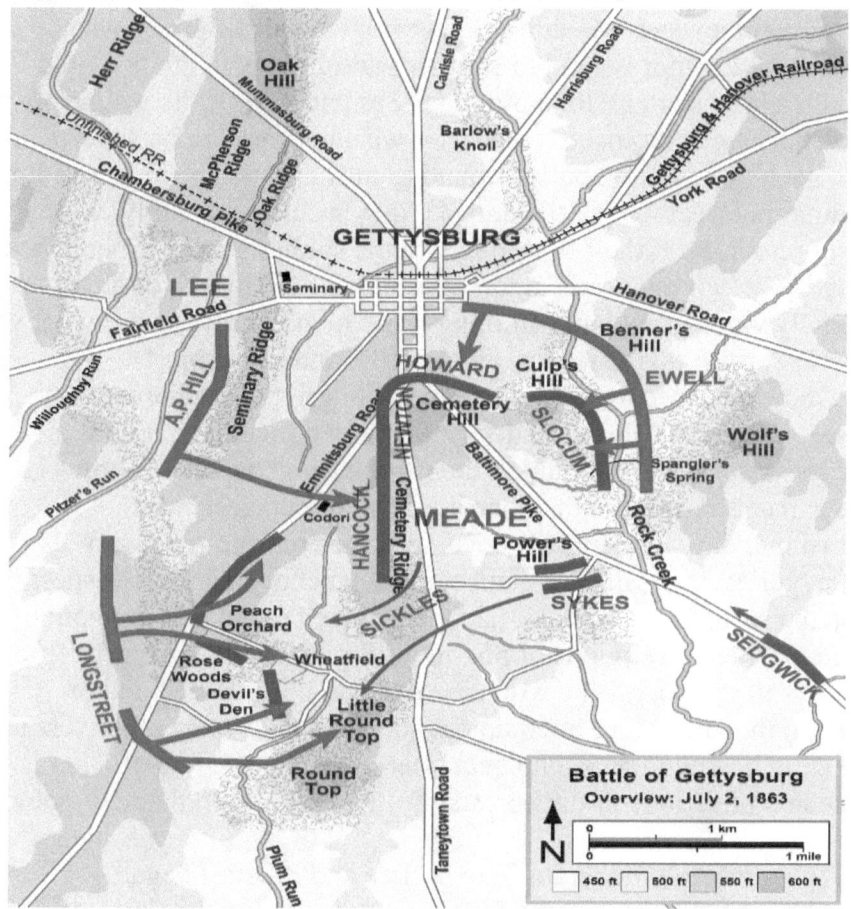

While the battle raged on, Henry's hospital tent was located in a relatively safe area about 100 yards south of Cemetery Hill, in the triangle formed by the intersection of the Baltimore Pike and Taneytown Road. Slocum's troops to his east, Howard's troops to the north, and Hancock's troops on his west, served as a protective barrier to the attacking Confederate forces. His field hospital's ambulance with two stretcher bearers made a couple of trips every daylight hour to the fields of battle to find and load onto the ambulance wounded Yankee soldiers, to transport them to the hospital tent. With well over 100,000 soldiers engaged in battle that day, there were thousands of dead, dying and wounded men littering the fields, staining the dry grass and ground red with their blood. The ambulance driver would periodically stop, disembark with the stretcher bearers, and walk among the bodies on the ground. When they saw a Union soldier with wounded limb or what appeared to be a minor wound to another part of his body, they would put him on a stretcher and load him on the ambulance. If the wound was to the head, chest or stomach [except for what appeared to be superficial wounds, such as a grazing bullet wound to the head or hip, causing a lot of bleeding, but treatable by the doctor], they would reluctantly, with a feeling of remorse, do their best to ignore the soldier's cries for help and pass him by. When they came upon a wounded Reb, in a fit of anger they occasionally would kick him, shouting something like: "You got what ya deserve for startin' this here war, ya bastard", and move on.

Once more, Henry was overcome with grief at the horrors he witnessed, the cries of the wounded (many of whom cursed him as a butcher and a devil for amputating their limbs), and he and his crew became exhausted as more than one hundred amputations were performed that day. As darkness enveloped the area and made any further surgeries impossible, a blanket of melancholy and helplessness set upon the crew. None of them had the stomach to get any food out of the wagon. Whether religious or not, they all prayed to God for the horrific war to end soon. The wounded that had been treated and/or operated on that day, were lined up outside the tent in rows of ten. Henry and the crew boarded the wagon and, after a couple of hours of tormented recollections of the horrors they had witnessed that day, they fell asleep.

That night, Confederate General Lee and his staff began preparing a plan of battle for the following day. During the first two days of battle, the Rebs had been unable to penetrate the defensive line of the Union forces, although General Longstreet's divisions had succeeded in pushing back the southerly portion of the Yankee line from Emmitsburg Road about a mile in an easterly direction in a line running from Hancock's divisions along Cemetery Ridge southward a mile to the high ground known as Round Top. Thus far, in a costly and ferocious two days of battle, neither side could claim victory, both having suffered nearly an equal number of casualties. Recalling his successes against far superior forces at Fredericksburg and Chancellorsville, Lee still believed that, under his command, the Army of Northern Virginia was invincible. He determined that Longstreet's divisions should attack the entire westerly Union line from its northernmost position along Emmitsburg Road to its southernmost troops on and east of Round Top, with three of Longstreet's divisions concentrating their attack against Union General Hancock's forces along Cemetery Ridge in an attempt to break through the northwest Union defensive line.

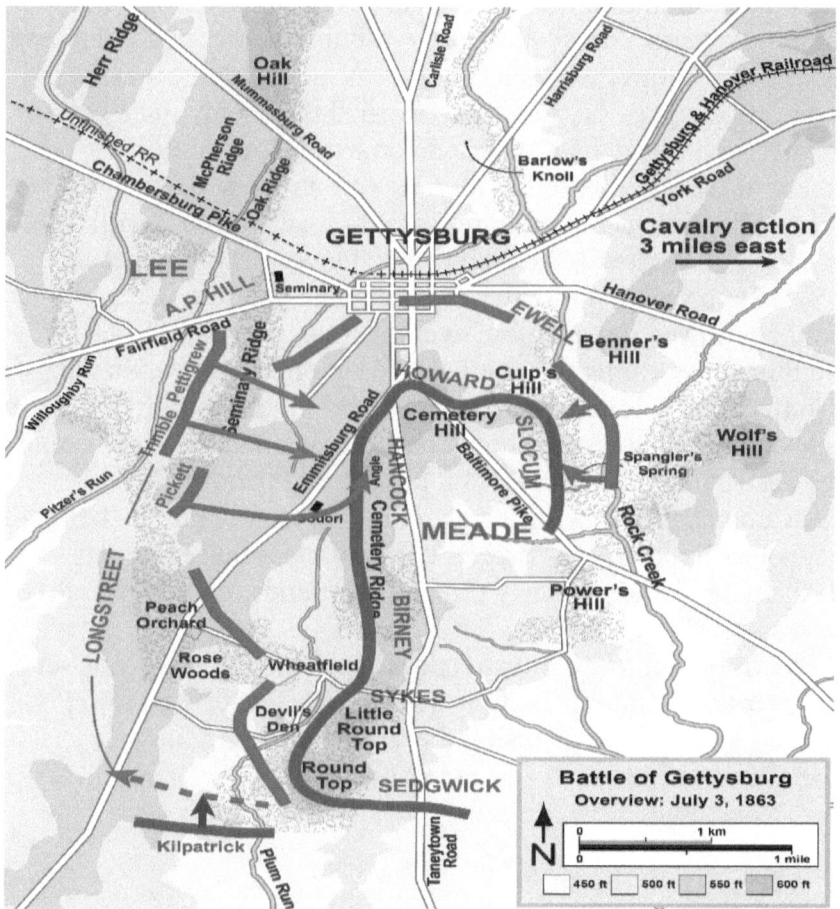

Meanwhile, Lee intended for Ewell's divisions to attack Generals Howard's and Slocum's Union divisions on the northernmost and eastern sections of the Army of the Potomac's lines. Realizing that most of the Yankees' army was located in strong defensive positions on higher ground facing about a mile of low-lying open fields and terrain with fences and other obstacles for the Reb Army to cross before reaching the Union lines, Longstreet argued against the plan, which he was certain could not succeed. He said to Lee:

"General, I have been a soldier all my life…..and…know what soldiers can do. It is my opinion that no fifteen thousand men ever arrayed for battle can take that [Cemetery Ridge and Cemetery Hill] position."

Lee had been educated at West Point, where he learned the battle tactics of Napoleon: infantry formations of several lines of one hundred men marching towards enemy positions, with the first row shooting and then kneeling down to reload their muskets as the second row moved forward shooting, and so on, until they reached the enemy lines with fixed bayonets and began hand-to-hand combat. But with the development of the rifled barrel, with a maximum range of over 500 yards and an effective [accurate] range of 300 yards [more than five times the range of muskets], the Napoleonic tactic was no longer feasible, as an approaching infantry crossing nine hundred yards of open field would be mowed down before ever reaching the enemy. Lee had witnessed this in the killing of thousands of Union infantry advancing against Confederate soldiers firing from behind a stone wall in the Battle of Fredericksburg and knew or should have known that the Napoleonic tactic was obsolete and disastrous. But his ego and belief in his invincibility and desire for a decisive victory apparently got the better of him. He ignored General Longstreet's constant pleas that his troops would be massacred and callously ordered thousands of Confederate troops on a suicidal mission.

Lee firmly rebuffed Longstreet's advice, and the stage was set for the South's disastrous attack the following day, which caused it to lose the battle, was a prelude to its losing the War, and would for over a century be memorialized as "The Lost Cause."

CHAPTER 24:

LEE ORDERS THOUSANDS OF REBS ON A HOPELESS SUICIDAL ATTACK

As the bright yellow sun rose in the east on the morning of July 3, Henry and his crew awakened and stepped out of the wagon. The temperature was already in the mid-70s and, within a couple of hours, would reach nearly 90 degrees. The air was so humid that moderate activity would cause one to drip with perspiration. The field hospital tent was still about one hundred yards south of General Howard's troops entrenched at the top of Cemetery Hill. The Union commanders believed it was in a protected area, midway between Hancock's troops on the west and Slocum's division on the east, in the hook area of the army's fishhook configuration defensive position.

Because the Army of the Potomac was surrounded on three sides by Confederate troops preparing to attack, Henry had been unable, without crossing Rebel lines, to transport to the train depot or the nearest divisional hospital, any of the wounded that he had treated the previous day. Five soldiers that had successfully been treated for flesh wounds to their limbs, had returned to their units for duty. Ten with inoperable wounds to their stomach, chest or head, who had been given opium to ease the pain while dying, had departed this world overnight. John Massey and the stretcher bearers buried them in shallow graves about fifty feet south of the tent. The remaining approximately 85 wounded were still lying on the ground in eight rows of ten and one of five, in what was thought to be a safe location, fifteen feet southeast of the field hospital. Once every hour, nurse Alice hunter would spend about fifteen minutes bringing them water and tending as best she could to their needs.

The nearest source of fresh water, Rock Creek, was to the east, behind enemy lines. But its tributary, a stream, ran in a westerly direction, about four hundred yards south of Henry's tent. Massey and the stretcher bearers made several trips there carrying empty pails, filling them with water, and returning to the tent, where they filled an empty barrel with fresh water. They made hot coffee with the water, and that, together with a slice of hardtack and some hot cornmeal mush, was their breakfast.

Lee had planned for General Ewell's Second Corps, which the previous day had captured the Union's abandoned defensive positions near the bottom of Culp's Hill, to attack and capture the Federal defensive positions at the top of the hill. But shortly after daybreak, as the Rebs began their attack, Union artillery bombarded their positions on lower Culp's Hill and, four hours later the Union troops still held their positions and the Confederates abandoned their attack. Lee also had planned for Confederate artillery to be in place early that morning on the west side of the fishhook line and begin a bombardment of the Union's center line, but the artillery was not ready until more than five hours later.

Meanwhile, Henry's ambulance with two stretcher bearers rode up the southern side of Copp's Hill, loaded wounded onto the ambulance and transported them to the field hospital tent. Henry had once more set up the operating table outside the tent, near the entrance. By 1 p.m., only thirty wounded had been brought to the field hospital for treatment, many of them had sustained just flesh wounds, which the Major cleaned, stitched close, and then sent the soldiers back to their unit. Only sixteen of the wounded had severe injuries to a limb that required amputation. So, Henry, Massey and nurse Hunter were relieved that the pace of surgeries was much slower and they had more time to make certain that the outcome would be the best possible. That was to change drastically that afternoon.

By 1 p.m., more than 150 Confederate cannons were in place along Emmitsburg Road from Peach Orchard northwards for two miles, to near its intersection with Taneytown Road. For the first time in the war, the Confederates had far more cannons [over 150] in place and ready to bombard the Union positions than the Army of the Potomac had in place to fire on the Rebs [80 cannons]. But all of the Rebs artillery were smooth bore, less accurate and with far less effective range than 30 of the Union's cannons, which had rifled barrels capable of accurately striking troops more than 500 yards distant. Another major advantage of the North's artillery was that some fired partially hollow shells, filled with small metal balls and an explosive that would detonate upon impact, sending shrapnel in all directions, capable of killing as many as ten soldiers at one time.

The thunderous sound of all those cannons firing at each other's positions was almost deafening. The cannonballs landed with such force that earth, rocks and pieces of trees, plants and troops they struck shot out in all directions, leaving fires and smoke at the point of impact. Less than fifteen minutes after the bombardment began, the hills occupied by the Feds and the positions of both sides became enveloped in smoke, making it difficult for each side to see if their artillery had hit the opposing force's positions. To take advantage of that, and to preserve ammunition for the anticipated Reb infantry attack, Union General Hunt ordered the cannon to gradually cease firing, to give the Confederates the impression that they had successfully knocked out the Union's artillery batteries.

Henry and his crew thought that the rows of treated wounded lying on the ground near the tent were in a safe place, protected by the federal troops on three sides. But within an hour after the thunderous bombardment of Union positions began, due in part to poor gun placement, defective munitions, and some inept artillery troops, Confederate shells often overshot Union positions. Henry, Massey and Hunter were startled by a loud noise as a couple of shells landed on the row of five of the wounded arrayed on the ground near the tent. Those poor souls were killed instantly, their heads or other major body parts crushed, as skin, flesh and bones went flying in all directions, splattering onto a dozen others of the wounded, who let out terrified screams. For a about a minute, the dry grass underneath the victims burst into flames, which within minutes petered out, leaving behind billows of smoke and the odor of burnt flesh. Henry grabbed some bandages, a bottle of whiskey, a scalpel and needle and thread, while Massey ladled a gallon of fresh water into a pail. The two of them and nurse Hunter then rapidly walked over to the row of five wounded that had been struck by the cannonballs.

"There's nothing we can do for these poor souls except bury them as soon as possible. Their skulls have been crushed and their bodies burnt beyond recognition.," Henry said.

The three medical personnel then turned to the other wounded who had been splattered with blood, skin and body parts and were pleading for help and to be moved away to a safer place.

The Major, Hunter and Massey dipped cloths into the pail of water and washed away the spattering from the faces and bodies of the terrified wounded, giving some of them a sip of whiskey in hopes it might calm their fears. Henry ordered the stretcher bearers to drag the five dead bodies about twenty feet south, dig a shallow grave, and bury them in it. He ordered Massey to drive the ambulance wagon about a quarter mile west, just beyond Taneytown Road, to ask General Hancock for five wagons with horses to transport the 80 wounded to the nearest division hospital. As Massey approached within one hundred yards of where Hancock, astride his horse, was riding back and forth behind his troops on Cemetery Ridge, supervising their defense, a colonel, the General's aide, stopped John's wagon.

"I'm John Massey, a medic from Surgeon Major Freeman's field hospital back there [pointing]. I want to talk to General Hancock. We need five horses and wagons to transport to the nearest division hospital about eighty wounded soldiers that Major Freeman has treated. They're lying on the ground between your troops and General Slocum's. It's not safe there. Five have already been killed by artillery fire."

"Sorry about that, John. Even if we had wagons and horses, we couldn't spare them now. As you can see, we're under heavy bombardment by Reb artillery. The Johnnies surround our army and are attacking on three sides. The only way your wounded could make it outta here is by going south towards Baltimore or Washington, which would be a long trip, and there's no guarantee that you wouldn't encounter hostile troops on the way. The wounded are safer where they are. Maybe tomorrow, if the shelling and attack have stopped, you can take them to the nearby train station in Gettysburg, which would be a lot safer and faster ride than a wagon."

Discouraged, but realizing that the colonel was right, John turned his wagon around and rode back to the field hospital and related to Henry what Hancock's aide had said. About 3 p.m., the bombardment ceased, as nearly 13,000 Confederate infantrymen, in a line nearly a mile long, started marching across three quarters of a mile of open fields to attack Hancock's divisions on Cemetery Ridge in what came to be known as Pickett's Charge [although he was but one of three Reb Generals whose divisions made the attack]. Suddenly, the Yankee artillery came to life, pummeling the Johnnies with barrages of shells, including many of the hollow ones filled with small metal balls and explosives that killed as many as ten soldiers upon impact.

Witnessing the devastation to his troops, General Longstreet implored General Lee to call off the attack, calling it suicide. But Lee steadfastly refused. He had a reputation for a hot temper, and Longstreet's constant pleading irritated Lee to the point where the Rebs' First Corps Commander gave up, but could not bring himself to order General Pickett to start the advance. When Pickett asked his commander if it was time for his division to advance, Longstreet was unable to speak the words that would send much of his division to certain death, simply bowed his head, which Pickett took to mean "Yes".

Was General Lee so desperate to be victorious in Gettysburg that he lost all sense of reason? Did he really believe that he was the most brilliant general and that his army was invincible? Was he so arrogant that he refused to listen to the sage advice of others? We can never be certain why this commander, once revered by his troops and feared by enemy armies, chose to force the men under his command into a suicidal attack. Lee never wrote his memoirs, his officers that led the charge were casualties or failed to write any report, and Pickett rote a scathing report, but Lee ordered him to destroy it. What is certain is that, as the Rebs marched across the fields, it was as if they were walking into the jaws of death. More than half of the 13,000 Johnnies were mowed down, first by Yankee cannon-fire, and then, as they came within 500 yards of the Union infantry that was crouching behind a four-foot high stone wall, a nearly constant barrage of rifle and rifled musket fire decimated the attacking Rebs before they reached the Union defenders. It was the reverse of what had occurred to Union troops during the First Battle of Fredericksburg, when more than 6,000 of them lost their lives in attacking Confederate infantry positioned behind a four-foot high stone wall. Lee had witnessed that, but either forgot about it or didn't care when his troops were faced with a similar situation. But the Union defenders at Gettysburg did remember. Some of them joyfully said things like: "It's like shooting a flock of ducks sitting on a pond." Many who had been at Fredericksburg shouted: "Fredericksburg—them dumb ass Johnnies is getting the crap beat out of them, like happened to us at Fredericksburg."

For a brief time, some of Pickett's men actually made it to a portion of the wall called "The Angle", and some of the defenders fled. The Rebs captured two cannons and turned them to fire on the Yanks, but realized there was no more ammunition for the artillery. A fierce counter-attack by a Union regiment forced the Johnnies to retreat from what came to be known as the "high water mark" of the Confederacy. The surviving Reb troops retreated back to their lines near Seminary Ridge, and that ended the three-day battle. The Union sustained only 1,500 casualties that day, whereas Lee's army sustained nearly 7,000 casualties in 'Pickett's Charge'. General Lee's insistence on that attack that was doomed to failure from the start and his failure to heed the advice of the commander of his First Corps, General Longstreet, had turned what until then was an indecisive battle in which the South had sustained fewer casualties than the North, into a humiliating defeat. Union General Meade's forces had struck Lee's Army of Northern Virginia with a devastating loss from which it would never fully recover. To add to the sad news for the South, the following day the Confederate's Vicksburg garrison surrendered to General Grant, and shortly thereafter the English decided against recognizing the Confederacy as a nation.

Heavy rains came on July 4, when the two exhausted armies gathered much of their wounded from the battlefields. Major Henry Freeman finally got the horses and wagons he needed to carry the wounded to a waiting train that would deliver them to hospitals in Washington. That evening, Lee's army, including an over a mile-long wagon train of supplies and the wounded, protected by cavalry, began its long retreat back to Virginia. Although Meade's exhausted army followed, it failed to aggressively attack and attempt to crush the Army of Northern Virginia. Lincoln became irritated at Meade because of this, especially when Lee's army reached the safety of the south side of the Rappahannock River. General Pickett held Lee in contempt after Gettysburg, but in later life apparently developed a sense of humor about the events of July 3, 1863. When asked why 'Pickett's Charge' failed, he replied:

"I'm not rightly sure, but I think the Yankees might have had something to do with it."

As for the battlefields in Gettysburg after the armies departed, they were left in a mess, with several thousand wounded and dying Confederate soldiers, 8,000 dead Reb and Union soldiers, and the carcasses of several thousand dead horses. Putrefaction already had begun setting in and creating a horrible stench. It was left to the residents and over a thousand volunteers to bury the dead and clean up the area before the dedication of the cemetery and Lincoln's Gettysburg Address occurred months later.

CHAPTER 25:

HENRY RETURNS TO CAMPBELL HOSPITAL

When their wagon reached Baltimore, Henry, Alice Hunter and John Massey decided to take the B & O train to Washington, D.C., since it would be much faster and more comfortable than the horse-drawn wagon. They gave the driver and the two stretcher bearers instructions to bring the wagon to the Medical Corps Headquarters ambulance yard in D.C., and then boarded the train at Baltimore Depot. The trio arrived in Washington at 5 p.m. on July 10, 1863. Since it had been nearly two weeks since any of them had eaten a decent meal, Henry offered to hire a cab to go to Shoemaker's Restaurant on E Street NW and treat them to dinner.

"It's got the reputation of being one of the finest restaurants in the city. I've been there only once, but the food was delicious. A German immigrant runs it and the menu has a large selection of German cuisine and, of course, an assortment of German beers. I had the sauerbraten and it was delicious and the meat was very tender. I'm sure you'll like it."

Massey quickly replied, "Say no more, Major. You convinced me. Thanks for the generous offer. It'll be a welcome change from the crappy salt horse [meat] and desiccated [dehydrated] vegetables and weevil-infested hardtack the army's been feeding us the past couple of weeks."

Hunter enthusiastically agreed.

Outside the train station, Henry hired a horse and buggy to take them to Shoemaker's Restaurant. This time the Major did not act like a country bumpkin. He negotiated with the driver and paid him fifty cents for the fare. When they arrived at Shoemaker's, Henry asked the driver to return at 7 p.m. to take them to Campbell Hospital. The three friends then entered the restaurant, were seated at a table covered with an embroidered linen tablecloth, on top of which the waiter put three place settings, silverware, glasses and cups.

"They sure treat us like big bugs [important people]", exclaimed nurse Hunter.

The crew each selected their meal and a glass of beer from the menu. An hour and fifteen minutes later, after enjoying their savory repast, Henry paid the five-dollar charge for the meals, and they went outside where they found the cab waiting to take them to Campbell Hospital. Arriving at Campbell at 7:30 p.m., tired out from days of travelling, they each retired to their quarters. Henry lit a candle and read a letter from his wife that had been delivered and left on his desk while he was away. He decided to reply before going to bed.

> *July 11, 1863*
> *Campbell Hospital, Washington, D.C.*
> *My dearest Liz,*
> *I found your letter when I returned to my quarters a half hour ago. You wanted to know why you hadn't heard from me for some time, and how I was doing. I can tell you that I am now well, but very tired. You see, two weeks ago I was ordered to report to the Army of the Potomac in Gettysburg, Pennsylvania. The Confederate Army of Northern Virginia had invaded the North and was expected to do battle there. After an uncomfortable two-and-a-half-days' journey in a wagon, over mostly dirt and gravel roads, John Massey, nurse Alice Hunter and I arrived at Gettysburg late in the afternoon of June 30 and met up with a division of General Howard's XI Corps about one mile north of town. Before we could set up our field hospital tent, Reb General Jubal Early's divisions attacked and Union General Barlow ordered us to drive our wagon two miles south, past Gettysburg, and set up our tent on the south side of Cemetery Hill. We did as ordered and, by the morning of July 1, we found ourselves in the center of a half circle of the northernmost Union lines, protected by General Hancock's divisions on the west, General Howard's on the north, and General Slocum's on the east.*
>
> *What happened next was three days of living Hell, as about 165,000 troops furiously battled in the fields and hills south of the town, as the Reb army surrounded our troops on all but the*

southern side of our lines. They made repeated attacks against our troops' positions, but for the most part, failed to break through the Union lines. Both sides suffered many casualties. Our ambulance made trips to the scenes of battle throughout the morning, picking up the wounded and bringing them to our field hospital, where we treated and operated [amputations] on the poor brave young men. The weather was hot and very humid, with perspiration pouring off our bodies as if we had been standing out in the rain. About fifteen feet from the entrance to our tent, in the oppressive outside air, a pile of bloody, discolored arms, legs, feet, flesh and blood that I had severed from the terrified and screaming young soldiers during surgery, began to pile up, attracting flies, larvae, beetles and other vermin, and gradually giving off a putrid odor.

We were unable to transport to a divisional hospital the recovering wounded troops that we had treated, because we lacked adequate wagons and our army was surrounded on three sides. So, we placed the recovering soldiers in rows on the ground. By noon on the third day of battle, Lee's artillery opened up a tremendous, deafening barrage of cannon fire. A couple of errant shells overshot the Union lines and landed on a row of five of the wounded, crushing, dismembering, and burning them. It was a horrifying scene that I will never forget. In a final desperate attempt to prevail, Lee sent some 13,000 men on a suicide mission, crossing open fields, to attack Union troops entrenched behind a long stone wall. Our troops massacred half of them before Lee discontinued the battle and withdrew into the town. The following day, amidst heavy rains, each side gathered up its wounded. By the morning of July 5, Lee's defeated army was in retreat back to Virginia, General Meade had our army follow some distance behind, and both armies left thousands of dead soldiers and horses lying on the battlefield.

This is the first time that I have described the horrors of battle in my letters to you. I want you to understand how and why my attitudes and beliefs have changed dramatically. When I first expressed a desire to join the army, it was due to a feeling of patriotism, the firm conviction that secession was an act of treason. I firmly believed the South's hostile actions to preserve slavery were evil, that our side was in the right and God would therefore make certain that the War would be over shortly. At training camp, when I realized I was not cut out to be a fighting infantryman and was reassigned to the Medical Corps, I was overjoyed at the prospect of getting on-the-job medical training and surgical experience. But now, after being through two horrendous battles, where the casualties on both sides were more than twice the population of our hometown of Cleveland, I have no wish ever again to work as a battlefield surgeon. I have come to appreciate your parents' Quaker beliefs more. Surely it would be preferable to reach a peaceful resolution of this War. My ambulance driver and stretcher bearers have told me that about ten percent of the dead Confederate bodies they have encountered in their trips to the scenes of battle have been shoeless, wearing tattered clothes. The South apparently is unable to properly outfit its servicemen, many of whom come from families too poor to supply them with the necessary clothing. Yet these poor misguided young men are giving up life and limb in a fool's errand: preserving an abominable system run by wealthy and callous landowners that enslaves members of the human race.

I have come to hate Southerners who have caused this horrible war in an effort to preserve slavery. I also have come to hate those who support that evil and seek to kill Union soldiers. If God were in one blow to strike dead those Southerners, I would shed no tears. In fact, I would be overjoyed. I realize this is not a Christian attitude, but that is how I now feel.

Please forgive me for my lengthy diatribe. What I have seen and done during the past few months has been both enlightening and depressing, and given rise to a feeling of hatred of Southerners. I miss you very much. I long to return to Cleveland and the happy, peaceful life we had there. Please write soon. Your letters cheer me up.

With all my love, always and forever,
Henry

CHAPTER 26:

THE HOSPITAL ROUTINE IS A WELCOME RELIEF AFTER HENRY'S BATTLEFIELD EXPERIENCES

Henry had his first good night's sleep in a couple of weeks. He woke up refreshed at 7 a.m., got dressed and walked to the Mess Hall for a breakfast of bacon, eggs, coffee, and a slice of hardtack [without the weevils]. At 8 a.m., he entered the office of Colonel Corcoran to report for duty. John Massey and Alice Hunter had entered the office a couple of minutes earlier and were seated in chairs in front of the colonel's desk.

"Sit down, Major Freeman. Now that the three of you are here, I'll give you your assignments. But first, I want to thank all of you for your battlefield service. I have a telegram from General Hancock that I received yesterday. Let me read it to you."

> *"Colonel Corcoran,*
> *I am writing this to advise you of the outstanding service during the recent Gettysburg Campaign by three of the employees of Campbell Hospital: Surgeon Major Henry Freeman, his assistant John Massey, and nurse Alice Hunter.*
>
> *Their field hospital tent was set up behind the northernmost section of the Union lines, equidistant from my troops on the west, General Howard's on the north, and General Slocum's on the east. It was thought that they would be able to carry out their work of tending to the wounded and performing necessary surgeries in a protected area. However, within a short time the Rebel artillery began pounding our lines with a constant barrage of shells, some of which overshot their targets and landed near*

*the field hospital tent, killing five of the wounded soldiers who
had been recovering from surgery.*

*Through the entire three days of battle, your employees worked
tirelessly during the thirteen hours of daylight, gathering the
wounded from the battlefield, tending to their wounds, skillfully
performing hundreds of surgeries with an extraordinary rate of
success, while ignoring the dangers to their own lives. I commend
their bravery, devotion to duty and tireless efforts to save as
many of our brave wounded soldiers as possible.*

*I would appreciate your posting this telegram in a prominent
place in Campbell Hospital, so that all of the patients, their
visitors, and the medical personnel at Campbell can learn of
these heroes' achievements.*

Sincerely,
Major General Winfield S. Hancock"

After reading the communication, the colonel congratulated the
three of them, ordered Massey and Hunter to Ward E, and told Henry he
wanted to discuss something with him.

"Major, how would you like to be appointed Chief Surgeon of
this hospital? You would perform all of the major surgeries and train and
supervise the doctors performing all other surgeries."

"Thanks for the offer, sir. But I'm not sure I'm qualified to train
doctors or perform ALL of the major surgeries."

"Nonsense, Henry. With your experience and skill in performing
hundreds of surgeries under extreme battlefield conditions, you are
eminently qualified for the job."

"Even if that is true, Colonel, I think I'd prefer the slower pace
and more normal work of being the doctor in charge of Ward E. There
was a time when I might have jumped at the opportunity, but after the
hellish pace and rather depressing work during two battles, I think I'd
prefer a break and return to my former job."

"All right, Henry. I can understand your reluctance to accept the
offer. You can return to your work in Ward E."

Within a couple of days, the news of General Hancock's telegram
praising the work of Henry, Massey and Hunter had spread throughout
the hospital to doctors, nurses, patients and their visitors. The three were

looked upon as angels of mercy, and Henry was considered to have risen to the pinnacle of his profession. Whenever doctors or nurses had a question about proper diagnoses of, or treatment for, a patient's condition, they would seek Henry's advice. Patients who required major surgery would ask that Henry perform, or at least supervise, it. Not only did the major get great satisfaction from his new status in the hospital, but he also was very pleased at the results of some of the improvements in hospital care that he had established before leaving for the Gettysburg campaign. Several doctors and nurses told him:

"After the Army agreed to your demands and authorized the hiring of an additional employee for each ward, whose duty was to empty bedpans and clean up soiled bandages that littered the floors, the detailed medical records that we keep show that the rate of dysentery spreading to other patients decreased by more than 50 percent. We're not sure why, but it seems likely that your improvements in sanitation had something to do with it."

At the time, medical science was unaware of the existence of bacteria or that they and various unknown microscopic parasitic organisms, caused and spread disease. But thanks to Henry's insistence on prompt hygienic disposal of feces, the surroundings [food, water, hands of persons touching bedpans, etc.] were less likely to become contaminated, thereby reducing the spread of disease.

Over the next several weeks, Henry wrote a couple of letters to his beloved wife, telling her of his success in improvements in sanitation and treatment of patients which caused him to conduct his work with renewed enthusiasm and a heightened sense of satisfaction. He ended each letter with:

"I pray that this horrible war will be over soon. I miss you terribly and long to hold you in my arms again. I hope you and our parents are all well. Please write often, my dearest. I look forward anxiously for each of your letters to arrive. They bring great cheer to my lonely heart.

With all my love, forever,
Henry".

It was late in July, 1863, when Henry received a letter from Elizabeth in reply to the letter he wrote the night he returned to Campbell Hospital from Gettysburg. It read in part:

"My dearest Henry,

I was saddened by your recent letter about your experiences at Gettysburg and how they changed your attitude towards Reb soldiers. It pained me to read that you apparently have discarded your Christian teachings of love and forgiveness and replaced them with hatred, retribution, and a wish that God strike them all dead. I admired you when, a couple of months ago, you told me how you cared for a lonely, shunned wounded Reb in your ward. Your compassionate attitude and love for your fellow man was justified by the words and actions of Mrs. Lincoln who said the wounded Reb was a human being in need, that she had relatives in the Confederacy, and she hoped that one day peace will come and we all will live together as friends and fellow citizens.

I was also disappointed to read that you no longer were willing to be a battlefield surgeon. You are a skilled surgeon who, in two battles, has saved many lives. But until this war is over, there will be many more battles and many more wounded soldiers in desperate need of medical care. The Powells have been friends of my parents for years. One of their sons, Eugene Powell, joined the 81st regiment of Ohio Volunteer Infantry in September, 1861. He was a corporal on April 28, 1863, in the Battle of Town Creek, Alabama, when he was severely wounded. The Union Army had a shortage of competent surgeons at that battlefield, deep in Confederate territory. Gene lay on the ground, near the regimental hospital tent, for many hours before the surgeon could administer to his wounds. Our army won the battle that day, but Eugene lost his life.

I am sure there will be many more brave soldiers wounded in battles before the War is over. If you are called to serve as a battlefield surgeon, please answer the call. I realize you would prefer never again to go through the stress and horrors of battle. But think of Eugene and the many other brave soldiers who are depending on you to save their lives.

Darling, you are the bravest, most compassionate, kind, moral, and skilled person that I know. Please don't let the evil of a relatively small percentage of Southerners change you, your character, and your beliefs.

****

With all my love, and may God keep you safe,
Your loving wife, Elizabeth"

With tears in his eyes, Henry took out of his coat pocket, the photograph of his wife, kissed it, held it close to his heart, and silently swore to comply with her wishes. His feeling of hatred was lifted from his heart like a heavy weight taken from his shoulders. Once more, there seemed hope for peace and happiness in the world.

CHAPTER 27:

HENRY AGREES TO SERVE AS SURGEON IN UNION ARMY'S CAMPAIGN IN THE DEEP SOUTH

During the first month after returning to Campbell Hospital, Henry was kept busy administering to the needs of the patients in Ward E. He liked the shorter hours of work, far fewer surgeries, less stress and more relaxing pace than during the Battle of Gettysburg. The patients seemed more appreciative of his medical treatment, possibly because there was rarely any need for surgical amputations and Henry experienced a high rate of success in outcomes. Each morning he looked forward to work and hoped he would spend the duration of the War as a doctor at Campbell Hospital. Sadly, events were about to change the course of his military career.

The Union Army had finally brought the war to Confederate territory in the southwest. Reb General Braxton Bragg's army was entrenched in Chattanooga. Union general Rosecrans' Army of the Cumberland had taken up positions in the nearby hills. Chief of Staff General Halleck and President Lincoln both were pressuring Rosecrans to engage Bragg's army in battle. Rosecrans kept delaying until he had adequate supplies and troop reinforcements, since this was one of those rare occasions when the Reb Army outnumbered the Union troops. Major Arnold McMahan of the Ohio 21st infantry Regiment, attached to Rosecrans' army, was dispatched to Washington, D.C. to obtain much needed medical supplies. Rapidly-growing pharmaceutical companies like Pfizer, Wyeth, Upjohn, and Powers & Wrightman were all located in the northeast. The largest concentration of military hospitals in the world was located in Washington. Pharmaceutical companies customarily shipped the military's medical supplies to D.C., from which they were distributed to the various battlefields.

The morning of August 29 was another hot summer's day in the Capital. The air was still, with no breeze and high humidity. The pungent odor of sewage floating in the canals and swamps, and infrequently collected garbage, wafted through the open windows, permeating the atmosphere of the hospital wards. Virtually all of the occupants prayed for cool breezes or rains to wash away the disgusting odors. While making his rounds shortly before noon, an orderly approached and told the major that Colonel Corcoran wanted to see him immediately. As he entered Corcoran's office, Henry saluted the colonel and an Army Major who was standing in front of his desk.

"Henry, this is Major Arnold McMahan of the 21st Ohio Infantry, currently encamped in southeastern Tennessee. He and some of his men are here to pick up medical supplies, eight horses and four wagons that are badly needed by General Rosecrans' Army of the Cumberland, to which the 21st Ohio Regiment is attached. He has a request for you. I'll let him explain. I just want to make it clear that it is a request, not an order. It is solely up to you whether or not you go along with it."

Major McMahan then turned to Henry, told him of the imminent battle situation, and said:

"We expect there may be a large number of casualties. We have a shortage of experienced battle surgeons, and cannot enlist the aid of doctors in the area of anticipated battle, since we're in Confederate territory. We have heard of your reputation and experience, and hope that you will return with us to serve as a surgeon attached to the Ohio 21st Regiment."

Henry had his fill of battlefield surgeries. He never again wanted to experience the intense, fast-paced surgeries and seemingly unappreciative name-calling by frightened wounded soldiers that he had experienced in Chancellorsville and Gettysburg. Henry stared blankly into space for a moment, not wanting to leave his pleasant duty at Campbell Hospital. But then he recalled the plea of his beloved wife in her last letter to him:

"If you are called to serve as a battlefield surgeon, please answer the call, because our brave soldiers need your help."

So, despite his preference never to return to battlefield surgery, Henry felt he could not turn his back on an urgent request to help young soldiers from his home state who were giving their youth, health and lives for their country.

"Major McMahan, I had hoped to fulfill the remainder of my three-year's enlistment as a doctor in this hospital. But, I cannot turn my back on the needs of Ohio soldiers who may be wounded in battle. Just one question: If I accept, how long will I serve with the 21st?"

"Just until the battle ends. I'm sure it will be less than one month."

"That's fine. When and where do you want me to report for duty?"

"We've already got the horses, wagons, and medical supplies. We can leave as soon as you have gathered your belongings and medical bag."

"I'll meet you back here, ready to leave, in thirty minutes."

One half hour later, Henry returned and rode in one of the wagons on what was to be a ten day, six hundred miles long trip through the eastern border of West Virginia, across the southeastern part of Kentucky, and southward in Tennessee to Chattanooga.

In the afternoon of September 9, as Major McMahan's party approached within a couple of miles of Chattanooga, they encountered several Union pickets who told them that, the previous day, apparently fearing an imminent attack by General Rosecrans, the Reb army had departed from Chattanooga and was fleeing south into Georgia, headed towards Atlanta. In fact, Bragg's army had camped about twenty miles south of the city, hoping to draw the Union Army into pursuing it and then attacking the Yanks when their supply lines are stretched thin and their army is on hard-to-defend open ground. When McMahan's group reported to headquarters in Chattanooga, he was ordered to travel south about eighteen miles to Steven's Gap, a low point near the center of Lookout Mountain, Georgia. There he was to join up with General Negley's Division, which included the 21st Ohio. Henry's group accomplished this by noon on September 11.

Early in September, one week after Henry left Campbell Hospital to join the 21st Ohio regiment in Tennessee, a letter arrived from Henry's wife, Elizabeth. Colonel Corcoran placed the letter in his desk drawer, intending to give it to Henry as soon as he returned, which he expected would be in about a month. The unopened letter said in part:

"My dearest Henry,
I was going to wait until your next leave to tell you the wonderful
news in person. But since that might be months from now, I do

not want to wait any longer to tell you the exciting news. It seems that during the time we spent together during your leave in late May, I became pregnant with child. Father estimates our baby will be born next February. If it's a boy, I think we should name him "Henry, Jr."

CHAPTER 28:

THE BATTLE OF CHICKAMAUGA

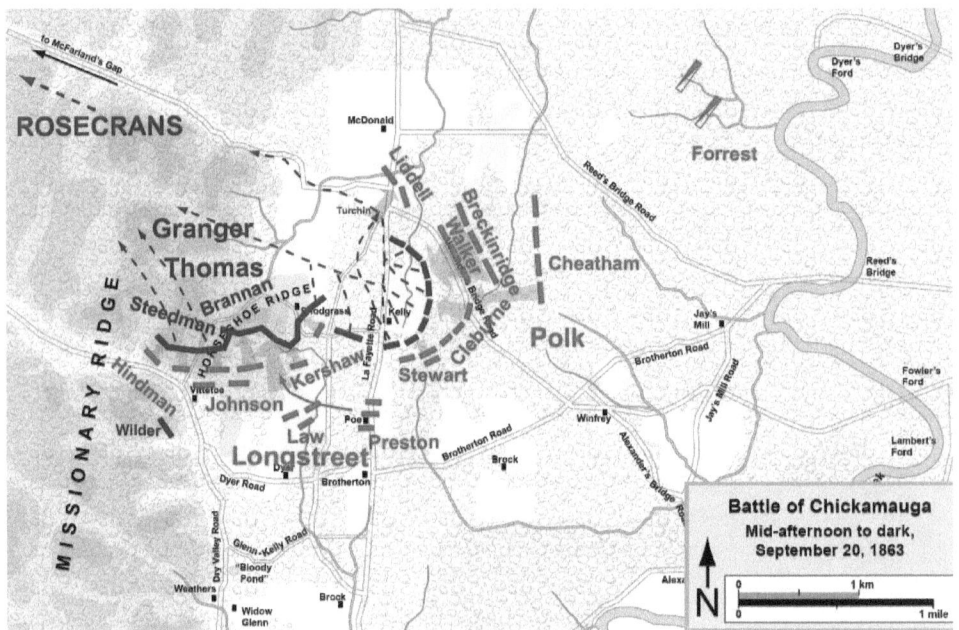

Battle of Chickamauga
Mid-afternoon to dark,
September 20, 1863

Meanwhile, Reb General Bragg had been ordering several subordinate generals to have their troops attack various sections of Union General Negley's XIV Corps while they were still dispersed over several miles, before they could consolidate their forces. But due to personal animosity and jealousy, several of the confederate generals disobeyed his orders, making up excuses why they could not begin an attack. Over the next several days, both armies began consolidating their positions, moving to what they believed were more strategic deployments, and the Reb Army received reinforcements giving it substantial numerical superiority over the Yanks.

Henry's medical staff included a male nurse, two stretcher bearers, an ambulance with a driver, and the covered supply wagon in which he came from Washington. He was not given a tent to set up for a field hospital. He was told that, unlike the previous battles he had been in, here the Union Army expected to be on the move, pursuing and engaging in battle Bragg's retreating Confederate Army. [Unbeknownst to the Yanks, in fact Bragg was not retreating, but trying to entrap Rosecrans' army.] He was told that the battle lines would be fluid, subject to frequent advances or retreats, and therefore Henry would have to set up the operating table in the open, in front of the wagon, so that he would be prepared to relocate promptly any time it became necessary. Over the next several days, they accompanied General Negley's division, which included the 21st Ohio Regiment, as it finally moved on September 18 into position south of the Union Army, at Crawfish Springs. On the first morning of the Battle of Chickamauga, September 19, 1863, most of the action took place several miles northeast, near Chickamauga Creek, so Henry and his crew had very little to do. Shortly after noon, Negley's Division was ordered to relocate to the northern edge of Horseshoe Ridge, the northernmost section of the Union line, which they accomplished by 1:00 p.m. on September 19. Within a half hour on that day and throughout September 20, the battle resumed, with attacks against the north end of the Union line, counterattacks by Rosecrans' army, and huge casualties for each side.

Henry's wagon was stationed a couple of hundred feet northwest of Negley's troops, just beyond Horseshoe Ridge. Due to a misunderstanding of an ambiguously written order, a gap was opened up in the Union line. That afternoon, Reb General Longstreet took advantage of the Union error, as some of his brigades penetrated the Union line. A couple of Union brigades fled in fear until a senior officer ordered them to hold their ground and set up defenses at Horseshoe Ridge. A Reb division attacked the southernmost portion of the Union line, killing General Lytle. His leaderless division and other units retreated in panic. Seeing that, Rosecrans decided to withdraw his army to Chattanooga. Brigadier General John Brannon had been requesting that Negley send to him at Horseshoe Ridge the 21st Ohio Regiment. Its 535 men had been issued five-shot Colt revolving rifles, a new, untested in battle, but devastating weapon.

Late in the afternoon of September 20, Reb General Longstreet's men made 25 assaults against the Union soldiers on Horseshoe Ridge, but were driven back after suffering many casualties from the devastating firepower of the 21st Ohio's Colt rifles. Despite occasional malfunctions, the fast-reloading Colt five shot revolving rifles sprayed bullets so rapidly at the oncoming Rebs that they thought there must be an entire Union Division at the top of the Ridge. During those assaults, Union Generals Thomas and Brannon and most of their troops retreated towards Chattanooga, leaving the 21st Ohio and two other regiments to defend against the Rebs' assaults. Finally, the Union's defenders ran out of ammunition. After a brief attempt to hold off the Rebs using bayonets, the remaining 116 defenders were forced to surrender.

The Battle of Chickamauga was the second bloodiest battle of the War thus far, second only to Gettysburg. Total casualties suffered by both sides in the two days of bitter fighting exceeded 34,000 soldiers, including several senior officers on both sides. Among the Confederate officers killed was Brigadier General Benjamin Hardin Helm, the brother-in-law of Lincoln's wife, Mary Todd Lincoln. The President and his wife mourned his death in secret, so as not to raise the ire of Union citizens during the War against the South. Chickamauga Creek lived up to the English translation of its American Indian name: "The River of Blood". For two days, the once peaceful scene had been transformed into Hell on earth.

Henry and his crew had been busy since the previous afternoon, gathering the wounded and bringing them to the hospital wagon; operating on those whose lives they might save; cleaning the wounds of, and sedating with opium, those who could not be saved, and leaving them to die. The surgeon and his aides worked at a frantic pace, refusing to withdraw with most of the retreating troops. They vowed to remain as long as there were wounded soldiers needing their help, but sent those whom they had treated or operated on, in wagons along with the retreating soldiers. Early in the evening of September 20, about the same time as the 116 members of the regiment found themselves without any more ammunition, surrounded by Reb soldiers who were demanding they surrender, Henry and his crew were approached by a Confederate captain and a dozen members of his company, all on horseback. The Reb officer shouted:

" Yanks, throw down on the ground any weapons y'all got, we're takin' y'all prisoners."

Henry replied:

"We don't have any weapons, Captain. We're in the Medical Corps. So, leave us alone and let us care for the four remaining wounded soldiers lying here on the ground in front of us." [Henry pointed to the four wounded he had operated on who were left there by the recently departed last wagon of the retreating Army because there was no more room for them.] The Reb captain dismounted from his horse, climbed inside the wagon, picked up an object from a nearby table, and emerged from the wagon waving the pistol he had found on the table.

"Acknowledge the corn [admit you're not telling the truth], Major. You tryin' to bullshit me that this is some kind of doctor's instrument?"

"Look, Captain. All of us Medical Corps officers are issued a firearm for our own protection, not to engage in battle with the enemy. As you can see, I didn't have it on me, and I'm wearing a green uniform—not a Union Army uniform, but one of the Medical Corps."

"Yeh, well why are all your so-called helpers wearing the blue uniforms of the regular Union Army?"

"That's just because they are regular Army soldiers assigned to assist me during battle. So, let us all go free or exchange us for Reb prisoners, as is the custom."

"Guess you ain't kept up with the status of prisoner parole and exchange. Early in May, the Confederate Congress proclaimed that captured Negro troops in the Union Army should be put to death or returned to the authorities of the states where they are captured, to be punished in accordance with the law of that state. To get even with the South, the Federal's War Department ordered prisoner exchanges to be halted. It refused to recognize that the Negroes are slaves, chattel belonging to their white owners. So y'all are our prisoners. Y'all made a mistake in not fleeing like rats on a sinking ship, with the rest of the Yank Army. Now, load the wounded lying here on the ground, onto your wagon. Then climb onto the wagon and put your hands behind your back so we can tie them to make sure you cannot escape. If y'all don't, we'll shoot you on the spot."

Henry's thoughts were once more flooded with hatred for the Reb soldiers who considered the Negroes less than human and had started the treasonous war to preserve their horrible institution of slavery. He wished he had had his pistol with him when the Reb captain had approached. It would have given him a feeling of satisfaction and revenge to shoot the captain and as many of his fellow soldiers as he could, even if it cost Henry his life. But then he realized there would be nobody left to care for the four wounded soldiers. Even worse, without any ammunition, the 116 remaining members of the 21st Ohio Regiment might have been shot and killed by the Rebs. So, reluctantly, Henry and his crew did as they were ordered. Then, with Reb Cavalry soldiers on each side of the wagon and one serving as driver, urging the horses forward, Henry and his crew began a 110-mile long journey to a Southern prisoner of War camp in Atlanta. The Reb Captain said with a smile:

Yanks, y'all are going on a journey to the beautiful deep South. Enjoy the scenery and our 'Southern Hospitality'".

The Reb captain ordered a Confederate private to sit next to the driver on the bench in front of the wagon, to guard the prisoners. He was young—19 years of age—with a fair complexion, brown hair and medium build. He turned to the prisoners and said:

"Get as comfy as y'all can, Yanks, cuz it's gonna take us a few days to reach Atlanta."

"What's your name, private? How long you been in the service?" asked Union corporal Jenkins, one of the captives.

"What for do ya want to know?" replied the Reb.

"Just curious. You look kinda young to serve in the front-line cavalry."

"I ain't as young as I look. I'm 19. I joined the cavalry a year ago cuz I knows all 'bout horses. I grew up on a horse farm in Tennessee. My name is Zack Reynolds."

"Mind if I ask a personal question, Zack?"

"Go right ahead. Not sure I'll answer it, but go on and ask."

"Before you joined the Reb Cavalry, did you or your family own any slaves?"

"You foolin'? Us own slaves," Zack said, laughing. "We ain't wealthy plantation owners. We just got a small horse farm, raisin' 'bout five horses at a time. When we sells one, we buy a young colt or filly to raise. There's my mom, dad, two brothers and a sister. We works hard, growing just enough taters, corn, peanuts and greens to feed us. Y'all could buy a farm like ours with what you could get from selling about a half-dozen slaves in good physical condition. Less than a quarter of Southerners own slaves. Them is mostly plantation owners and rich merchants."

"Then why in hell did you join the Reb Cavalry to fight and kill your Northern countrymen, just so as to preserve the abominable custom of slavery?"

"It ain't 'just to preserve slavery'. Most of us poor soldiers don't have much education. Maybe as many as one out of ten cain't even read or write. But the smart educated Southerners—the successful ones—warned us that if we give in to the North, they will destroy our way of life—force us to free the slaves, educate them, train them for jobs. That'd kill our agriculture. They'd work for less, so the poor whites would lose their jobs. All us Southerners wanted was to lead our lives as we pleased, like we'd done for over a hundred years."

"You poor fools. You've been conned by wealthy slave-owners into a lost cause; one you cain't win."

"What d'ya mean by 'lost cause'? We whipped ya Union Army in Chickamauga."

"That was just one battle. The Union has more people, more factories, guns and food than the South. And it has Almighty God on its side, what with you Rebs trying to preserve the enslavement of your fellow man. It is only a matter of time before the South loses the War."

Having just come away from a victorious battle, and having captured prisoners, the Reb soldier turned a deaf ear to the Union soldier's warning. He said:

"I ain't got the smarts to argue with ya, Yank. Talk to our Captaln. He can better explain why you're wrong, and we's just doin' our patriotic duty."

The Union soldier turned to Henry and whispered:

"No point wasting my breath talking to that dumb ass. It's like the old saying: 'A man convinced against his will is of the same opinion still.'"

CHAPTER 29:

ON THE JOURNEY TO IMPRISONMENT IN ATLANTA

A little more than two hours later, as the sun began to set, they stopped by the clear waters of the Conasauga River near Tunnel Hill, Georgia, the site of a Western & Atlantic Railroad tunnel. The Reb Captain said:

"We all can camp here for the night. Men, fill your canteens with fresh water from the river and let your horses drink their fill." Turning to Henry, he continued: "Major, we'll cut you and your crew loose from the ropes on your wrists so's y'all can fill some buckets of water and carry them back to your wagon for y'all and the wounded to drink. But if any of ya try to skedaddle [run away], my men will shoot the lot of ya, understand? Not that y'all could get very far if we didn't kill ya, since y'all are in Confederate territory."

As Henry was filling a pail of water at the nearby stream, he noticed a Reb private several feet away from him approaching the stream on wobbly legs. The Reb kneeled down to fill his canteen. As the Confederate soldier started to stand up, his legs shook as if under strain from a great weight. The Reb dropped his rifle onto the ground and fell down face first into the stream. For the moment, Henry's years of training in helping people caused him to forget that the man was his enemy. Instinctively, the major dropped his pail, rushed over to the Reb and raised his head out of the water. As Henry pulled the soldier away from the stream, a nearby Yank soldier angrily said:

"Why in hell are you helping the enemy, Major? Grab his rifle and let's flee?"

"That would be a really stupid move," Henry replied. "The Rebs would shoot us before we got very far, and even if we did escape, where could we go? We're deep in Confederate territory."

"Well, I still don't understand why you are helping save the life of an enemy soldier."

"He is a fellow human being in need. In Campbell Hospital I watched Mrs. Lincoln come to the aid of a Reb soldier. She said she hoped the Rebs would treat captured Yanks with like kindness."

As the ill Confederate soldier began to regain full consciousness, he lifted his head and said to the Major in a weak voice:

"Thanks, Major. I don't know why I fainted. I felt so weak...."

"I am a doctor; my duty is to help the injured and sick. I just could not stand idly by and watch you drown."

The Confederate Captain had witnessed the incident. He walked over to Henry and said:

"Thanks, Major. I guess you Yanks are not all bad after all. By the way, my name is Burnside....Captain Jed Burnside."

Henry said: "We are just normally peaceful, kind folks, just like you. It's unfortunate that the few wealthy slave owners suckered the rest of you Southern folks into leaving the Union and starting a war against your fellow Americans, so as to preserve the evil institution of slavery.

In an attempt to justify what Henry had insinuated was an act of treason by the South, the captain said:

"In Georgia, there were more than 400,000 blacks out of a total population of over a million people. The rest of the Confederacy was about the same. None of us here Rebs own slaves, Major. We were told that the Northerners intended to force their ways on us, control our lives and take away our rights. Our leaders said that the Yanks intended to crush our economy and impoverish us. They said that, if the slaves were freed, the majority of whites that were working in the mills, stores, jobs like carpenters and such, would become unemployed, because the darkies would be willing to work for much less. And the plantation owners and farmers would go broke because they no longer could afford farm laborers."

"That was just a bunch of bullshit that the rich slave-owners fed you. A son of a slave-owner wrote a book called "The Impending Crisis of the South", in which he showed that slavery was actually ruining the economy of the South. Too bad very few Rebs ever read it or heard of it."

Henry observed that the ill soldier was still unable to stand up. He asked the Captain if he could examine the Reb to try to determine what was causing his illness. Henry dipped a cloth into the pail of cold water and began gently wiping the soldier's brow. The Captain agreed and helped Henry remove the Reb's trousers so that he could examine his legs. There were blotchy red hemorrhages on both legs and swollen knees. His joints were stiff and he complained of pain when the Major tried to bend the soldier's knees or move his ankles. In response to Henry's request, the Reb opened his mouth, exuding putrid breath. The doctor observed a couple of loose teeth and bleeding gums. Henry asked the Captain:

"How long has it been since this soldier had any fresh vegetables or citrus fruit like limes or oranges?"

"At least two months. Not since about 8 weeks before we left Chatanooga. Why do you ask?"

"Because this man has a bad case of scurvy. He needs fresh vegetables or, preferably, a lemon, lime or orange as soon as possible. If he does not get that, his condition could become irreversible and he could die. And if you and your men have lacked such food, most of you will probably come down soon with that disease."

The Reb Captain turned to one of his men who was filling his canteen with fresh water.

"Corporal, I saw a small farm about a mile back there. Ride out there and ask the farmer to give you a three-gallon burlap bag filled with fresh vegetables, lemons, limes or oranges, if he has any. Tell him we need that for a very ill soldier."

The corporal mounted his horse and rode away.

"How come you Yanks ain't got scurvy, Major?"

"We have some dehydrated vegetables, and we had some fruit that General Barlow's men gave us just before the battle at Chickamauga. But we have run out of most of that. So, if we do not replenish our supplies within the next couple of months, we will probably start coming down with scurvy, also."

About one hour later, the corporal returned with a sack filled with carrots, potatoes, and a couple of dozen limes and oranges. Henry asked the corporal to cut one of the limes in half and give it to the ill soldier to chew on. Within a few days, the Reb private's condition began to improve and he and his comrades thanked Henry for saving his life. From then onward, those soldiers began treating their captives more like friends than enemies. The Reb Captain said to Henry:

"When we get to Atlanta, we are gonna have to lock y'all up in the City Jail that's temporarily serving as a prisoner of war camp. But I will make sure that you and your men get adequate food and that you can continue to provide medical care to them, provided that you agree to care for any of my men that need it, Major. You see, we Confederates have a severe shortage of medical personnel."

"That's a deal, Captain. But how long do you think we will be kept in that jail? When can we be exchanged for Reb prisoners held by the Union?"

"That's up to your General Grant. He's the one who suspended the prisoner exchange program so as to hurt the South. The stupid ass did not realize he would be hurting captured Yanks even more, 'cause the South doesn't have enough food and medical care for its own troops, let alone captive Yanks."

On the road to Atlanta, the Yank prisoners ate their desiccated vegetables, hard tack, and beans. Captain Burnside observed them eating the large, off-white, several inches thick, cracker-like food and asked the Major if he could try a piece. Henry handed him an eight square inch piece and watched as the Captain, after a few minutes struggle, broke it in half.

"This is like a piece o' wood," he said. He suddenly jumped backwards, throwing the hardtack on the floor of the wagon, as several live weevils began crawling out from inside the cracker. "I ain't gonna eat this crap. It's fulla worms."

Henry and a couple of his crew laughed. "You get used to it", Henry said. "You have to soften it with water. Those things are weevils, not worms." Then he jokingly said: "It's Yankee ingenuity. They make it so that if you drop a piece, it crawls back to you."

The Captain and the nearby Rebs all joined their captives in a laugh at the occurrence and Henry's explanation. Digging into a cardboard box by his feet, the Reb officer took out a handful of peanuts and handed some to the Yanks.

"Y'all try these southern goobers. They are crunchy, tasty, fresh and worm-free. They are a staple food of us Confederates."

The Major and his men crunched on the tasty nut-like food, and exclaimed:

"Thanks. These beat our sheet-iron crackers any day of the week."

The Rebs then ate some Johnnie Cakes [corn bread]. Having 'broken the ice' with his Captives, the Captain apologized for not sharing the corn bread with the Yanks because he had just barely enough for his men. After ordering his soldiers to stand guard a couple at a time for two hours each, the soldiers and their captives retired for the night. The following morning, they continued on their journey.

CHAPTER 30:

ATLANTA: THE INDUSTRIAL CENTER OF THE SOUTH

Four days later, the Captain's cavalrymen and their prisoners approached a bridge that crossed a wide river.

"This here is the Chattahoochee River, the northern boundary of the great city of Atlanta," the captain said to Henry. A short distance from the other side of the river, you'll see why Atlanta is one of the greatest industrial cities of the South; probably not much different from Chicago or other of the North's big cities."

In fact, although Atlanta was the fourteenth largest city in the South, it had a population of only about 20,000. The only city in the entire confederacy with a population of more than 50,000 was New Orleans, where 168,000 people lived. The North had eight cities with more than 100,000 people, ranging from 112,000 in Chicago to more than 850,000 in New York City. Unlike the agricultural South, most of those large Union cities were bustling with factories, commerce and railroads. Atlanta was located in the deep South. When the War began, it was anticipated that Atlanta would be far from any scenes of battle. It was at the confluence of four major railroads. Most of Georgia had rich, fertile soil that produced a wide variety of crops, from cotton to peanuts, peaches, vegetables and fruit. During the war, factories were built for manufacture of guns, ammunition, railroad tracks and trains, iron, cannons, and military uniforms. Warehouses were constructed to hold munitions, armaments, food and supplies.

As the Rebs and their prisoners entered the sprawling city, they passed several large factories, including the Winship Foundry, Atlanta Machine Works, and Atlanta Steam Tannery, on their way to the Fulton County Jail, which served as a holding area for as many as 175 captured Union Soldiers. They were told that they would remain there until a proposed large prisoner-of-war camp was constructed about 130 miles south, near Anderson Railroad Depot, Georgia. It was originally named Camp Sumter, but later became known as Andersonville Prison. Over the next four months, Henry and his men were held as prisoners in the Jail. Henry was given a large cell for himself, in which the guards placed his operating table, his medical instrument bag, some of the medicines, bandages and anesthetics from his wagon. A small sign reading: "INFIRMARY" was placed on the door to his cell. The Major served as the jailhouse doctor, treating sick and wounded prisoners, as well as some Reb soldiers needing medical care.

Sometime in October, 1863, Henry was told by one of his captors that a Confederate Colonel would soon be departing on a mission to meet with a Union Exchange Officer to discuss the possibility of renewal of prisoner exchanges. Henry asked if he could give the Colonel a letter to Elizabeth, his wife, who Henry was certain would be worrying what happened to him. The Colonel agreed, so Henry wrote the following letter.

"My dearest Elizabeth,
I am certain that by now you are fearful of what may have
happened to me. Please do not worry. I and several of my aides,
along with four wounded who we were treating, were captured by
the Reb Cavalry at the end of the Battle of Chickamauga. They
took us to Atlanta, to be imprisoned in the Fulton County Jail,
which serves as a temporary prisoner of war camp for about 175
Union soldiers. Along the way, a Reb private collapsed and fell
face first into a stream. I saved him from drowning and found he
suffered from an almost terminal case of scurvy. I treated him,
restored him to health, and our captors were extremely grateful.
They began treating us more like friends than captured enemies.
We found that they were not such a bad lot, after all. None of
them owned slaves, and it seems they were conned by the small
percentage of Southerners that are slave owners, into believing
that it was their patriotic duty to protect their economy and their
way of life, to engage the North in this awful War.

We've been treated fairly well. I've been allowed to care for my
men, including the wounded four soldiers, and have occasionally
treated some of our captors when they have become ill. There's a
shortage of medical supplies in the South. It has no

pharmaceutical companies—they are all located in the North, between Baltimore and Boston. The Union's blockade of Southern ports has prevented British and French ships from delivering medical supplies to the South. As a result, the Rebs have turned to home-grown herbs in an attempt to treat illnesses. A very few of them help, but most are useless and some even cause more harm. The food rations are small—the South is having difficulty feeding its own troops. But some—like goobers [peanuts] and "Johnnie Cakes" [a tasty corn bread] are much better than the board-like and weevil infested hardtack the Union Army fed us.

We've been told that, some 130 miles south of here, the Rebs are constructing a huge prisoner of war camp, capable of holding 10,000 prisoners, with a hospital, kitchens, a stream with fresh water running through it, and wood barracks for the prisoners, in an open area surrounded by pine tree woods, near the Anderson railroad depot. We're anxious to go there. We don't get out in the fresh air, here in these dark and dusty jail cells.

I miss you terribly, and keep your photograph in my shirt pocket, next to my heart. If the prisoner exchange is resumed, maybe I'll be home soon.
Give my love to our parents. I love you more than life itself.
With all my love,
Henry"

CHAPTER 31:

RELOCATION TO CAMP SUMTER

D uring their stay at the Fulton County Jail, Henry and his fellow
prisoners were unaware of the progress of the War. They were
aware that the Union Army had suffered a disastrous defeat at
Chickamauga. But they were in the dark about what transpired in the
months after that. When the South had a victorious battle, the guards
cheered. But late in November, the cheering stopped and the faces of
many showed a look of despair. While they would not reveal anything
about the recent events of the War to their prisoners, Henry had the
impression that the tide of battle had begun to turn against the South.
Reinforcing this belief was the fact that the younger guards were reassigned to front-line companies and replaced by middle-aged, elderly
and disabled soldiers. Finally, in early December of 1863, one of the new
guards—a middle-aged Reb soldier with a gimpy leg that he said
resulted from a shrapnel wound in the Battle of Chattanooga—told
Henry that Union General Grant's troops had defeated the Confederates
in the Battle of Chattanooga. The Reb Army retreated. The Reb soldier
with the shrapnel wound said he, together with about a thousand
wounded and ill Confederate troops, had been transported in cattle cars
by train to Atlanta, for treatment in one of the many buildings [former
schools, warehouses and hotels] that had been hastily converted into
hospitals. Henry relayed this encouraging news to his men, and soon the
Union prisoners began smiling and cheering with renewed hope for an
end to the War.

In mid-February, 1864, many of the prisoners overheard the
guards mentioning that the Reb Army and City leaders were considering
building strong fortifications surrounding Atlanta, to aid in repelling an
anticipated attack by approaching Union forces. That gave rise to rumors
spreading among the prisoners, that they might soon be freed, paroled

[set free on condition they not rejoin the Union Army in its fight against the South], or relocated to another prisoner- of-war camp. About a month later, Captain Burnside unexpectedly visited Henry in the jail.

"Major Freeman, I wanted to be the first to tell you that, on April 10,1864, you and the rest of the prisoners will be transported by rail to Camp Sumter, the recently opened prisoner-of-war camp located 139 miles south of here, near Anderson Depot. Construction is still ongoing, but it's supposed to have wooden barracks, kitchens, latrines and a hospital. It's in an open clearing surrounded by thick pine woods. It should be a welcome change from this crowded, dirty, musty old prison. About 25 men under my command will be taking you to your new quarters."

Henry thanked the captain for the news and said he and his fellow prisoners would be looking forward to the move. The news spread rapidly to the other prisoners, most of whom welcomed the change to new, cleaner, surroundings, and the possibility that they would be able to walk out into the fresh open air and sunshine.

The morning of April 10, 1864, the 176 prisoners were awakened shortly after sunrise. Through a small opening at the bottom of each cell, the guards served them a light breakfast of Johnny Cakes and coffee. The guards then opened their cells and let them out one at a time, securely tying a rope around each man's wrists while they stood in the corridor, until there was a line of eight bound prisoners. Then they would proceed to the next cells and follow the same procedure until there were twenty-two bound groups totaling 176 prisoners. Captain Burnside and 25 of his men armed with rifles then escorted the captives outside the jail and marched them about one mile to the Atlanta railroad depot. Despite the ropes binding their wrists, the prisoners enjoyed their walk in the pleasant 68-degree fresh air on this sunny spring morning. It was the first time in six months that Henry and the others had been outside of the old jail. Henry inquired of Captain Burnside whether he would be allowed to continue treating prisoners at Camp Sumter, since Burnside had ordered him to leave his equipment and few remaining medical supplies at the jail, and only permitted him to take his medical kit with him.

"I ain't rightly sure," the captain replied. That all is up to the new commandant of Camp Sumter, Captain Wirz. But seein' as how we Rebs got a real shortage of medical personnel, I reckon he will welcome your help."

When they reached the depot, the captain ordered the men to halt alongside a track on which there was a short train of seven cars: a locomotive and four cattle cars sandwiched between two passenger cars. Four of the Reb soldiers opened the sliding doors of the four cattle cars. Six groups of the bound prisoners were ordered to walk up wooden planks to board each of two livestock cars. The remaining 80 bound prisoners were then divided into two groups, each of which was ordered to board one of the empty cattle cars. A Reb sergeant then issued a stern warning:

"You Yanks are to remain in the cars until we reach our destination, in about four and a half to five hours. Anyone trying to open the doors or escape will be promptly shot. Sorry, we ain't got no food or water for you during this short trip."

The doors were pushed shut and bolted. The cavalrymen then boarded the passenger cars, about half of them in each car.

As the train pulled out of the depot and started its journey to Anderson Station, several captive soldiers in each cattle car loudly complained:

"This car smells like cowshit. Why in Hell didn't the Johnnies give us passenger cars to ride in?"

Several of the men, including Henry, responded:

"Don't complain. You'll only have to put up with the stench for about four hours. It's a lot better than being forced to walk 139 miles to our destination."

The train whistle pierced the air and a puff of white steam rose from the locomotive's smokestack as the train slowly pulled out of the station. It began to pick up speed, reaching about 31 miles per hour. About four and a half hours later, at about 3 o'clock in the afternoon, it arrived Andersonville station in southeast central Georgia. Captain Burnside and his men disembarked from the passenger cars. Four Reb soldiers placed a couple of wide wood planks leaning up against the cattle cars, slid open the doors, and ordered the prisoners to disembark. Henry told the Captain that he and the other prisoners' mouths were parched, so Captain Burnside had his sergeant hand a four-gallon empty pail to each of three of his men and order them to go to a nearby stream and fill the pails with fresh water. When they returned, the sergeant handed each a tin cup to use to give Henry and the other prisoners a drink. About an hour after arriving at the railroad station, the prisoners having quenched their thirst, the Reb captain ordered each row of eight prisoners with wrists tied to line up in a column of 22 rows. Twelve Reb soldiers with rifles at the ready were on each side of the column, and one Reb soldier was in the rear. They began to march about three hundred yards to the south gate entrance to Camp Sumter. Most of the prisoners didn't mind marching in the warm humid weather. They anxiously looked forward to the camp with promised wood barracks, kitchen, hospital, clean surroundings with lots of fresh air and sunshine. Even if the prisoner exchange program was not revived, it seemed like a pleasant way to spend the remainder of the War.

Unbeknownst to them, the South's ambitious plans for the camp were never achieved. Within an hour, they would be shocked by the reality of the horrible conditions they would have to endure.

CHAPTER 32:

HISTORY AND DESCRIPTION OF CAMP SUMTER, AND ITS NEW COMMANDANT, HENRY WIRZ

The railroad depot was near a small village with one house and several small wooden structures [possibly storage sheds or stables]. There were no paved roads. The soil appeared to be sandy, not the rich agricultural soil found within a couple of miles of that location. It was a bright sunny day, with the temperature about 75 degrees, but felt much hotter due to the high humidity. A few hundred yards east of the depot was a large clearing of 100 acres, surrounded on three sides by thick woods of tall pine and hemlock trees. Within that clearing was a stockade, 16 acres in area, surrounded by a wall of pine logs 12 feet in height. About 120 feet from the wall was an inner wall of pine logs 18 feet high. On the outside of that pine wall, at intervals of 30 yards, were square platforms rising 6 feet above the wall, with a wood roof held up by four poles. These were the guard platforms, from which the Reb guards, armed with rifles, had a clear view of the stockade's inner grounds. Fifteen feet from the inner wall was a line of small wood posts, four feet apart from one another, three feet in height, encircling the entire inner stockade. The prisoners called it the "dead line", because if any prisoner went beyond that line of wood posts, he would be shot. A stream flowed in an east to west direction through the midpoint of the stockade. During rainy periods, it would often overflow its banks, making the ground very muddy for a distance of fifty feet on each side of it, and causing the nearby latrines to spill human waste throughout the overflow area. The resulting swamp-like area became a fertile breeding ground for mosquitos, flies, fleas and other vermin, which rapidly infested the entire camp grounds.

About 100 feet from the southwest corner of each wall [inner and outer] were the south gates. 400 feet north of them on each wall were the north gates. Fifty feet from the south side of the outer wall were several large tents, and the same distance from the west side of the outer wall were a dozen tents, all of which served as barracks for the guards. Also, on the south side was a very large tent that served as a temporary hospital while the wood structure was being built. The prisoner of war camp had originally been planned to hold a maximum of 10,000 prisoners. But due to the North's suspension of the prisoner exchange agreement in mid-1863, the number of Union soldiers held prisoner by the Rebs rapidly increased. By mid-April, 1864, when the train carrying Henry and the others arrived at Anderson Depot, the number of prisoners at Camp Sumpter had swelled to more than 16,000. To accommodate them, several hundred slaves were busy extending the stockade walls to surround an additional ten acres.

With severe shortages of food and supplies, and much of its railroads captured or destroyed by the Union Army, the South was unable to adequately clothe, feed or supply its own troops. It found it impossible to provide adequate food or shelter for Yank prisoners. So, the prisoners had a pint or less of frequently worm-infested corn mush [including the cob], two ounces or less of uncooked, often rancid, meat, and occasionally a few peanuts for their daily rations. Their only source of water was the polluted stream that ran through the center of the camp. While there was a clean stream located north of the inner wall of the compound, any soldier crossing the dead line—even just by sticking out his arm—in an attempt to reach that water, was promptly shot. In fact, some of the guards became so bored that they took a perverse pleasure in shooting prisoners.

CAPTAIN HEINRICH [HENRY] WIRZ

Historians have written inconsistent stories about the early life of Henry Wirz. Much of the confusion has been caused by tales spun by Wirz himself in an apparent attempt to gild his banal early years and career. He claimed he had attended the Medical School of Zurich University in Switzerland, emigrated to America in 1849, practiced medicine in Kentucky for several years, then moved to Louisiana where he had a thriving medical practice until 1861. That year he joined the Louisiana Infantry of the Confederate army as a private, and was promoted to Captain allegedly for heroism in the Battle of Seven Pines in May, 1862, in which he was wounded and lost the use of his right arm.

Thereafter he was assigned to the staff of General John Winder, head of Confederate prisoner-of-war camps. The truth was much different.

In fact, Wirz was born in Zurich in 1823. He did dream of one day becoming a doctor, but his parents were too poor to send him to medical school. So, he trained as a weaver, at which he worked for several years. He married and had two children. He borrowed money to help support his family, but was unable to repay the loan, and, in 1847, was sentenced to four years in prison for that 'crime'. Within a year, his sentence was commuted on the condition that he leave Switzerland. His wife refused to relocate herself and the children outside of Switzerland, and divorced him. Henry Wirz emigrated to the United States, worked for five years at a textile factory in Lawrence, Massachusetts, saved up enough money to move to Kentucky, where he obtained employment as a doctor's assistant. In 1854, he married a widow, Elizabeth Wolfe, who had two daughters. They moved to Louisiana, where Wirz worked for plantation owner Levin Marshall as a superintendent and doctor. At the outbreak of the Civil War in 1861, he joined the Louisiana Infantry. There is no record substantiating his claim of being wounded in the Battle of Seven Pines. But it is true that he somehow lost the use of his right arm [at least one historian claims it was as a result of a carriage accident]. It is also true that he was promoted to the rank of Captain and assigned to the staff of General Winder, who in late March, 1864, appointed Wirz commandant of the new prisoner-of-war camp known as Camp Sumter, but referred to by inmates as 'Andersonville Prison'.

CHAPTER 33:

ENTERING THE GATES OF HELL

A s the column of prisoners escorted by Reb soldiers approached Camp Sumter, Henry observed the many tents located near the south and west outside walls of the stockade. Dozens of Confederate soldiers were standing or walking around outside and in and out of the tents. He inquired of Captain Burnside:

"What's the reason for all those tents outside the camp walls?"

"I'm not certain. This is the first time I've been here. My guess is they are the sleeping quarters for the guards, and that big tent may be the hospital."

"I thought you said there would be wooden barracks and that a hospital was being constructed."

"That was what I was told was the plan. I'm not sure what was actually constructed."

"Well, Captain, if the guards don't have wooden barracks, seems to me that it's likely that neither do the prisoners inside the walls."

"Maybe so, Henry. We'll know soon enough when we go inside the gates of Camp Sumter. Before we reach the gates, I'm going to have one of my men cut the rope that's binding your wrists. I want personally to introduce you to Captain Wirz as a doctor and surgeon who is willing to treat the guards as well as the prisoners. If he sees you without any restraints, he's more likely to feel y'all can be trusted to provide proper medical treatment to our Reb soldiers, and not take advantage of your freedom of movement outside the camp, to try to escape."

When they reached about fifty yards from the outside gate, Captain Burnside told his sergeant to wait there with the prisoners and their escorts. He and Henry were going inside the stockade first, to meet Captain Wirz.

"As soon as we're done with the meeting—probably within a half hour—I'll order our men and the prisoners to march into the compound." The captain and Henry then approached two guards in front of the South Gate. Burnside told them he was bringing 176 prisoners from the Fulton County Jail, and said he wanted to speak to Captain Wirz. They opened the gate, let Burnside and Henry inside, where a Reb guard said he would escort them to commandant Wirz's office, which was a couple of hundred feet north of the gate, in a small wood building in front of the eighteen-foot high pine log wall surrounding the stockade where the prisoners were held.

Captain Wirz*

Upon entering Wirz's office, the commandant got up from a chair behind a large pine desk. He was rather short, maybe about 5 feet 7 inches tall. His uniform was rumpled and looked like it hadn't been cleaned in months. Henry momentarily chuckled to himself as he observed Wirz's grey Confederate soldier's cap that looked as if he had just sat on it. He had a thick black moustache and an even thicker triangular shaped Van Dyke beard that partially hid a stern, "don't mess with me", almost threatening facial expression. Henry felt an uncomfortable chill run up his back as Wirz's piercing eyes focused on him, looking him up and down. Burnside saluted and said:

"Captain Wirz, I am Captain Burnside, reporting with 176 Union prisoners that are being transferred here from the Fulton County Jail in Atlanta. I and 25 of our Confederate soldiers under my command arrived by train about an hour ago. My men and their prisoners are waiting outside the South Gate to Camp Sumter."

Wirz raised his left arm to salute Burnsaide. Henry noticed that the commandant's right arm was dangling by his side. He assumed that Wirz had lost the use of that arm as a result of a battlefield injury. In a loud voice with a thick German accent, Wirz said to Burnside:

"Who is that Yankee officer on your right?"

"I brought him in to see you, Sir. He is Surgeon Major Henry Freeman of the Union Army Medical Corps. He is a very capable and experienced surgeon. I believe y'all could make use of his services in treating any sick or wounded guards, as well as the prisoners."

"How do I know I can trust this son-of-a-bitch Yank to treat or perform surgery on my men. I don't give a damn what he does with the prisoners. But you don't really expect me to trust this Yank son-of-a-bitch to furnish medical aid to my soldiers."

"I trust him…He saved the life of one of my soldiers a few days after we captured him and his fellow Yanks. During his months at the jail in Atlanta, he treated many sick and wounded Confederate soldiers, as well as Yank prisoners. If you've got a shortage of medical personnel in this here prison, like I suspect, you might welcome the help of an experienced and capable surgeon."

Focusing his gaze on Henry, Captain Wirz said:

"We've got a few, mostly elderly, not very capable, doctors who come here part time. They do their best with what little drugs, medicines and medical instruments we have available. But with hundreds of guards and now more than 16,000 prisoners, they can't do much. The South ain't got enough food for its own soldiers. Them that's in battlefields often get just one meal a day. Many have tattered uniforms, at least one out of every ten has no shoes. But they keep on fightin' you damn Yanks. And here at Camp Sumter, feeding the enemy got no priority with General Winder. He's the officer that is in charge of all the Confederate POW camps. The prisoners don't get much to eat. They sleep out in the open, exposed to the winter cold, summer heat, and year-round rains in this stinkin' place in the middle of nowhere. So, yes, Major Freeman, I'll let you treat our Confederate guards as well as the prisoners. I'll assign you to a tent outside the stockade for sleeping quarters. You can eat with the guards. Their food is just a little better than the prisoners' slop, but at least it ain't always infested with vermin. But I'm warning you. I'll know if you're not doing your best treating the guards. I'm a doctor, educated at the University of Zurich, Switzerland. I practiced medicine for years in Kentucky and Louisiana. If I find you failing to use proper medical procedures or not treating sick guards properly, I'll see to it that you're beaten 'til your fuckin' body cries out in pain, do you understand?"

The commandant's demeanor and stern warning momentarily startled Henry, causing the hair on the back of his neck to stand up. Quickly recovering his composure, the Major said:

"Yes Sir, captain."

Captain Burnside then said:

"Captain Wirz. I don't understand. You said there's over 16,000 prisoners. They sleep in the open, exposed to the elements. I saw the plans for Camp Sumter. It was intended to hold a maximum of 10,000 prisoners. There were supposed to be wooden barracks, a kitchen, a hospital was to be built…lots of other things. What happened?"

"Captain Burnside, when the North decided it would be to its advantage to end the prisoner exchange agreement, the South was suddenly swamped with thousands of prisoners and nowhere to put them, not enough food to feed them. This camp was built with mostly slave labor. But soon after it opened, we found the 16 acres was not enough. So, we are extending the stockade to include another 10 acres. This place is so crowded that the prisoners are massed so close together that they barely have room to lie down. Many of them relieve themselves right where they are, so the ground stinks of shit and piss. Flies, fleas, ants, roaches, mice, rats and all kinds of vermin love those conditions and multiply like crazy. When the rains come, the sandy soil becomes like a swamp, and the human excrement spreads all over the Camp, polluting the stream that is their only source of water. Sickness and disease spread like wildfire, and each day dozens of prisoners die. Their bodies are thrown in a ditch, lightly covered over with dirt. I've begged my superiors for food, clothing, barracks for the prisoners. But my pleas have fallen on deaf ears. With conditions like that, the only way I can enforce discipline is to act tough, threaten those who disobey the rules, punish severely any who try to escape."

Wirz emphasized his last comment by pointing to a diagram of the camp that was hanging on the wall. He showed Henry the dead line, which, if any of the prisoners crossed, they would promptly be shot by one of the guards stationed on the platforms that were 30 yards apart on the outside of the 18-foot high wall. The meeting was over, and Wirz told Burnside to have his men bring the prisoners inside the South Gate. Once they were lined up in an orderly fashion, the commandant said he would give them an introduction to the prison similar to what he had just discussed. Then he would order them to enter the stockade through the South Gate on the inner wall. It would be up to each of them to find their own space inside the stockade. Henry watched as Wirz threateningly brandished his revolver in his left hand as he began talking to the prisoners. The Major observed the disappointed and somewhat fearful look on the faces of the prisoners as their dreams of serving out the remainder of the war in clean, comfortable surroundings were dashed. Upon viewing the deplorable, overcrowded conditions of the camp, the new camp prisoners were heard crying out phrases like:

"Oh my God, this is hell on earth".

Henry, standing next to Captain Burnside outside the gate, could see only a small portion of the campgrounds. But as he watched the 175 Union soldiers marching into the prison camp, he reflected on Captain Wirz's description of life inside the stockade and thought

"Poor souls. If they are here too long, none of them may survive."

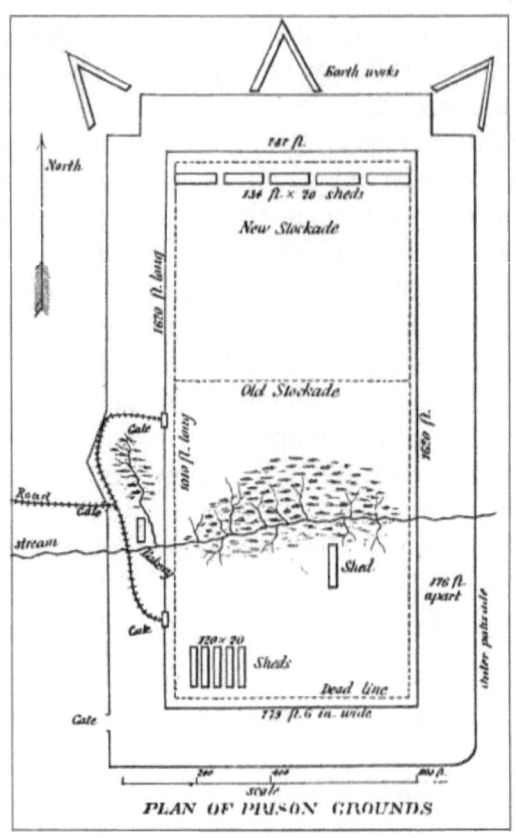

PLAN OF PRISON GROUNDS

CHAPTER 34:

A PLACE OF DEPRIVATION, DISEASE AND DEATH

Henry's sleeping quarters were located in a tent outside the outer wall of the stockade, near the South Gate. His bed was a wooden board raised, by a small wood block on each corner, about three inches off the sandy ground. He shared the tent with three guards who Wirz assigned to assist Henry in his work as the only Union doctor treating the prisoners. He was given the following routine work schedule:

Each morning he was to spend four hours going inside the stockade, accompanied by the three-armed guards for protection as well as assistance, examining and treating as many sick or wounded POWs as possible. Those too ill to be left in the enclosure could be removed to the hospital tent, if there was room to accommodate them. Eight prisoners that had been selected by the guards as trustworthy and in good physical condition, were assigned as body bearers to accompany Henry on his rounds inside the stockade. They were to take to the hospital tent the very ill POWs selected by Henry for hospitalization. They also were to carry the bodies of dead POWs to trenches located about 300 feet outside the stockade walls. There the bodies would be tossed into the ditches and covered with about a foot of dirt. As consideration for performing those duties, the eight prisoners were given sleeping quarters in a tent outside the stockade walls, near the guards' tents, and ate their meals with the guards in the nearby dining hall/kitchen. They thus had better food than the rest of the POWs, more sanitary and comfortable living quarters, and less exposure to vermin, disease and illness.

Obviously, Henry could only examine or treat a small percentage of the prisoner population in four hours. Nevertheless, at the end of that time, he was to exit the stockade, go to the hospital tent, and examine and treat patients there. The hospital tent had one hundred beds for the patients, and three nurses on duty at all times, with rotating shifts. Two elderly confederate doctors [neither had much surgical experience], Dr. Hamilton and Dr. Story, worked about four hours each day providing basic medical care, examining patients, dressing their wounds, occasionally prescribing medication or drugs if available. For the most part, there were little or no medicines or drugs available for the POWs. The Reb doctors considered all of the POWs their enemy and had little empathy for their pain and suffering, so they rarely prescribed any medication or drugs, anyway.

On Henry's first morning at Camp Sumter, he awoke about 7 a.m. and accompanied his tent-mates to the dining hall tent for breakfast. There wasn't a cloud in the sky and the bright sun had already begun to raise the ambient temperature to 70 degrees. Henry turned to one of the guards and said:

"It's early morning and it's already warm. Guess it's going to be a hot day."

"Enjoy it while you can, Major. This here area gets over 45 inches of rain per year, and April is one of the wettest months. When the rains come, this here crappy soil quickly turns to mud. That's one of the reasons our bed boards are raised several inches above the ground."

"Do the prisoners inside the stockade have bed boards inside their tents?"

The guards all laughed. Irritated, Henry asked what was so funny. One of them responded:

"Them Yank POWs ain't got no tents, except maybe a shirt or blanket held up by sticks or pieces of wood, if they're lucky. And almost none of 'em have boards to lie on. They's lyin' on the sandy, often muddy, ground that's crawling with ants, roaches, beetles, worms and who knows what else. That's why the eight body bearers are so happy carrying and burying the dead. In return, they gets to sleep out here in tents and eat better food with us, 'stead of the rotten slop the other POWs get."

Henry felt both anger at the guards uncaring attitude towards the prisoners, and anguish for the mistreated POWs. He struggled to overcome a feeling of guilt, that he had much better living conditions than the rest of the captive Union soldiers. He silently prayed to Jesus—even begged God—to bring a quick end to this horrible war so that the soldiers could return safely home to their loved ones.

For breakfast, Henry ate 'cush' , which was beef and cornmeal fried in bacon grease; about 3 ounces of fatty bacon; a small Johnnie cake; and a mug of Reb 'coffee', which really was not coffee, which was not available due to the Union blockades, but was a drink made of chicory, okra, bran and dried apples mixed with hot water. After breakfast, he, the three guards, and the eight body bearers walked over to the stockade and entered through the South Gate. Despite having been told some of what to expect, Henry was shocked by what he saw upon entering the stockade for the first time. There were two unpaved streets running into the camp; one from the South Gate and one from the North Gate. Near the center of the stockade, running from east to west, was a slow-moving stream, dark brown in color from all the excrements, garbage and filth that flowed into it during the frequent rains. That disease and death producing water was the source of drinking water for the prisoners. Throughout the camp there were a total of more than forty holes dug by prisoners, using tin plates, wood sticks and their bare hands, in an often-futile attempt to reach an underground pool of fresh water. Some prisoners used such diggings to conceal attempts to dig a tunnel under the walls of the stockade. That always had one of two results: 1) another prisoner informing the guards in return for an additional portion of food or other favors; or 2) rains came, turning the sandy soil into mud, which washed down into the hole, covering and asphyxiating the digger.

Over a distance of about fifty feet on the north and south sides of the stream, the earth had become a sticky swamp due to the frequent rains that caused it to overflow its banks. No prisoners could occupy that area. Throughout most of the rest of the campgrounds, half-naked prisoners were crowded together with barely enough space to lie down at night. They had used their shirts, coats, blankets--if they were lucky enough to have any—with sticks for support, as make-shift tents for partial shelter from the elements. Henry observed that the skin of most of the POWs was covered with dark mud and brown sand from lying on the ground to sleep at night. Vermin—roaches, ants, beetles and worms—were often crawling on the prisoners' bodies, which kept many of the POWs busy picking or flicking them off onto the ground.

As Henry began making his rounds, he noted that the physical condition of the prisoners ranged from robust [those who had been imprisoned for less than a month] to sickly, weak and emaciated [those who had been imprisoned for several months or longer]. He was only able to cursorily examine about one hundred inmates during the four hours of his day that were allocated to that work. Of those, ten percent were suffering from dysentery, many so badly that they would defecate right where they slept, being physically too weak to walk several hundred feet to the latrines. That served to increase the stench, pollution, vermin and disease that pervaded the campgrounds. Another ten percent had lost so much weight from poor nutrition and lack of adequate food that the outline of their rib cage and other bones was clearly visible. That, plus their loose and wrinkled skin, gave them the appearance of living, walking skeletons. A similar percentage of the prisoners Henry examined exhibited acute symptoms of scurvy, including loose and discolored teeth, putrid breath, and multiple hemorrhages on their legs. The guards assisting told Henry that the hospital tent was nearly full and could accommodate at most twenty more patients. So, with deep regret, the Major selected the twenty prisoners of those he had examined who were in the worst condition but that he thought might recover with proper care and treatment, for the guards to escort to the hospital tent.

As he was making his rounds, Henry observed the body-bearers carrying to the South Gate the bodies of twenty-five prisoners who had died during the night, which the bearers then carried to the trenches 300 feet away from the stockade walls, and then hurled them into the ditch. Henry said to one of the guards assisting him:

"If the conditions don't improve, hundreds of these poor prisoners will soon be dying every day. I'm going to speak to Captain Wirz and demand that he provide more and better food, some sort of tents or shelter, and proper medication for these poor souls who are so unfortunate as to be held captive here."

"If I was you, I'd be careful what you say to our commandant, Major. Captain Wirz has a short fuse—a vile temper. If'n you ain't careful, he's just as likely to throw you into the stinkin' camp with the rest of the Yank POWs. If y'all feel ya gotta bring those conditions to his attention, I'd advise y'all to BEG him, not 'demand', and be willin' to accept whatever he decides."

Upon reflection, Henry realized that the guard was right. He thanked him for the advice. Upon entering the hospital tent after leaving the stockade, Henry was told that there were several guards with complaints of minor injuries or illnesses, waiting for Henry to examine and treat them. After doing so, about an hour later, Henry walked to Captain Wirz's office and, in a somewhat timid manner, described to him the appalling conditions he had observed inside the stockade, the deleterious effects they and inadequate food were having on the inmates, and, heeding the admonition of the guard, said to Wirz:

"Captain, you are a war hero, an accomplished administrator, as well as a medical doctor who has devoted much of his career to helping heal the sick and saving lives. I realize my fellow Yanks that are imprisoned here are, to your eyes, the enemy. But they are human beings, and as such deserve proper treatment, as I hope and believe the Union Army is administering to the Confederates that are held in prisons in the North. I beg you, in the name of God, please get the Reb Army to furnish them with adequate shelter, more and nutritious food, and medication. Otherwise, I fear that thousands of those held captive here— and perhaps all of them—will succumb to starvation, illness and disease."

Wirz, silently, but somewhat impatiently, let Henry finish his supplication. He responded, in a calm voice at first, but with increasing volume as his face became flushed with anger:

"Do you think you are telling me something I don't already know? Don't you realize I have several times asked General Winder for more food, clothing and shelter for the prisoners, medicine and doctors? His consistent reply has been that the Yanks caused this problem when they suspended the prisoner exchange program. The South does not have adequate food and clothing to supply its own troops, and now your President refuses even to talk to Confederate representatives about reaching a peaceful settlement to this abominable War. The North has blockaded all of our ports, so medicine and supplies cannot reach our shores. You are asking me to do something that is not possible. Your fucking General Grant doesn't give a shit if all of the Yank prisoners in this and the other Confederate camps die. His aim in ending the exchange program is obviously to prevent the release of thousands of Confederate troops held prisoner by the North, to prevent them from rejoining their units and continuing the fight for freedom from the Union. He is the one you should be asking for aid to save the inmates' lives."

Despite Henry's growing contempt for Wirz, much of what the commandant said rang true. Wirz's temper began to flare like a volcano on the verge of erupting. The Major recalled the guard's admonition when Wirz menacingly said:

"I ain't got to take this crap from you cocksucker POW. Maybe you'd prefer to join your comrades in the stockade, 'stead of enjoying the comfort and better food you get living in a tent outside the camp walls. Of course, the inmates would suffer, 'cause, without medical supplies and the assistance of the guards, you would'na be able to provide medical services to the POWs. Then ya'd really have something to complain about."

"No, sir, Captain. I'm sorry. I didn't mean to upset you or sound like I was accusing you of not caring or neglect. I was just trying to improve the conditions of the men interned in Camp Sumter."

The commandant seemed to calm down after Henry's apology. He said:

"Tell ya what I'm gonna do. You compose a letter to General John Winder, the officer in charge of Confederate prison camps. Tell him of the lack of adequate food, clothing and shelter, and how that's affecting the prisoner's health and causing many to die. Respectfully request more and better food, etc. I'll sign it and send it on to the General. I'm not sure he'll respond. I am certain that if he does, it'll be, in essence, 'we can't furnish those things to our own troops, so there's no way we can provide them to our captured enemy.' That should satisfy y'all that I have done everything possible to improve the Yank POWs condition."

Henry was surprised, but pleased, at the Captain's offer. Maybe he wasn't such an evil man after all. He thanked Wirz and said he would have the letter ready for his signature the following morning. The Major exited the commandant's office and returned to the hospital tent to examine and treat more patients.

That evening, when he retired to the tent he shared with the guards, Henry thought of his wife, Elizabeth. He wondered if she had ever received the last letter he wrote, in which he informed her that he would be moved to Camp Sumter. In it, the Major described what he had been told of the plans for a clean, well-constructed, POW camp, and how he and his fellow captives were looking forward to their new quarters. He wondered if the folks back home had heard of the horrendous conditions, and life-threatening treatment of the POWs, in Andersonville Prison.

CHAPTER 35:

THE DEAD LINE

The next morning, immediately after breakfast, Henry went to Wirz's office and gave him the letter to General Winder that the Major had composed. The Commandant read it approvingly, signed it, and ordered a sergeant of the guards to make sure that it is delivered to General Winder as soon as possible. Henry then joined his three guards who assisted him in making his rounds of the camp.

Shortly before sunrise, a light rain began falling, as dark clouds moved into the sky above the camp. By the time Henry entered the gates of the camp, so many black clouds had gathered that they shut out much of the rays of the sun, giving the area the appearance of night-time darkness. The drenching rain turned the sandy soil into sticky mud, making it difficult to walk. Most of the inmates, cold and wet from exposure to the elements, huddled together in large groups, not realizing that doing so facilitated the spread of disease. The polluted, vermin-infested, muddy soil flowed over their feet, many of which were shoeless, and a variety of vermin living in the mud began crawling up the legs and trousers of the POWs. Henry observed the eight body-bearers busily gathering and laying by the South Gate exit, nearly one hundred lifeless bodies of inmates who had expired last night and that morning from exposure to the elements, starvation, and various diseases.

One of the POWs that Henry examined that morning had a nearly foot-long bleeding bruise on the upper left side of his back. As Henry cleaned it with a cotton ball dipped in alcohol and placed a bandage over it, he asked the prisoner how he got that injury. The prisoner replied that he had been sleeping under his tent, made of a blanket held up by two sticks, when he awoke to see a couple of prisoners who belonged to an evil group known as 'The Raiders', standing over him and stealing his blanket. When he began to get up in an attempt to stop the theft, one of them struck him on the back with a wooden club. He told Henry that there were about a couple of dozen POWs that were members of that group, and that they preyed on other prisoners, stealing their food, clothes, blankets, and anything of value, often beating or even murdering those who resisted. The guards were aware of the group of criminals, but failed to do anything to stop them. Henry said he would talk to Captain Wirz and hoped he would put an end to such abuse and punish the perpetrators.

Henry kept his promise. He did complain to Wirz about the criminal actions of "The Raiders.' But for some time, the Commandant did nothing, saying their actions showed that many of the Yanks were criminals who apparently loved hurting others and stealing, and they probably had joined the Union Army because they would get pleasure out of inflicting pain and harm on people of the South, who simply wanted to be left alone to run their own lives without threats from the more populous North. He was not willing to risk injury or loss of life to his guards by trying to round up and prosecute "The Raiders'. More than a month later, the band of criminals had grown in number to fifty, they had committed many more violent acts, including more than a dozen murders, and the guards reported that they were afraid of some of the more physically powerful members of the group, many of whom had acquired weapons such as clubs or knives fashioned out of tin plates.

Wirz began to take heed of Henry's pleas and warnings that unrest caused by the group might result in hard to control riots or even mass attempts to escape. He ordered his guards to organize a group of a dozen inmates who were in good physical condition and anxious to protect their fellow POWs from abuse by 'The Raiders'. Six armed guards were to accompany them as they rounded up the criminals and bound their hands and feet with ropes. The sergeant of the guards was to select three POWs who were lawyers before enlisting in the Union Army, to serve as judges. They were then to hold trials of the six organizers of 'The Raiders', and, if they were found guilty—as Wirz was certain they would be—the defendants were to promptly be hanged in a place where all of the POWs, including the remainder of 'The Raiders', could see. The dozen inmates who had rounded up the criminals were from then onwards to serve as an internal unarmed police force, and given double rations of food as compensation. When all that was done, the violence and criminal acts against POWs ended.

The POWs had no idea as to how the War was progressing. Wirz and the guards did not mention any battles that the Rebs lost. Shortly after the first of July, many of the guards shouted and cheered, and several proudly and joyously told Henry and some of the prisoners that 50,000 Confederate troops under General Joseph Johnston had just defeated an army twice its size, namely 100,000 Union soldiers commanded by General William T. Sherman, at Kennesaw Mountain, Georgia. Many of the North's soldiers that were captured in that battle were taken by cattle car trains to Andersonville Prison, along with other Union soldiers captured in other battles, swelling the number of POWs there to more than 33,000. The number of guards had increased proportionately, also, and by now numbered over 3,000. With no increase in food rations, large numbers of POWs went without any food for three days during that month. While making his rounds on several rainy days in July, Henry observed, at various times, a total of a dozen inmates approaching the dead line at a location where, a few feet away, pools of fresh rainwater had accumulated in a twenty-foot-long gully. Holding a tin cup or pail in one hand, they each stretched out their arm beyond the dead line in an attempt to get some of the fairly clean water. They obviously were not trying to escape. Nevertheless, one or more of the guards stationed at a nearby guard post above the inner wall of the stockade, whether in hatred or for their amusement, shot the thirsty POWs, killing them.

With worsening conditions and increased overcrowding of prisoners in the camp, the mortality rate of the POWs increased to nearly 2,000 per month during July, August and September of 1864. Henry began to suffer from depression because of that and his feeling of helplessness in being unable to improve the food rations, shelter and health of the POWs. To make matters worse, he did not receive any letters from his wife or other members of his family. He worried that they might be unaware that he survived the Battle of Chickamauga, not know that he was imprisoned at Andersonville, or even worse, he worried that sickness or accident had befallen them.

CHAPTER 36:

THE FALL OF ATLANTA BRINGS NEW HOPE FOR THE PRISONERS

On September 3, 1864, while Henry was making his rounds inside the stockade, one of the guards, with tears in his eyes and an aura of sadness in his voice, told Henry that Captain Wirz had received a telegram that morning stating that Atlanta had fallen to General Sherman's Union Army, and that Reb General Hood had retreated. He said it seemed like the South could not hold out much longer; that it would probably have to surrender within a year. Despite a cloudy sky threatening rain, Henry felt like there was a burst of sunshine on a warm and beautiful day. He exclaimed to the guard:

"That's great news for the prisoners. Now the South has no good reason to keep the Yank prisoners here, and the North has no motive to refuse to exchange prisoners."

Immediately after completing his rounds, Henry rushed to Wirz's office. He said he had heard the news of the fall of Atlanta and expressed his opinion that now General Winder might agree to contact the Union exchange officers and attempt to trade captured soldiers with the Union. To Henry's surprise, Wirz said he had the same thought, except that he didn't want to wait for Winder to reply to that suggestion before he would act. He said to Henry:

"You know, Major, maybe there is something you can do to alleviate the situation. Today, I want you to go back inside the stockade and select five prisoners who are in good physical condition and seem trustworthy, to be ambassadors of peace. Bring them to me for an interview. If I agree with your selection, I will release them to travel, accompanied by ten Confederate soldiers, to General Hood's encampment outside of Atlanta, and ask him to arrange a meeting with Union General Sherman to discuss a renewal of the prisoner exchange program. To encourage the Yanks to agree, the five POWs can tell him of the hardships and deaths that the suspension of the exchange program has caused to the Yank POWs. Maybe the Union will listen to them and decide to restore the program, so that both sides can empty out most of their prison camps."

Henry agreed that Wirz's suggestion might work. He promptly returned to the inside of the stockade and selected the Yank 'ambassadors'. Wirz then had ten of his soldiers accompany them on a trip by rail and then horse drawn wagons, to General Hood's camp. On September 10 and 11, Hood had the 'ambassadors', accompanied by the ten guards, meet with General Sherman in an attempt to exchange Andersonville prisoners for captured Reb soldiers. But, after hearing of the extremely poor physical condition of the POWs, realizing that he was being asked to release recently captured able-bodied Rebs who might rejoin the Confederate forces still fighting the Yanks, Sherman refused. Finally, one week later, on September 18, an exchange of several hundred sick and invalid prisoners begins, but less than two weeks later it stalled.

General Winder was aware that, in late July of 1864, Union General Stoneman, who had been ordered to lead his troops south of Atlanta to destroy the Reb railroad facilities at Macon, Georgia so as to cut off supplies to Confederate General Hood, had disobeyed orders and attempted to ride south to Andersonville to free the Union POWs. His undertaking failed when he and some of his men were captured by Reb troops. But by late September, 1864, after Atlanta had fallen to the Union, Winder feared that a Union Army attack on Andersonville might be imminent and likely would succeed. He therefore ordered Captain Wirz to relocate all but 5,000 of Andersonville's inmates to a prison in Millen, Georgia and one in Columbia, South Carolina. Relieved at the prospect of ridding himself of responsibility for almost 85 percent of the prison population under his command, Wirz promptly began carrying out that order. By early November, the number of prisoners had been reduced to 5,000. With the decline in the prison's population, the South furnished far less food to the camp. As a result, each prisoner's rations consisted of ten ounces or less of corn mush, two ounces or less of rancid bacon, and a couple of cups of 'coffee' per day. Many still succumbed each month to the ravages of starvation, dysentery and scurvy. But despite the polluted water and soil, because there was more open space for each prisoner to occupy, they were not crowded together, so disease did not spread as rapidly among the POWs. The guards found four empty barrels outside of the camp kitchen. Henry had the barrels placed in locations inside the stockade near the areas occupied by large numbers of the POWs. There they would collect rainwater during the frequent storms, so that at least some of the inmates would have some fresh water available.

In Washington, President Lincoln, who was up for re-election, was pleased to learn that Atlanta had fallen. At last, victory for the North and restoration of the Union seemed to be within reach. In Chicago, at the Democratic National Convention, its nominee, McClellan, realized that, contrary to his party's platform, peace would only come if the South, voluntarily or by force, were to rejoin the Union.

On November 22, 1864, some civilians who were fleeing south from the Atlanta area, stopped momentarily at Andersonville and told Captain Wirz that, one week earlier, Union General Sherman had his troops set fire to the city. About one month later, on December 23, 1864, Captain Wirz received a telegram stating that General Sherman's army had just captured the city of Savannah. Realizing that the War was lost, the commandant summoned Henry to his office.

"Major, I have just received news that Savannah has fallen to the Yankees. I doubt whether the South can hold off total defeat for more than a few months. You have been a model prisoner, providing medical services to the Confederate guards as well as the POWs. You have expressed many times how you long to rejoin your wife and family. I have decided to offer you the opportunity to do that. I will send you, accompanied by a couple of guards to make sure you will not be stopped by any Reb patrols on your way, south to Savannah. There, Sherman's troops can arrange for your passage back to Ohio."

For a few moments, Henry reflected on the offer and his desire to reunite with his wife and family. But he also thought of his duty to care for the remaining POWs, who might have as long as a year to wait for the Union to defeat the Rebs and free the prisoners. Reluctantly, he said to Wirz:

"Thank you, Captain. But I respectfully decline your offer. I could not, in good conscience, leave the remaining 5,000 inmates without any medical care. I will wait here, continuing to help the POWs, until the Union Army arrives to free all of the prisoners. I feel certain that day will come soon. The only way I would accept your offer would be if you were to give all of the captives their freedom now."

"I am sorry you feel that way, Henry. I am a Confederate officer. It would be contrary to my orders—treason—for me to free all of the POWs I have been ordered to keep imprisoned here."

Henry exited Wirz's office and returned to attending to the patients at the hospital.

CHAPTER 37:

HENRY AND MOST OF THE PRISONERS ARE FREED

Telegraph lines connecting the South to the North had been cut and/or disrupted since early 1863. With very rare exceptions, there was no delivery of mail from the South to people in the North, or vice-versa. One of those exceptions occurred in October, 1863, when Henry succeeded in having a Confederate Colonel, who General Hood sent to General Sherman to negotiate resumption of prisoner exchanges, deliver to the Union General a letter to his wife, Elizabeth. By mid-November, the letter finally reached her in Cleveland, Ohio. Having worried for months about Henry, she anxiously tore open the envelope and read his letter. Tears welled up in her eyes as she read about his incarceration in the Fulton County Jail and realized that he was unaware of the fact that she was carrying his baby, who would be born within a few months. But she felt somewhat relieved as she read that he was to be transferred to Camp Sumter, a new facility under construction with clean wood barracks, a kitchen, lots of fresh air and sunshine. Months later, when Henry was relocated to Camp Sumter, he had no way of communicating with Elizabeth. His wife assumed that he was in pleasant new surroundings, awaiting the end of the War. While popular newspapers in big Northern cities like New York did carry some stories about reports of horrible conditions at Andersonville Prison, and summaries of a few of those reports ultimately were published by a local newspaper in Cleveland, it never occurred to Elizabeth that Camp Sumter and Andersonville Prison were one and the same. That was probably fortunate, since in her pregnant condition, it would have been worrisome, and probably deleterious, if she had been aware of the truth.

In late February, 1865, the local Cleveland paper published a story about a Union soldier who had been wounded, captured by the Rebs and imprisoned at Andersonville Prison, the name inmates gave to

Camp Sumter. The article said that, after the fall of Atlanta, the prison commandant had relocated about 25,000 of the prisoners to POW camps further south. After Sherman captured the City of Savannah, some of those prisoners who suffered wounds requiring continuing medical care, had been sent to Savannah, turned over to Sherman's troops, and transported by ship to the North. That soldier returned to his home in Cleveland to recuperate. In an interview by a reporter, he told of the atrocious conditions at Andersonville, but praised the medical treatment he had received from another prisoner, Surgeon Major Henry Freeman. Elizabeth finally realized the horrible conditions of her husband's incarceration. She contacted the newspaper, which gave her the address of the soldier who was the subject of the article, and visited him at his home. She spent a couple of hours with him as he related tales of his incarceration, treatment of the prisoners, and Henry's providing medical care to the POWs. He assured her that Henry appeared to be in good health, although the Major had told the soldier that he lost twenty-five pounds during his incarceration. Henry also told the soldier that he slept outside of the stockade and had somewhat better food and cleaner water than was provided to the POWs. Elizabeth returned home with the weight of her worries lifted and hope for Henry's return home in good health.

The next day, she went to the post office and asked the postmaster:

"If I wrIte a letter to my husband who is a POW in Andersonville, could it be delivered.?"

The postmaster said that it could be delivered to General Sherman's army, which occupied Savannah, and that he was fairly certain that the General could find a way to deliver the letter to Andersonville, since it appeared the War was almost over. Elizabeth took her baby to a photographer's studio in Cleveland and had a photograph taken of her holding Henry, Jr. She then wrote a letter to her husband and brought it to the Post Office for delivery to General Sherman in Savannah. The letter said in part:

> *"Dearest, I have some wonderful news for you. On February 23 of last year, our young son, Henry, Jr., was born. He has your features and is now a healthy, handsome, twenty-pound baby boy. I have enclosed a photograph of me holding him. We both anxiously await your return home.*

Your loving wife,
Elizabeth".

    In late March, the letter finally arrived at Andersonville prison. Henry was overjoyed at the news. Although he was anxious to return home, he still felt he could not abandon the nearly 5,000 remaining prisoners who would be left without any medical care if he were to go free now. The governor of Georgia had released thousands of the Confederate Army's Georgia Militia to return home; there were rumors that General Grant was cornering Lee's Confederate Army of Northern Virginia; and a month earlier Grant had agreed to resume prisoner exchanges in the amount of at least 3,000 per week. Henry felt certain that it would be at most only a few weeks before he and the thousands of prisoners remaining at Andersonville would be set free to return home. A few days later, after a struggle between his feeling of duty to care for the remaining POWs and his intense desire to return home to his beloved wife and for the first time to meet his young son and hold him in his arms, Henry resolved that, if he ever again is offered his freedom, he would accept the offer.

    In early April, 1865, in a series of battles in Virginia, the Union Army finally broke the back of the Confederacy, leaving the Army of Northern Virginia without the will to continue the fight. In the Battle of Five Forks, General Sheridan routed the Confederates. One day later, on April 2, 1865, Grant defeated Lee in the Battle of Petersburg, Virginia. Four days later, the Union Army was victorious in the Battle of Sayler's Creek, as a result of which General Lee realized that defeat was imminent. Finally, on April 9, 1865, Grant's Amy surrounded Lee's Army of Northern Virginia in the Battle of Appomattox Courthouse. The once arrogant and proud General Robert E. Lee was forced to concede defeat and surrender. The president of the Confederacy, Jefferson Davis, fled, but a few weeks later was captured, charged with treason, and imprisoned in chains. Weeks later, bail in the amount of $100,000 that had been raised primarily by southern supporters, was paid for his release. He was never brought to trial.

    By April 12, word of Lee's surrender reached Andersonville. Commandant Wirz, in accordance with an agreement reached between Grant and Confederate Exchange Officers, made preparations to immediately release 2,500 prisoners. About 1,500 who were deemed physically able to tolerate the journey, were to be taken to a parole camp near Vicksburg, where they would await transportation to the North. Another 1,000 prisoners, who were seriously ill, would be turned over to Union troops to be escorted to the nearest medical facilities or to the coast, where hospital ships could bring them North. Although 2,500 prisoners would remain at Andersonville, Henry felt certain that they would be freed within a few weeks in the next prisoner exchange. He missed his wife and family, longed to hold Elizabeth in his arms once more, and was anxious to see his baby. So, he agreed to accompany the 1,500 POWs being transported to Vicksburg. They arrived at the parole camp on April 15, joining the nearly 1,000 other paroled prisoners from a camp near Selma, Alabama, already at the parole camp, awaiting transport to the North. During the next several days, until a boat was available to bring home the former POWs, they finally received adequate food, fresh air, sunshine and, for those physically able, exercise to improve their physical condition.

CHAPTER 38:

NORTH TOWARDS HOME ON THE RIVERBOAT 'THE SULTANA

A Mississippi River steamboat, the Sultana, had been constructed in 1863 and, for two years had been carrying troops and cargo between St. Louis and New Orleans. On April 17, its Captain, J. Cass Mason, stopped at Vicksburg enroute to New Orleans, where he was to pick up some cargo and passengers. He also intended to distribute one hundred Cairo, Illinois newspapers that had a couple of pages-long story of the shooting of Abraham Lincoln at Ford's theater on April 15. Telegraph lines from the North to New Orleans had not yet been restored, so residents of 'the Big Easy' were unaware of Lincoln's assassination. While his boat was docked, an acquaintance, Colonel Robert Hatch of the Union Army, who was the head quartermaster of the troops stationed at Vicksburg, had a meeting with Mason about a proposal that he said would be very profitable for both of them. Hatch had been authorized to obtain transportation to the North for the occupants of the parole camp, most of whom came from Ohio, Illinois, Michigan and West Virginia. The federal government would pay $10 per officer and $5 per enlisted man to the steamboat captain who would carry the parolees north to Cairo, Illinois, and Cincinnati, Ohio. Col. Hatch knew that Mason had money problems. Hatch told him that Mason would make a considerable profit as he would be transporting upwards of 1500 paroled Union soldiers, and said that he expected Mason to pay Hatch a kickback. Mason happily agreed to pay the bribe. He would make more than four months profit in one trip. Hatch was anxious to get the kickback, which he estimated would total considerably more than one year's pay from the Army. Captain Mason planned to take on the parolees as passengers as soon as he returned from New Orleans.

On April 21, 1865, upon the Sultana's arrival in New Orleans, it took on one hundred cattle, a load of sugar, seventy-five passengers, and then proceeded up river, making its regular stop at Vicksburg, where it was to pick up the paroled prisoners. While the boat was being tied up at the dock for the night, an engineer discovered that a boiler was leaking. A mechanic was brought onboard to repair it. He said a ruptured seam had to be cut out and replaced, and that other repair work was required, all of which would take several days. Realizing that several days delay would mean that Colonel Hatch would find other boats to carry the soldiers home, Mason told the mechanic to just hammer the ruptured seam back into place and rivet on a metal patch. He thought that temporary repair job might hold up until they reached Cairo. If the boat stopped there for permanent repairs, the soldiers would already be on board, and Mason would not lose the payment for transporting them to Cincinnati.

The temporary [which today might be termed "Mickey Mouse"] repairs were completed in less than one day, during which time the paroled prisoners were loaded on board. They numbered almost 2,000, many of whom were physically very weak and/or ill, due to imprisonment in the Confederate POW camps. The Sultana had a legal capacity of only 85 crew and 376 passengers. With more than 2300 persons on board, the Sultana was carrying in excess of five times its legal capacity. Virtually every inch of available space—in the cabins, hallways, and on the decks--was crowded with passengers. Those who had boarded the Sultana in New Orleans and occupied the cabins became upset and angry when they found the hallways so teeming with former POWs that the passengers had difficulty opening their cabin doors or making their way down the halls to the dining area. They complained to crew members who simply shrugged their shoulders and said: "Ain't nothing we can do about it."

Henry was squeezed in among many hundreds of ex-prisoners of war on the forward section of the upper deck. Weakened physically by illness and lack of adequate food during their term of imprisonment, and packed as tight as popped kernels in a bag of popcorn, they supported themselves in part by leaning against one another. Despite the cool night air, Henry and the other ex-POWs began perspiring and their legs and feet began to feel numb. Gradually, a mild odor developed into the stench of hundreds of perspiring human beings, especially heightened by the fact that many of the former POWs had not washed for several days.

It was midnight when the Sultana cast off from Vicksburg and began slowly proceeding North. Spring rains and melting snow from the Northern states through which the Mississippi River and its tributaries flowed, had flooded the mighty Mississippi with icy-cold water, causing it to overflow its banks, and creating a powerful current against which the steamboat had to struggle to move upstream. Two days later, at 5 p.m. on April 26, 1865, the Sultana arrived at Memphis, where the crew unloaded some of its cargo, including about 120 tons of sugar. One of the Sultana's officers told Henry that the boat was scheduled to arrive in Cincinnati in the afternoon of May 1st. Henry disembarked and walked to a telegraph office in the town. There he was told that telegraph lines to the North had just been restored. He sent his wife the following telegram before returning to the boat:

"Memphis, Tennessee, April 26, 1865
My dearest Elizabeth, along with other former POWs, I am on
the steamboat Sultana, transporting us home. Expect to arrive at
the docks in Cincinnati in the afternoon of May 1. It will be great
if you, our baby, and my mom and dad can meet me there. I miss
you all terribly.

Love, Henry"

Henry boarded the boat and slowly made his way to the forward part of the top deck. As he stood there waiting for the boat to resume its journey, a soldier standing next to him said:

"You'd a think the army would provide more comfortable transportation home for us, after we fought for our country and suffered the Hell of POW camps. Packing us all in so close is like more Hell."

Henry sympathized with the soldier. It was uncaring and disgraceful for the Army to treat its men so heartlessly after they had served their country so valiantly and endured horrendous hardships. But Henry did not want to openly encourage the soldier's complaints, fearing that others might join in and create a panic. So, he said to the man:

"Look on the bright side, soldier. I know you've been through Hell and this isn't a pleasant trip. But consider it a journey from Hell almost to Heaven, because in a few short days you will be home with loved ones."

During the six hours the boat was docked at Memphis, several of the former POWs who were in good physical condition, decided to disembark to go sightseeing in the town. They failed to return before midnight, when the Sultana left to continue its journey upriver. When they finally returned to the dock about fifteen minutes after the boat had departed, they were disappointed. They began arguing among themselves about which one was to blame for their late return. Many who had consumed alcoholic beverages during their sojourn in town began pushing and shoving others. A couple of the physically stronger men broke up the shoving match, preventing it from developing into a brawl, reminding the group that they could arrange for passage on the next boat to Cincinnati. Although disappointed that evening, the following day they were to rejoice, feeling they were among the luckiest people on earth.

During its time docked in Memphis, the Sultana's boiler was found to be leaking once more, and the mechanic made more temporary repairs. Straining against the strong current, it took the sternwheeler two hours to travel just seven miles beyond Memphis. Henry thought he could almost hear the ship's boilers groaning as they struggled to produce more steam to move the boat faster. The men in the boiler room were urged to fire up the coal in the furnaces as much as possible, to cause the boilers to increase the steam pressure so as to move the boat forward against the strong opposing current. That, plus the low water level in the boilers due to continuous leaking from the "Mickey Mouse" patches, resulted in a huge explosion, with columns of steam ripping apart the upper decks, flinging hundreds of passengers into the cold river water. One of the large smokestacks crashed into the hole created by the explosion, and the other collapsed forward onto the upper deck, crushing and burning scores of crowded passengers. The remaining upper deck caught fire and collapsed, dropping many passengers into the now burning boiler room below. The couple of hundred passengers remaining on the forward part of the crumbling and burning upper deck panicked like people running from a lava flow when a volcano erupts. They pushed their way to the front edge of the steamboat and leaped or were shoved overboard into the water below.

Within seconds, Henry found himself in the water, dazed and with a ringing in his ears. He was uncertain whether the force of the explosion or the onrush of panicking passengers, or both, had caused him to be thrown overboard. But, looking up at the boat's demolished and burning hull, he was certain he had only survived because he was hurled from the boat. As he looked around him, leaking oil and burning wood from the broken ship lit up the area. He saw hundreds of soldiers clinging to each other in large groups, many in such weakened condition that they gradually sunk below the surface, pulling others down with them. Henry quickly decided that the only way he might survive would be to avoid the groups of survivors clinging desperately to each other, like clumps of branches, plants and mud floating aimlessly on a fast-moving river during a hurricane, and to swim towards shore. With some difficulty, he finally was able to remove the coat of his uniform, so as to facilitate his attempt to swim to shore while avoiding the floating debris and numerous pockets of fire on the surface of the fast-moving river. Unable to swim northwards to shore because of the overwhelmingly strong current, he began swimming southward, attempting to avoid the fires, debris and groups of passengers clinging hopelessly to each other. When he was but a few feet from shore, a large piece of wood hurled downstream by the current, hit Henry on the side of his head, knocking him unconscious and propelling his seemingly lifeless body onto the nearby river bank.

Many of the ex-POWs who had been hurled, or jumped, into the icy cold water did not know how to swim, or were too weak physically to swim with the fast-moving current. Desperately grabbing onto other survivors or floating debris, most of them eventually drowned, often bringing others down with them into the icy depths. In the light caused by the fires in the debris and oil floating on the river's surface, onlookers on shore could see the heads of hundreds of passengers bobbing up and down in the turbulent water, arms often flailing hopelessly, until they finally disappeared under the water. Hundreds of men clung to sections of the bow of the boat that still remained above the water, but as fire reached them they either were fatally burned or slid off into the water, desperately trying to find a piece of floating debris on which to cling. For several hours, small boats docked in Memphis cast off in search of survivors. Those boats and a steamboat that was several miles north of the site, traveling south, picked up more than 700 survivors, who were rushed to hospitals in Memphis. Unfortunately, about five percent of those died within days, succumbing to severe burns and/or their physically weakened condition. Because the crew had not made a list of all the POWs that had boarded in Vicksburg, it was not possible to determine the exact number of those who perished in the disaster. However, the Army estimated that approximately 1,700 passengers had died in the sinking of the Sultana. If that count was correct, the incident was the worst maritime disaster in United States History. The sinking of the Titanic 47 years later resulted in 1512 deaths.

There were several reasons why the Sultana disaster was not well-publicized at the time. The front pages of the newspapers were still filled with stories of Lee's surrender a couple of weeks earlier; Lincoln's assassination eleven days earlier and the capture of John Wilkes Booth a few days after he shot the President; the surrender of Confederate General Joseph E. Johnston and his army, the last major Reb holdouts, the day prior to the sinking of the Sultana; and the fact that the Army preferred not to spread news of the disaster which had been partly caused by tremendous overloading of the steamboat in a war-profiteering scheme of army Colonel Hatch and Sultana Captain Mason. The colonel resigned from the military days later and, by then a civilian, could not be subjected to prosecution by court martial. Captain Mason died in the explosion, and thus could not be prosecuted in a civilian court. An army Captain Williams, who had actually directed the POWs to board the steamboat, was a popular officer and graduate of West Point, and there was no evidence he had been involved in the bribery, so his superiors chose not to prosecute him. The result was that no one was ever prosecuted and convicted for involvement in the disaster.

Not yet aware of the sinking of the Sultana, on April 30, 1865, Elizabeth, her baby, and Henry's parents traveled by train to Cincinnati where, the following afternoon, they and hundreds of relatives of other POW passengers awaited the arrival of the steamboat. A band of local high school children was playing patriotic music in anticipation of the arrival of the boat. At 3 p.m., a boat arrived and about 100 ex-POWs disembarked. The boat's captain announced that there had been an explosion aboard the Sultana on April 27, that many of the POWs aboard had lost their lives, a few hundred had been injured and were still being treated at Memphis hospitals, and that the Army would soon be notifying family members of those who had survived and those who had lost their lives. After desperately searching for Henry among those who had disembarked, like dark clouds gathering before a storm, Elizabeth and Henry's parents began to despair, until Henry's father said:

"You know, we shouldn't give up hope. Maybe he's recuperating at a hospital in Memphis. We should know in a few days, when the Army notifies us."

Encouraged by that thought, the group returned home.

The remains of many of the victims were never recovered, apparently having sunk into the muddy bottom of the river or washed way downstream by the fast-moving current. A couple of weeks later, the coat of Henry's uniform was found where it had washed up onshore about a hundred yards from the site of the disaster. The army presumed he had been killed in the explosion, and sent a telegram of condolence to his wife, which arrived on May 15. Henry's wife and his and her families all were saddened at the news and grieved at the loss. However, being informed that his body had not yet been recovered, they held onto a slight glimmer of hope that he had somehow survived. What was certain was that Henry's description of the boat ride on the Sultana as a "journey almost to Heaven" was wrong. Like his journey to Andersonville, it was a journey to Hell on earth.

EPILOGUE

Elizabeth and her newborn son remained at Henry's parents' home during the next year. They clung to that hope that Henry might still be alive with the intensity of an eagle holding its prey in its claws after swooping down on a rabbit, refusing to acknowledge that Henry was likely deceased.

Early in May, 1865, when the Union Army freed the remaining prisoners held at Andersonville, the soldiers and an accompanying photographer were shocked at the horrible conditions at the camp: the filth and vermin throughout the stockade in which the POWs had been forced to live in the open, exposed to the elements; the polluted stream that provided the prisoners' source of water; the emaciated condition— skeleton-like appearance—of about one-third of the survivors; and the illnesses and malnutrition suffered by many. Outside of the camp, they were horrified by the make-shift graveyard [shallow trenches] that held the remains of more than 13,000 of the approximately 42,000 prisoners who had been incarcerated there during the 14 months that Andersonville had been open.

Angered by the mistreatment of Union POWs, the Union Army soldiers took Captain Wirz prisoner and had him transported back to Washington. There he was tried by a military tribunal for war crimes, including murder and conspiracy to injure and cause harm to Union POWs. During the two-months-long trial, his defense attorneys contended that Wirz was a scapegoat, that he had done his best trying to provide adequate food and shelter for the prisoners. But his defense attorneys were prevented by the court from presenting some exculpatory evidence and witnesses. Wirz, who contended he had unsuccessfully pleaded with his superiors to provide better food and living conditions for the prisoners, was found guilty on all counts. His sentence was death by hanging, which took place on November 10, 1865. The day before his execution, Wirz's attorney received an offer from a member of the

President's cabinet to commute Wirz's sentence if he would implicate Jefferson Davis in the horrendous treatment of the Union POWs. Wirz refused, saying he knew nothing of Jefferson Davis and even if he had, he would not commit treason by testifying against the former Confederate President just to save his own life.

The more than 600,000 casualties suffered by the North and South due to advanced and more deadly weaponry led the nations of the world to abandon Napoleonic battle tactics and revise the methods of waging war. Unfortunately, it also encouraged development of more devastating weaponry and ultimately led to the development of weapons of mass destruction.

The necessity of supplying large numbers of troops with armaments, food, clothing and transportation, led to the even more rapid pace of the industrial revolution, especially in the North, and improved methods of mass production, such as the manufacture of identical interchangeable parts. The increase in productivity led to a more than doubling of the number of American millionaires during the War, although some war profiteers became rich by providing the military with shoddy parts.

In medicine, the demand for various drugs to combat disease and injuries, led to huge growth of formerly tiny pharmaceutical companies. Some, like Pfizer, ultimately would become world leaders in drug manufacture, producing billions of dollars of pharmaceuticals per year. The field of medicine, which had changed little in several hundred years prior to the War, entered the modern age with improvements in sanitation, surgery, and, within a couple of decades from the end of the War, the discovery of microorganisms by Pasteur and others, and their relationship to disease.

Although Lincoln had freed the slaves, many Southerners deeply resented that, considered the Blacks less than their equals. Southern states enacted laws making racial intermarriage a crime, Southerners founded organizations like the Ku Klux Klan that attempted to subjugate blacks by segregation, denial of the right to vote, and threats, rapes, burning of residences, torture, lynching and other forms of murder during the next 100 years, until passage of the Civil Rights Act in 1965. During the 50 years following that Act, many Southerners' hatred of and/or prejudice against blacks was demonstrated by further attempts to deny them voting rights, formation of white supremacist groups, secretive denial of employment and housing opportunities, and the open and revered display of Confederate battle flags and monuments to heroes of the Rebellion. It was only during the past couple of years that the governing bodies of several southern states began to take down Confederate battle flags and some monuments to Rebel heroes. Some Southerners began to realize that General Lee, Jefferson Davis and other Rebel leaders had committed treason in starting a war against the Union so as to preserve the abominable institution of slavery. But hate-mongering ultra-right media served as an inspiration to hate-filled and/or deranged white supremacists to murder innocent blacks. When a black was elected President of our country, some ultra-right-wing media and bigoted whites falsely questioned whether he was born in the United States. We have come a long way towards fairness and equality in our nation since the Civil War. But we still have a long way to go before all races will be treated equal.

The musical 'South Pacific' highlighted one of the basic causes of bigotry, in a song that said while one is still very young, he has to be taught to hate those people his relatives hate. If only the peoples of this world would adhere to the pronouncements of Jesus in Matthew 22:36-40, including 'Thou shalt love thy neighbor as thyself', there might be an end to discrimination and war. It is a difficult path, but mankind's very existence depends on it.

NOTES